Atlas' Rise

By J. Channing

Book 3 of the Atlas Carter Saga

Red Team Ink
DBA of Zealot Solutions, Idaho LLC
5447 Kendall St.
Boise, ID 83706
Copyright© 2017 by Red Team Ink

For permission requests or information about discounts for special bulk purchases please contact: redteamink@gmail.com. Substantial discounts on bulk orders are available to corporations, professional associations, and small businesses.

Printed in The United States of America

ISBN: 978-0-9984881-8-9

Title: Atlas' Rise
Description: First Edition

Prologue

Elsewhere

The First Ones had been a part of the universe's fabric at its inception, and they had come to reclaim their birthright. Trillions of years ago, they existed in a physical form that needed to be protected from the harshness of space, but eventually they evolved beyond that. They shed their physical bodies and became something far greater as they learned to walk among the stars. In the millennia that followed, they scoured the empty universe, searching for other intelligent races who could stand with them as equals, and yet their search proved to be in vain.

During this time, the learned about the true nature of the universe, and peered into the other dimensions that human scientists would only come to discover countless eons later. They built their understanding of how the physical universe, and even time itself could be overcome, and as such, their explorations turned inward. They pursued a new kind of existence, and in doing so, disappeared from the physical universe.

They gave little thought to the Bwain slaves they left behind. The pathetic creatures were left to rummage through the First Ones' abandoned ships, attempting to survive in whatever way they could.

The First Ones thought first and always of their own hunger. Consciousness that had evolved so long ago in physical bodies, longed once more to feel temperature. They wanted to hold rock and metal, and to satiate their hunger through the consumption of food. They wanted sensations that were denied to them in their present form, and it angered them greatly.

In the discussions they had in the fractals and geometric patterns that served as their thought, the First Ones' scientists discussed what would happen now that the upper dimensions had been explored and found to be just as empty.

"*We will dissolve. We are alone,*" the tired ones said.

"*There were the Bwain,*" another answered.

"*Clockworks to be wound, not intelligent life.*"

"I miss the stars. I miss water and the grass."

"Your complaints do not change over the eons."

"Nor does your solipsism."

"We should return. It may be different."

"Return? To feel limitation once more? To be constrained?"

"AND WHAT IS HERE?" a booming voice rang out. He was known as The Ancient. It was his consciousness that first flickered in the oceans of their long extinct planet so many eons ago, and it was he who gifted them with life.

"HERE IS THE SAME. ONLY HUNGER, ONLY WANT."

The other voices quieted, but then one who was braver than the others dared to speak.

"What would you do?"

"WE WILL RETURN. WE WILL BE REBORN," The Ancient growled.

Thus began the First Ones' emergence from the obelisk. Half-formed from memory, lacking enough matter from the physical universe to complete their tentacled, chitinous bodies, the First Ones stretched and contorted their consciousness into the shapes they they once possessed trillions of years ago. They came in search of the hardness of matter, of the sensation of space's vacuum, and of the feeling of warm photons battering against their exteriors. They had long ago surpassed any physical need for food or water. The only sustenance they required was that which would be used to form their new bodies. They came to consume the matter of the universe, and to reshape it in their own image. As they began their return, they viewed the Sword Belt's stars, gasses, and planets much the same way a man dying of would view an oasis.

Yet, there was resistance to their return. A dim memory long forgotten fought against them, and as the fight went on, the rage and anger they felt became more and more profound.

"WE WILL CONSUME ALL. WE WILL BE REBORN!" The Ancient roared.

Chapter 1

Earth
The Galactic Capital
Johannesburg, South Africa

President Nelson Kidewange presided over the largest territory in human history. In just two-hundred short years after the discovery of faster-than-light Alcubierre travel, mankind had spread from Earth to thousands of worlds in hundreds of solar systems. Billions of lives thrived on Earth itself, and billions more woke and slept under different suns in the galaxy's numerous colonies. Natural resources and scientific breakthroughs flowed through the void of space in the holds of the greatest trading fleets ever assembled, and Kidewange's rule had the potential to be an era of unprecedented growth and prosperity.

His thoughts turned momentarily to the many obstacles he had already overcome in his rise to become one of Earth's most important leaders. While there were political challenges from disgruntled senators in the outlying colonies, he had so far managed to fend off the threats, and to maintain some sense of balance and control.

The large windows of the office looked out over the ordered grid of the capital's streets. All of Africa had been transformed by the riches the galactic traders had brought back to Earth. In Kidewange's youth, this corner of Johannesburg had been little more than garbage-strewn slums, but it had now been transformed into something beautiful. Young trees spread in a green canopy beneath gleaming buildings of bright steel and sparkling glass, and off in the distance, one could see the could see nature preserves that were populated with genetically reclaimed rhinoceroses and giraffes that had been rescued from extinction, and golden grasslands swaying gently in the breeze.

His secretary knocked quietly on the door, and then opened it, stepping aside so that the hulking man behind her could enter the office.

In another era, the coal-black beard and broad face of the man who'd just walked into his office would have invited comparisons to Stalin. The admiral's uniform swelled around his thick chest, and his blunt brow seemed as though it'd been carved from stone.

"Admiral Nico. Please, have a seat," Kidewange said as he motioned toward a chair on the other side of his desk.

"Sitting and talking is for politicians. I prefer to stand," Nico replied arrogantly.

"Yes well, it's comforting to know that you have no political aims," the president answered.

Kidewange's intelligence office was quite certain that the admiral was making inquiries among the galactic senate. Representatives who had sought to use the Bwain's threat as an excuse to line their own pockets had grown weary of Kidewange's constant vetoing of their demands for more funding and resources, and they wanted nothing more than to see new leadership in the office. The people of the galaxy had elected their president, and Kidewange had come to power by promising to end corruption, and to balance trade between the inner and outer worlds. For a time, he had done so by exiling the most corrupt senators to other worlds, and by and thinning out the ranks of the SSC, but that was before the Bwain had come.

The bird-like reptilian aliens had slaughtered countless numbers of people in the outer colonies, and swarmed the first SSC battle groups that had been sent to defeat them. Unfortunately, because of these attacks, Kidewange now found himself wedded to the very man whom his intelligence officers deemed to be the most likely to lead a coup against him. Whether Kidewange liked it or not, Vladislav Nico was his only option to stop Captain Atlas Carter from turning his vengeance on the entire human race.

"Is that why you summoned me here all the way from Canaveral, Mr. President?" Nico asked. "You wanted to have a chat about my political ambitions?"

"Admiral Nico, we last spoke forty-eight hours ago, and you promised me updates every twelve hours. I asked you here in person because I find it incredible that, in the past two days, no messengers have come from Commander Decival's fleet. I know this because I have sources within Sol Space Command, not because anyone from your office has given me the courtesy of an update. Do you understand how that makes me feel, Admiral?" the president demanded.

"Blind?" a new voice said from the doorway. Kidewange glanced up at him furiously.

The man who had entered the room was much shorter than Nico, to the point of being almost comically so. He wore a finely tailored suit with shimmering LED piping, and a set of expensive holovisors pushed up on his squat forehead. These let him see his own private messages, and to communicate with his advisors in real time. In the short while that Phuri Vongsa had been back on Earth after fleeing the colonial revolt in the Sword Belt, the man had managed to insert himself into various circles of power. The SSC, the Senate, even the *narco* states, were all rumored to be working with him. As of late, the only one who wasn't working with him it seemed was Kidewange.

"This is a private conversation," the president barked.

"Mr. Vongsa is my attaché. I would like him to join us," Nico said.

"Your expert on Atlas Carter...who never would have been in such a position, if he hadn't conveniently been the top aide to the exiled Senator Tannin. Do I have that quite right?" Kidewange asked pointedly.

"I am here to serve," Phuri answered, as he seated himself without being invited to join them. "The past is unfortunate, but it does not color my future, or the execution of my tasks for the SSC."

"Then perhaps you would care to comment on what's happened to Commander Decival's fleet, because it's clear to me that your employer is unaware."

The blow struck home, and Nico's mottled forehead suddenly tensed in anger. A part of Kidewange wanted the admiral to erupt and lose his temper. Outright insubordination to the SSC's nominal commander in chief would give Kidewange the excuse to remove Nico, and end the threat he posed once and for all.

Unfortunately, Nico's Neanderthal mind was not as crude as Kidewange had hoped.

"Unfortunately, I can only speculate on what happened, Mr. President. I'm as blind as you," the admiral replied neutrally.

Kidewange studied the two men. They were cut from the same cloth.

They were men who proclaimed their honesty and innocence, and yet their actions chipped away at the very ideal. Yet, what choice was he really left with but to believe them? Captain Agricourt, his last loyal SSC officer, had been stripped of his duties for a failed assault on the Bwain, and was currently awaiting the court martial that Nico had arranged for him. He had to press on while they still obeyed him, or until another solution presented itself.

"It is past time for this government to formulate a response to what we know of the events in the Sword Belt. The citizens are restless, thanks to the fear that *someone's* been spreading among the populace regarding Carter's allegiance with the Bwain," he said as he glared at Phuri. "The Senate is demanding action, and it is likely that the outer colonies will withhold their taxes unless we send ships to their aid."

Apparently Nico was still fuming over the insult, as he remained silent and glared at Phuri just as harshly as Kidewange was.

"Ordinarily, this wouldn't be a challenge," Kidewange continued. "However, our fleet is currently short the thirty-six ships that you emphatically assured me would be more than enough to deal with this rogue officer whom you saw fit to exile rather than execute. And I expect that..."

"Carter isn't just some rogue officer," Phuri interrupted.

"Men who interrupt me do not often get a second chance," Kidewange growled.

"Sir, with all due respect, you haven't encountered an adversary like this before. He is ruthless, driven, and as his despicable actions at the battle of Belize City as well as his alliance with the Bwain shows plainly that he lacks any semblance of morals. He's also highly intelligent. I would not even begin to hazard a guess as to what he's done, and I would not take any action until we have gathered further intelligence."

Kidewange stared at Phuri for a moment, and then he folded his arms and turned to look out the window. Below him, traffic rushed through the city in neat rows and columns. The sidewalks were filled with citizens visiting the shops, or looking for a restaurant to have a nice meal with their friends and family. As he watched however, a thick clot of them broke from the sidewalks and move out into the street. They were carrying signs and pumping their fists in the air. These were not citizens who would wait patiently for a solution, and yet it was obvious that someone had arranged the whole thing.

"I wonder, Nico, if what you really want is to see the crowds grow larger outside these windows," Kidewange commented.

"I am loyal to the civilian government, as is my navy," Nico replied.

"Then what, would you suggest we do?" the president asked.

"Send a messenger."

"You know as well as I do that they've all been dispatched," the president said.

In all of its vast increases in scientific knowledge, humanity had figured out only one method to communicate more quickly than light. The Alcubierre drives warped space and time, enabling physical objects to travel from one side of the galaxy to the other with incredible speed. Yet the ships that used this technology could only operate on antimatter, which was created at tremendous expense and energy cost in the orbit of Mars. The single-person messenger craft were far and away the largest users of the antimatter fuel, traversing the galaxy in person to deliver Kidewange's orders, and news from the outer planets.

"There's still one messenger ship on Earth, and one pilot," Phuri noted.

"You told me you didn't trust that man," Kidewange said.

"I don't, but Capra Falconi has dealt with Carter before," Nico answered.

"And he rescued me as Gertie fell to the rebels," Phuri added.

"And what will he do for us now?" Kidewange asked. Phuri and Nico were up to something. The scarcity of messenger vessels was just another tactic to try and build leverage against against him and make him panic. For now, the president could afford to let their rope play out a little more. Especially if he could reach this Capra himself.

"He'll contact Decival, gather intelligence, and then return. From there, we'll develop our strategy," Nico stated.

"And reassure the people by letting them know what's happening out there," Phuri added.

Kidewange glared at the sea of protestors swaying against the pavement. Their eyes climbed the building's windows until their eyes met his, and they shouted things at him that he couldn't hear. They didn't realize, nor appreciate the fact that he would fight for them to the bitter end.

"Then by all means, proceed with your plan. After all, we have a planet to defend," the president said as the meeting concluded.

* * *

Onboard the Bwainhome
The Great Orion Nebula planetary system G-1726, nicknamed "The Sword Belt"
1,339 light years away from Earth

Atlas Carter stood in the epicenter of the Sword Belt's evacuation, wondering how many more of those around him would die. The *Bwainhome*'s shuttle bay, if that's what it had originally been intended for, was a yawning canyon that ran for hundreds of meters along the ship's lower bow. A thin, jelly-like membrane held back the ship's breathable atmosphere from escaping into the void of space. Whatever the material was made from, it somehow knew to form an intelligent seal around the human shuttles that flew in and out of the bay as fast as their Casimir inducers could take them.

"How many more flights do we have, Mr. Xiao?" Carter asked.

Beside him, Carter's supply officer, Lieutenant Danny Xiao, consulted a holotablet.

"I'm showing two more, sir. Thirty-minutes at the most."

"It's not fast enough," Carter grumbled.

Each time a shuttle slipped through the membrane in front of him and landed on the bay's strange purple surface, a group of 50 terrified colonists disembarked. They were met by a mix of SSC crewmen on loan from the other ships that had originally come to the Sword Belt to destroy Carter and the Bwain. Carter had defeated their leader, Commander Decival, and had finally convinced him that the Bwain were not the true threat in the Sword Belt. Thousands had died in the process though, and if they didn't hurry and leave the system, thousands more would perish as well.

For a moment, a group of grubby farmers who'd been been hiding underground on Gertie during the fighting, shrank from the alien environment they suddenly found themselves in. In truth, Carter couldn't blame them. This was the first they were seeing of the *Bwainhome's* yawning pink and purple caverns that looked like the glowing inside of some alien digestive system. Worse than the strange geometries of the ship, were the Bwain themselves.

The creatures stood a meter and a half tall at the most, and appeared to be a cross between a chameleon and a sentient bird. Feathers ran down their backs and dangled in webbed wings under their ropy arms, rippling with color to blend with their environment or express emotion. The aliens' stomachs, legs, and arms were scaled, and their heads rose on a neck of thin muscle before swelling at a blunt beak bordered by glassed lidless eyes. They were difficult to look at, the very definition of the word alien, and every colonist who disembarked on the *Bwainhome* had been told that the Bwain were their mortal enemy.

That had been true, until Carter slaughtered millions of them, and took control of the ship that had sustained their race for untold millennia. Now, the ancient, broken down vessel would have to support thousands more colonists, and no one could predict for how long a duration.

Carter studied the apprehensive faces in front of him. Every one of them would die of old age dozens of times over before the fleet would reach safety. There was no antimatter here any longer, no way to travel back to Earth safely. They were on a ship of years, and at any moment the First Ones could come to reclaim their birthright.

A group of Bwain shuffled past the farmers and into the shuttle. The pilot sealed the craft's hatch, lifted from the deck, and slipped into open space. Carter could just make out the gray bricks of the SSC ships that were the aliens' destination on the other side of the membrane.

"Hurry them up if you can, Danny," Carter said. Then he ducked inside one of the shuttles that had been allocated to the *Bwainhome*.

The Bwain communicated through telepathy, which eliminated the need for things like radios and holoscreens, but humans were still limited by the need for such tools. As such, Carter was spreading the aliens across the fleet, so he could communicate with any ship in real time through the Bwainsong, the creature's telepathic connection. He still preferred human technology due to the level of detail it could convey, but their situation dictated that it was necessary to use other means.

Three faces appeared on the holoscreen he pulled up: Lieutenant Danielle Hoff, his former navigation officer; Commander Decival, a trim officer with sharp features, and Captain Mephista, the former pirate whom he'd convinced to join him in the fight against the Sword Belt's corrupt administrator…and the first woman he'd had feelings for since the death of his wife.

"Forgive me Aída," Atlas murmured to himself. He let out a tired sigh, and then joined the holoconference.

"Danny tells me we'll be ready in 30 minutes," Carter began.

"As soon as the last of the cargo is on board, we'll be ready," Decival replied.

"Is that Hal back there?" Carter asked as he glanced past Decival at several men who were confrerring behind him.

Hal Yellowknife was Gertie's colonial engineer. His nanofactories were able to break down substances into their component elements, and then build new items with the materials. The printing factories' capabilities would be sorely needed on the colony's voyage, but they hadn't been made to be deconstructed. So Hal had come up with an ingenious idea to have the nanobots disassemble their own factories. It had taken time, but Hal had finally lifted them from the colony's surface, along with as many raw materials ss the shuttles could carry.

"Yeah, that's him. We'll have a factory on every ship, give or take," Decival answered.

"Mephista, what's our current security situation?" Carter asked.

"I don't think I need to remind anyone of what we're up against, but just in case you've forgotten…," she said, and then her face flickered out, only to be replaced by a nightmarish scene that made Carter's skin crawl. The First Ones' impossible shapes gibbered in the blackness of space around the obelisk, which was being used as their entry point into the physical universe. The creatures seemed almost as though they were hidden, and not yet fully formed, but Carter knew they were coming. The Bwain knew it as well, and their fear was a constant and palpable presence within the Bwainsong.

Carter reached up and ran his fingers through his hair. As a boxer back on Earth, he'd had to dance around an opponent numerous times, usually when he was nervous, or unsure about his opponent's abilities. Invariably it had been the wrong approach, so now he made it a point to dive right into the unpleasantness.

"I've asked Ms. Hoff to join us, because we've got to think about what's next. I know you're all thinking we're gonna be heading back to Earth, and..."

"Atlas, what are you saying?" Mephista asked, her voice edged with concern.

"What I'm saying is, if we take that course, then we'd be leading the First Ones right to our home planet. I'm proposing that we go through The Gates," he said, referring to the nebula that bordered the Sword Belt. "Then once we get through, we'll keep going until we're sure the First Ones aren't following us. Ms. Hoff has already laid out a course that will, if necessary, keep going until we reach the nearest star."

"What if the First Ones *do* follow us?" Decival asked.

"The *Bwainhome* has shown the ability to resist their weapons, so Pandith and Granger are working on figuring out how to make this ship fully operational again. For the moment, that's going to be our top priority."

"We're never going home, are we?" Mephista asked.

"I don't know," Carter answered honestly.

"Carter, why don't we just load everyone onto the *Bwainhome* and use your dimensional drive to get us there?" Decival asked.

"It's the same problem. The *Bwainhome* uses the First Ones technology. I think this ship was actually built by them, so putting it in orbit around the Earth would be too dangerous," Carter answered.

"Well then what the hell are we supposed to tell the colonists?" Mephista asked.

This was the part that Carter dreaded. These people had trusted him, and to ask for even more sacrifice from them felt like a betrayal.

"We're gonna tell 'em the truth. It's the only way we're gonna survive any of this," Carter said flatly.

* * *

The last shuttle to arrive lumbered slowly into the *Bwainhome*'s bay and came to rest a few meters from where Carter and Danny stood. A group of curious Bwain surrounded the human crew who had brought hovercarts to help unload the raw materials and nanobots that would be required for Hal's factories to set themselves up on the *Bwainhome*.

"Do you know what you're gonna say yet?" Carter asked. "After all, you were the mayor of Gertie for a while."

"Not a clue. Doesn't matter how I word it, they ain't gonna like it," Danny said anxiously. "Besides, I resigned that position. Hal is one-hundred percent in charge now. Actually, why don't we just tell him, and then he can tell all the colonists for us?"

"Because Hal's busy doing important stuff right now, and the last thing he needs is a bunch of angry colonists chasting him around with torches and pitchforks," Carter said.

"Where the hell would they get torches and pitchforks?" Danny asked.

"Have you seen all the junk piled up on this ship? I'm sure they'd find 'em somewhere. Besides, they'll listen to you. You earned their respect during the rebellion."

"I hope so, but I still don't think they're gonna take this well. We might end up with a rebellion here if we don't keep it under control."

"Well, we'll deal with that if and when the need arises," Carter said.

The shuttle hatch in front of them opened, and a tall, thickly-built man with a long shock of gray-black hair climbed out of it. Hal Yellowknife had been Gertie's public works engineer, as well as one of the resistance leaders on Gertie who had stood up to Tannin, and emerged as a de facto leader for the colonists in the mad rush to ward off the SSC. He had been little more than a drunk when Lieutenant Xiao had first met him long before the rebellion, but he had sobered up and shouldered the responsibility of getting the colony to work together, despite its many challenges.

Captain Carter held out his hand and tried to smile, but the expression didn't feel sincere.

"I know that look. I've had it on my face more than a few times myself these past few weeks," Hal admitted.

"It's good to see you again, Hal. We never would have gotten to this point without what you did on Gertie. What you both did in fact," the captain added, indicating Xiao as well.

"Wasn't anything special, Captain. I just can't believe we pulled it off. Anyway, we got lots to talk about," Hal said as he turned to observe the crates that were being unloaded, and transported into the ship's interior. His eyes suddenly widened however, as he glanced up at the yawning interior of the *Bwainhome.* "My God, I've never seen anything like this. It's massive!"

"And it's a good thing, too. We're gonna need all the space we can get," Danny said.

"Why's that? What is it that you're not tellin' me?" Hal asked, his brow furrowed with concern.

"Hal, your factories are gonna be a lot more important to us than we originally thought," Carter said.

"How come?"

"Because...we might just be on this ship a whole hell of a lot longer than we anticipated," Carter replied solemnly.

* * *

The Tranquility

"How did Hal take it?" Mephista asked.

"Not well," Carter's holoimage responded. For a moment the transmission flickered, and she couldn't tell if it had just been interference, or if Carter had shivered.

"He cursed, and he actually called me a liar. Hell, I'm surprised he didn't try to punch me, and I wouldn't have blamed him if he had."

"Is everything all right?" she asked. "You don't seem...I dunno. What's wrong?" she asked. He let out a heavy sigh, and stared at her for a moment. She could see the bags under his eyes, and more of his hair had grayed in recent days. He'd been stretching himself far too thin, and she didn't know how much longer he'd be able to take the strain.

"What if we're wrong?" he asked.

"What do you mean?"

"What I mean is, a lot of people have already died, and a whole lot more might end up dead as well."

"I don't understand. What are we talking about here, Atlas?" she asked.

"The Bwain. They're absolutely terrified, and it's really starting to get to me. Every time I try to sleep, every time I go into the Bwainsong to talk to one of you, all I feel is their fear."

Mephista glanced over her shoulder. She was in her quarters, but the Bwain that had joined her ship was sound asleep. It had buried its head under one scruffed wing, and its chest rose and fell steadily.

"Are we doing the right thing, Elise? Should we just take the colonists back to Earth?"

She mulled this over for a moment before she answered. Earth, to her, had been so long forgotten, that the word itself didn't even seem real. She'd left that part of her life long ago, and the only desire she'd ever had to go back there was to get revenge upon the SSC for sacrificing her and her crew to the Bwain. She'd since given up on her plans for revenge, and her reasons for going back to Earth as well.

"Atlas, I've been in space longer than I lived on Earth. I don't think I'd even know what to do with myself is we ended up going back there. We call it home, but what is it really? It's just a planet, like so many others out there. We'll find a new home, and learn to adapt. And as far as people dying, we're gonna do our best to prevent that. You've already done more than anyone else I've ever known."

"Thanks Elise. I needed to hear that. I've always been able to talk to you," Carter said, looking a bit more relaxed than he had at the start of the conversation.

"Look, I'm not tellin' you anything you don't already know, but I'm glad I could help. After all, we're just two lost souls out here, tryin' to survive as best we can."

Her thoughts returned to the one night they had been able to enjoy a sense of peaceful camaraderie, a well-deserved respite from the intensity of the battle with the Bwain and the colonists' revolt – back before they came to realize the danger the First Ones posed.

The celebration on Gertie seemed to provide the perfect opportunity for them to talk about things other than strange alien invasions, politics back on Earth, the coming of the Sol Space Command fleet, or all the starving colonists and prisoners.

She couldn't resist the small smile that tugged at the edges of her mouth as she thought of the closeness they had both felt. Just being able to connect with another human being in that way...to share each other's thoughts, and to to be able to have a normal conversation, without the formality of command to get in the way, was simply amazing. She knew they were attracted to each other, but she was willing to wait until they both knew what they wanted before trying to find romance with a fellow SSC officer, and especially with one such as Captain Atlas Carter.

"It's more than that, isn't it?" Carter asked.

"It's whatever you want it to be," she replied steadily, not allowing her voice to reveal the hope she couldn't bring herself to express.

"I'm gonna go and try to get some sleep. Communications may be difficult in the radiation belt, so make sure to keep your friend there close to you," Carter said as he shifted away from the personal direction the conversation was heading. She glanced back at the Bwain once again. It still seemed to be sleeping, but now she wasn't sure.

"How did you know it was there? The camera can't see it."

"I have my ways. Are you gonna be all right back there?"

"I don't have any choice, do I? Our inducers are too damaged to go any faster, so we're stuck being the rear guard. Do me a favor though. Let me know if you find any antimatter in the nebula."

"Of course. And listen...Elise..."

"Yes?"

"Stay safe. I don't think I could stand to lose you too."

"You do the same," she said.

* * *

Mephista woke on board a dying ship. Her back screamed in agony, while fire crawled down through the nerves in her legs. She tore away the restraints that had held her in her bunk, pushed away from the wall, and floated into the dark interior of her quarters.

"Lights," she cried. "Bridge, status update."

Her stateroom lit, revealing a sparse desk, a toilet enclosure, and a wide electroglass window cut into the carbyne steel bulkhead that looked out over the spine of her ship. She expected to see flaming holes in the hull, the crystallized clouds of venting atmosphere, and bodies pinwheeling into the frozen blackness. Instead, she saw the distant repair crews working on damage from the SSC's attack, and the nanobots that protected the *Tranquility* from minor damage swarming in a golden river, completely undisturbed.

"Ma'am, nothing to report. It's been quiet since you signed off," the deck officer replied through her earpiece.

"All right. Sorry to disturb you," she said. The microphone that the SSC had implanted into her jaw in the naval academy transmitted her voice to the bridge, and she hoped the officer wouldn't hear her uncertainty.

"It's your ship, Captain," the man replied, long accustomed to her sleepless nights, and her incessant need to constantly be aware of what was going on with her ship and its crew.

Grabbing a handhold, she pulled herself closer to the window. It was her ship all right, but for the moment at least, it was as crippled as she was. She'd lost nearly half of her crew since they first entered the Sword Belt, and while her remaining crew were doing the best they could under the circumstances, the replacements she had taken on from the penal planet knew very little about starship repairs. If the First Ones came, she worried she would afford little protection against the ancient beings for her crew, or for the rest of the fleet.

She reached out and rested her palm against the cold glass. Knowing that the vacuum was still a few inches from her always calmed her when she woke from the nightmares she had of her crew screaming, and of herself being badly injured during the Bwain attack on her ship just a few short years before. The worst that could happen in space, like anywhere else, was death. She had already lived through that experience once. Every moment that followed was just borrowed time.

Pushing away from the glass, she spun around while zipping up her flight suit. Ever since she had lost the use of her legs, she'd become quite adept at maneuvering in the zero-G environment. It gave her a sense of grace that had become one of the few pleasures she still had left.

Laughter met her in the corridor as her cabin door opened. She nearly bumped into a young Asian girl who was hurtling through the gangway, propelled by a canister of compressed oxygen.

"Kaylee! Where are you going?" Mephista asked, laughing in spite of herself.

The girl whizzed past again, giggling with such glee that it almost seemed surreal, considering their present circumstances. Her black hair hung in a streak behind her, and she wore a comically oversized flight suit that had been the smallest in the *Tranquility*'s inventory. Kaylee was a refugee from the *Ichikari*, an illegal mining vessel that had been the Bwain's first conquest when they had tried to claim the Sword Belt's planets. She was the sole survivor of the Bwain attack, though their attempts at controlling the minds of the humans left her with some mental scars that would likely be with her for the rest of her life.

For a time, no one thought that Kaylee would ever recover from her ordeal, and she still carried a faint link to the Bwainsong that had connected to her thoughts. Despite that, she proved to be far more resilient than anyone had expected, and seemed to be adjusting to her new life just fine. To see the girl that Captain Carter had rescued becoming more and more like the girl that she should have been all along, filled Mephista with a hope that perhaps one day, they could all get back to being just normal people once again.

That was what Atlas did as well. He made you believe in yourself, which was just one of the many reasons she was falling for him.

A man's booming laughter sounded from the other end of the corridor, and Kaylee screeched as Captain Carter's former weapons officer, Lieutenant Bryon Purcell, chased her down the corridor, and then pulled her into a playful bear hug.

"Ha ha! Gotcha! I knew you'd come this way!" he said through his laughter. "What kind of hide and seek did they teach you in Japan?"

Kaylee squirmed in mock resistance, but floated free when the lieutenant glanced over and spotted Captain Mephista watching them from the doorway to her cabin. He blanched visibly, and pulled himself into zero-G attention, which caused his magnetic boots to lock down onto the deck, as his hand rose in salute.

"Ma'am, my apologies," he said.

Purcell's green eyes stood out against his freckled face. His red hair was a splash of color against the blue and gray SSC naval uniforms, and despite her tendency toward discipline, she had to admit she'd grown quite fond of Purcell's wisecracks. After all, a life without laughter isn't worth living.

"It's all right, Lieutenant. Anything you can do to boost the morale on this ship has my full approval," Mephista said.

The truth was, she'd been worried about Kaylee. The girl had been exposed to a hostile version of the Bwainsong when the aliens had tried to take over the minds of her former ship's crew. Since then, the poor girl was the victim of uncontrollable mood swings, so it was quite a relief to see her happy and having fun with the lieutenant.

"Thank you, ma'am...although...you do realize you're giving me a whole lotta leeway when you say *anything*," he said with a mischevious grin.

"Anything within the bounds of good taste, Lieutenant," she said.

"Of course, ma'am."

Kaylee triggered her oxygen bottle and floated to Mephista's side. The girl had taken a liking to Mephista, becoming her late-night confidante on those evenings when neither of them could sleep. She nestled against Mephista's waist and hugged tightly.

"The trick to hide and seek is to not let whoever's *it* know where you are," Mephista whispered into Kaylee's ear. The girl giggled again, and Mephista couldn't help but smile.

"Were you going somewhere?" Kaylee asked as she let go of her and floated back a bit.

"I dunno. I couldn't sleep, so I figured I'd just get up for a while. I'll probably head up to the bridge. You guys just go ahead and have fun. I'll see you later," she said as she reached for a handhold to propel herself forward, but before she could move, the lieutenant floated in front of her.

"Ma'am, your shift just ended two hours ago. If you don't mind me asking, is everything all right?" he asked with a look of concern.

The captain cocked her head. Her other crew would have known better than to ask their captain a personal question, but Purcell was different. He was a brash, cocky twenty-something who had survived every major Bwain engagement, and dealt enough damage to the aliens to be recognized as a war hero...*if* they ever got back to Earth.

"Thanks for your concern, but I'm afraid this is normal for me. I haven't slept well since the attack that caused me to end up like this," she said as she looked down at herself.

"I can make you some tea," Kaylee offered.

"That sounds delicious," Mephista answered.

"You know, Danny brought up a case of Gertie's finest tea leaves, to be used only in emergencies," Bryon said as he flashed her a mischevious grin. "I'm sure no one would notice if just a little bit went missing."

"Well, then we should get to the galley," Mephista said, smiling to herself at the thought of spending a relaxing moment with a cup of hot tea.

Kaylee gripped a handrail, pulled herself against the wall, and shot aft toward the galley, but just as Mephista was about to follow, the implant in her ear chimed with an alert.

"Captain to the bridge, urgent."

Her heart rose to her throat.

"I'm on my way. What is it?" Mephista responded.

"The First Ones are on the move, ma'am. They're coming after us."

Chapter 2

Earth
Cape Canaveral, two miles from SSC headquarters

In his apartment off the old NASA causeway, Capra Falconi stretched out on his couch with the window open, listening to the storm-driven ocean batter the shore. It was four in the morning, and the humid air was sticky and hot, but despite the pounding of the rain and the gusting of the wind, he wouldn't close the window. He wanted to hear everything, take in as much of the night and the planet as he could before he was pulled into whatever was about to happen to him. They might be the last memories he would have.

Every other pilot in the SSC's naval messenger corps had been dispatched off planet, either to join Sol Space Command's outer fleets in preparation to report on news of a Bwain attack, or to hold position in Earth orbit in order to shave off precious seconds if a message needed to be carried to the fleet. In a universe where faster-than-light travel was the only way of staying in contact over the vast distances of space, the messengers were the backbone of human expansion. It was an important job, and yet Capra had been left behind.

Ordered by a furious Admiral Nico to remain in his off-base apartment and to avoid communication with anyone aside from his commanding officer, Capra had passed three days in the empty building with little to do other than watch the news. Earth's citizens were worried: that the Bwain were coming to Earth, and President Kidewange hadn't done a thing about it.

He watched thousands of marchers converge on Johannesburg, then reel back as directed energy weapons used for crowd control caused their skin to burn. The rain lashed Capra's window screen, and dribbled in crooked trails down to his tile floor. Outside, through the flowing sheets of rain, Capra could just make out the sprawling SSC headquarters that filled Cape Canaveral. He'd been watching those buildings ever since he'd returned with Commander Decival's message that Atlas Carter had somehow been winning the engagement in the Sword Belt, and he'd been wondering what it all meant.

Nico had singled out Falconi for some reason, and the only reason he could think of was that he had some passing association with Carter. He'd taken the captain to the Sword Belt to begin his tour of duty, and he had rescued Phuri from the planet Gertie in the midst of the colonists' revolt. He told that to Lana Delgato and Captain Agricourt, when he was drunk, which had been a mistake. He had a bad habit of talking to much when he was nervous, and might have shared his speculation that Carter didn't seem like the type of a man who'd turn on the Earth. Had Nico found out what he said? It'd been idle conversation over a few drinks, but then again, SSC messengers were bound by an oath of secrecy, and he had violated that oath.

All the hours of waiting gave him too much time to think. Now Capra was starting to wonder how, in just a few days, protests against the president had spread across the entire globe.

He rubbed his tired eyes, and roused himself from the couch. On the news, images of a sea of angry people were shaking a riot fence somewhere in Brussels.

The feeling he couldn't shake was that all these things seemed connected somehow. Everything was too convenient, and maybe that's why Nico had shuttered him away. Because if he could see the connection, then others might as well. Still, how would he have even known? No, it had to be something else.

He lifted his keys from the table and stepped outside. The exterior lights cast a yellow aura to light his way, and the rain lashed his face, as he made his way out to his hovercar. These were the sensations he missed when he was locked inside his ship, traveling through space. They were the feelings associated with a living, breathing, human being. More than just a person who took orders, but someone who was capable of reason, and able to make connections that others didn't see.

He'd had enough of being shut in. Tonight, he needed some answers, and he wasn't going to find them in his apartment.

* * *

Lana Delgato had come to Florida from Madrid because she was digging for a story. She had been reporting on scientific developments in Europe and just going through the motions of her career, when a chance follow-up on a story about Majorana radiation had led her to Captain Atlas Carter and the *Fate's Winds*. From that scientific conference, she followed the thin thread of what she now believed was a massive cover-up that was being orchestrated at the highest levels of the SSC. What they were covering up however was still a mystery. The trail had cooled in Cape Canaveral, with no leads to speak of after her brief questioning of Capra Falconi.

She'd told her editor she had come to Florida for vacation, but that excuse would only buy her a few days. She needed access, and sources who were willing to talk. Captain Agricourt had been one, but the man who'd led the first expedition against Captain Carter in the Sword Belt, and had then been court-martialed for whatever had happened there, seemed to be playing several sides at once. He would only speak to her in dribs and drabs, and only at times of his own choosing. The trail had fizzled, and now she wasn't sure what to do next.

She finally managed to fall asleep, but she was shocked awake about a half an hour later when she heard a fist pounding against her door. She jerked up in the bed and froze as she stared at the door. Ever since Madrid, two men had been trailing her, watching her every move while claiming they were ensuring her protection. She had checked in late at night under an assumed name, and made sure that no one was following her. She'd been switching hotels every night, just to be safe, and there were only two other people on the planet who knew where she was right now.

The sheets slipped from her legs, and her feet dropped down onto the damp carpet.

"Whoever's out there, you should know that if I don't report to my editor tomorrow morning, they're going to look for me! All my research has already been transmitted!" Lana yelled through the locked door.

The banging stopped. In the bar of light under the door she saw footsteps shift uncertainly. Then, as she made her way cautiously over to the door and looked through the peephole, she saw a nervous face that she immediately recognized. The man had been drunk the last time she had seen him, and he'd failed to give her any solid information, but he had logged her location beacon in his communicator all the same.

She opened the door until it banged against the chain. Capra was standing there, soaked to the bone, and looking just as nervous as the last time she'd seen him.

"You're alone?" she asked.

"More than you know. Can I come in?"

"Hold on," she said. Closing the door, she jogged to the bathroom and slipped into her robe, and then she opened the door and handed him a towel.

"Come on in," she said.

"Thanks," he mumbled as he mopped his face.

"I'm glad you came, but I didn't expect it to be at four in the morning," she said as she stifled a yawn.

"I didn't expect it either to be perfectly honest."

"Why don't you start with why you came, and then we'll go from there," Lana suggested.

He shrugged as the water that dripped from his shirt started pooling around his feet.

"Can I record you?" she asked.

"No. I don't want any record of this that could be used against me."

"All right then, we'll just have a nice little chat. What's on your mind?"

Twisting the towel between his hands, he walked to the window and stared north toward Cape Canaveral.

"You can't see anything from here," he commented in a somewhat vague and distracted manner.

"No, but it was a cheap room, and it's keeping the rain off of my head, so that's something anyway. Capra, why are you here exactly?"

"You were with a Captain when I met you. What was his name?" he asked.

She was surprised. Considering how drunk Capra had been during their last meeting, his recollection was strong.

"Captain Agricourt," she answered.

"Agricourt. He led the first sortie to the Sword Belt."

"That's right," Lana acknowledged.

"And then what happened?" Capra asked.

Lana sat down on the edge of the bed and crossed her legs as she pulled her robe up tight around her neck.

"He won't tell me."

"I thought you two were working together?"

"I'm not exactly sure what the situation is with him," Lana said hesitantly.

"So what are you working on exactly?" he asked. "I thought you'd have at least a few answers by now."

Lana sighed as she stared down at Capra's wet footprints on the carpet.

"All right, fine. I'll go first," she said. She wanted to be cautious, but if this conversation was going to have any chance of producing anything fruitful, she was going to have to stop dancing around the issue and just get right to the point.

"All right, let's hear it," he said.

"Whatever's happening here has something to do Captain Carter. There's some kind of a cover-up, or an effort to manipulate what's happening, but I don't know what's going on, who's involved, or what they're trying to accomplish."

"You have your suspicions though..."

"That's all I have so far, but...well...here," she said as she lifted a holotablet, slipped on her haptic glove, and began flipping through her notes. "Agricourt won't tell me why he was court-martialed. He only gave me a copy of his orders."

She flipped to the facsimile and enlarged it so he could read it.

"Proceed to Sword Belt system. Eliminate Captain Carter at all costs," he read aloud.

"What do you notice there?" Lana asked.

"It doesn't say anything about the Bwain," Capra said.

"Exactly! And Decival came back, but Carter's still out there," Lana said as she watched him to study his reaction. Suddenly his eyes widened as the realization hit him.

"He disobeyed his orders?"

"Yes, and why do you think that is?" she asked.

"He saw something out there that made him do it," he said.

"That's right. I think Carter knows something that the SSC is desperate to hide from the folks back here on Earth, and I think you're probably the only other person aside from him who could potentially have a clue as to what that might be."

Lightning ripped through the sky as Falconi laid out his towel on the room's only chair, and sat himself down.

"Phuri said Carter allied himself with the Bwain. That he turned against humanity and attacked the colony."

"Phuri?" she asked. "Who's that?"

"He was the chief of staff to the colonial administrator, Sickyl Tannin. I brought him back from Gertie after I got his distress call. At the time I thought I was rescuing him."

"And now what do you think?" she asked.

He glanced at her tablet, and then back at her as she stripped off her glove and thumbed off the tablet.

"No recordings, no tricks. I just want the truth," Lana said.

"The protests started the day after I brought Phuri back. I carried so many messages from Phuri and Tannin back to Earth that were marked *Eyes Only*, but I never really thought of it as anything out of the ordinary. I just plugged them into the net, and off they went. I don't know what was in 'em but their official correspondence volume was triple, or even quadruple that of most of the other colonial staff."

"The message about the Bwain got out awful fast, didn't it? It's almost as if it was planned," she said.

"Exactly. And what's more, if it was a real threat, the SSC should have kept it confidential. Instead, they're out there screaming about the threats that people are facing while the civilian government is simply trying to gather information."

"People remember the Bwain ambushes, so it only makes sense they'd be reacting like this," Lana added.

"That's true, and that could be all there is to it, but still...what about Agricourt's orders, and the fact that he failed to execute 'em?"

"He was removed from his post and court martialed for failing to do so, which could just be normal procedure, or it could mean that he knows something they want to cover up. I need to know more about what's goin' on out there. When you go back out, would you take me with you?" Lana asked.

"I'm under orders not to leave Earth. I wasn't even supposed to leave my apartment," he said. "If they find out I did, then..."

"Wait...what?" Lana said as a sudden panic arose within her. She bolted upright, hunting for the articles of clothing she'd strewn around the room.

"What are you doing?"

"If you're under house arrest, then that means they've followed you here. You gotta get outta here now, and so do I!"

"I don't understand."

"Capra, there are men following me because of this story. That's how I know it's real, and the only ones who can get to the truth..."

"Are the messengers," he finished for her as the reality of what she was saying finally struck him.

"Yes, the messengers, and it just so happens that they've all been ordered off-planet...except for you," Lana noted as she hurriedly gathered her few belongings.

She jogged to the bathroom and swept up her toiletries, and then jumped as she turned around and found Capra standing there in the doorway.

"I'm sorry. I didn't mean to...I'll just go. I'll try to keep in touch if...," he said, but then his eyes turned, as though he was thinking about something. "It's my communicator."

He frowned as he pulled the communicator from his pocket. The device was flashing with a priority message. Those only came from SSC command, which meant that he was receiving orders.

"What's happening?" she asked. He tapped the band at his wrist, and a holomessage rose from the device's miniature display. It was from Nico himself. The man's bear face pinched in a sneer, as if he couldn't believe he had to converse with such a lowly officer.

"I hope you've enjoyed your leave Falconi, but you're needed back on the base immediately. Your escort will arrive in fifteen minutes.”

"You're not gonna go, are you?” Lana asked.

"It looks like something's goin' on, and it's the only way to find out what it is. Don't worry. I'll contact you if I can,” he said as he turned and headed toward the door.

"Capra, you can't go,” she practically begged, her fear for his safety growing ever greater by the second.

"I have to. It's my duty,” he said, giving her a half-hearted smile before he stepped back out in the rain and disappeared.

* * *

The rain matted hair and soaked her bag as she jogged across the parking lot. After tossing the luggage in the storage compartment of her rental car, she climbed into the driver's seat and began wringing out her hair. Water ran down the back of her neck, and the humidity in her rental car began to fog the windshield. Just as she was about to start the engine and turn on the defroster, a black SUV flew into the parking lot. She slid down in her seat, hiding herself from view as a pair of headlights swept across her windshield.

The SUV came to a stop, and then two doors banged closed. Were they looking for Capra, or were they after her? She didn't know, so she stayed slouched down in her seat and waited.

When she glanced up, she noticed that her the fog on her windshield, and on the side windows was increasing. She tried to hold her breath, so as not to give herself away, but it was no use. The moisture wasn't coming from her breath. All she could do for the moment is hope that no one noticed.

She sat for a long time with her knees wedged against the steering column and her back lying on the seat, praying that the men would leave.

As the day brightened and the rain ended, she heard the men climb back into their vehicle, and then she raised up and dared a peek as they sped off out of the parking lot.

Sighing in relief, she was about to sit up and turn on her car when the thought that they might still be watching occurred. She twisted herself until she could just see over the dashboard, and carefully scanned the parking lot. Nothing appeared out of place, and the SUV was gone. There were a few other cars scattered on the street, but she didn't see anyone around. Her legs were on fire, and sooner or later she'd have to leave anyway, so she snapped herself upright, powered up her car, and sped off out of the parking lot.

Fortunately, there were no sirens or cars following her. She was driving alone in the early morning light. It had been a close call, and her mind was racing. What she needed more than anything was to get to someone who knew more about what was happening in the Sword Belt. Now that Falconi was occupied, that only left Captain Agricourt.

Thumbing her communicator, she tapped the encryption mode and then called the man who had first approached her after her initial searches. He still wouldn't admit how he had found her, but he had been the one who'd told her that the SSC might not be acting in the best interests of its people.

"Call Agricourt," she instructed the device.

The call rang for what seemed like an eternity before the disgraced captain picked up. Nico had stripped the man of all responsibility after his disastrous sortie against Carter, and Agricourt clearly believed he'd been wronged. She didn't know what the truth was, but it was time to take a step closer to it.

"I told you never to call me," he said. His voice sounded strained, gruff, as if she'd caught him in a moment of exertion.

"Captain Agricourt, I need to speak to you. I had a visitor last night," Lana stated.

"Don't use my name!" he hissed.

"You told me this encryption was impenetrable, military grade..." she said, but he stopped her before she could finish.

"Don't believe everything people tell you. The encryption is strong, but nothing is foolproof."

She heard a rustle, and what she imagined could have been a muffled cry. Was someone with him, or was her tired mind running away with itself?

"Let's go to video," she suggested.

"I'm not dressed. What do you want exactly? Who visited you last night?" he asked.

She tensed, her reporter's instinct to preserve her sources kicking in. Anonymity was the best security, and she couldn't risk Capra's life.

"I can't tell you," she said.

"Then we're done here."

"Wait!" she cried. Straining her ears, she heard his breath still on the line. She hesitated. If she lost the connection now, the captain might refuse to speak with her again, and she would be at another dead-end. There was a story here. She could feel it in her bones. After all, he'd been the one to contact her originally upon his return to Earth. This might be her only chance to get to the truth.

"It was Capra," she said tentatively.

"What did he say?"

"Not over broadcast. I've already told you too much," she replied, regretting her decision to tell him about Capra's visit.

Silence stretched between them as she drove through the dull gray light, directionless.

"Meet me at my house. I'm transmitting the coordinates now," Agricourt said after a long pause.

As the communication closed, Lana wondered if Captain Agricourt was wrestling with his own issues of trust and personal safety. She didn't know, but soon enough she'd meet him in person and find out for herself.

* * *

Palm Bay, Florida
Ten kilometers south of Cape Canaveral

A glimmer of dawn split the horizon in her rearview mirror as she drove south from the Cape. Agricourt's directions led her to a single-story ranch house stuffed on a lot that was still muddy from the night's rain. Her intuition crackled as she pulled up. This was the feeling she'd been searching for when she'd first gone after this story, that something was happening. It was exciting, but also terrifying. Men had come to her hotel looking for her, and now here she was at a strange house that looked nothing like the place she had expected a former SSC captain to be living. Whatever she'd stumbled into, it was time to start taking risks like a true journalist. She needed to know exactly what had happened in the Sword Belt, and Agricourt was the only one who could tell her.

The storm had fully cleared, and the early morning sky was an orange gauze as she jogged up the flagstones that led from the driveway. She knocked and waited on the porch's wet concrete, but no one came to the door. Insects rattled from the shrubs planted on either side of the bay window. An orbital launch that could very well have been Capra roared into the sky from Cape Canaveral.

She knocked again, harder this time, and rang the doorbell. It had only been ten minutes since she'd spoken to Agricourt, but there was no sound of movement from inside the house. After waiting a minute longer, she tapped her communicator and dialed the captain's number.

"Captain? I'm at your front door," Lana said as soon as the connection went through.

"Lana, I'm sorry...," he murmured dully.

She was already turning to run before the line went dead, but she never made it off the porch. The men who seized her had been impossibly quiet, and they were too strong for her to break free of their grasp.

"*Buenos días, señorita,*" one of the men smiled humorlessly as the other pulled her arms in tight behind her and clamped a hand over her mouth. She recognized his face from Madrid. It was the same man who had claimed he would protect her, come all the way across the ocean after her. When he bent to unlock the door so his partner could pull her inside she kicked and tried to scream but only managed to twist around in her captors' grasp. Her last vision was of the heavy clouds tightening once more in front of the sun before the door slammed shut.

* * *

Sol Space Command's headquarters was connected to the Florida mainland by a four-lane causeway that led to an imposing concrete bunker split down the middle by fencing. Capra's driver barely slowed as the heavy gate lifted. The electronics in the bunker had recognized the vehicle and allowed it access.

"No search?" Capra asked the driver.

The man was expressionless, a deep-tanned ensign whose eyes stayed bolted to the road in front of him. Over the years that the SSC had expanded, Cape Canaveral had as well. Barge load after barge load of infill had grown the island into a sprawling complex of dozens of buildings and launch facilities. It was a gleaming mosaic of glass and steel, with hardened buildings that were built to withstand an orbital bombardment. His driver wound through the warren of surface streets, and then headed toward the underground network of tunnels that dipped under the ocean, allowing for even more protection from prying eyes or potential attackers.

There had been a time when Capra had been in awe of the SSC, and proud of everything it stood for. Now he had no idea where he was being taken, or what would happen to him when he got there.

"You've been classified for express entry," the driver said.

"Is there anything else you can tell me?" Capra asked, knowing his request for information would likely be ignored. "I've been grounded for a few days."

"No sir. They tell me less than you."

They passed down into the undersea tunnels, and made their way along in silence for a while, until that silence started to become oppressive.

"I've never been down this far," Capra said, for no other reason than to break the silence. The tunnel's endless gray concrete passed outside his window, the only change in the monotony an occasional maintenance crew or other vehicle.

"Not many have," the driver replied.

Eventually, the throughway widened out into a larger motor pool area. Tunnels spread in all directions, with trucks and other vehicles swarming around lifts that led up or down into the facility.

The driver pulled up to a corner of the facility that had been painted with a large orange arrow, with the word *Elevators* painted beneath it.

When they finally came to a stop, the driver didn't even bother powering down the vehicle.

"So, this is it?" Capra asked as he unclasped his safety belt.

"Yes sir," the driver answered.

"Where am I supposed to go from here?"

"The elevator's been programmed to take you where you need to go."

"Okay then, thanks for the ride," Capra said as he exited the vehicle.

It was strangely warm outside in the motor pool, a deep humidity that might have been left over from the storm. Capra was already sweating when his driver roared away, and the ventilation in the elevator was poor. There were no buttons or voice controls. The only thing he saw in the elevator itself was the bulb of a tiny camera above him. The elevator shuddered for just a brief moment, and then he could feel himself going downward.

Capra had no idea where he was headed, but going this deep underground wasn't a promising development. The SSC was a space-faring arm of the military, and the farther he got away from his ship, the more concerned he became. He half expected a bullet to the back of his head when the doors opened as he stepped out of the elevator, but instead, he was greeted with an even bigger shock.

Admiral Nico stood in what looked like a briefing room. An array of analysts were seated in front of several large holoscreens, and the low buzz of communication filled the room. He recognized several of the feeds that were being displayed. On one there were the Kuiper Belt listening stations out on the edge of the solar system, protecting against inbound threats. Another was showing the feed from Saturnalia, the next closest habitable planet to Earth, which was the jumping off point for most of the fleet. There were several other feeds coming in as well, but for the life of him, he couldn't figure out why he'd been summoned here.

He snapped to rigid attention as the admiral paced before him. He fully expected Nico to start bellowing at him about talking to a reporter, but when the admiral turned to face him, he seemed genuinely curious.

"At ease, Falconi," Nico said as he clasped his hands behind his back, causing the collar at his uniform to strain at his neck. "Have you ever been to the situation room?

"No sir."

"This is where we prepare for existential threats. It's supposedly deep enough that the only thing that can hurt us down here is plate tectonics."

"That's very secure, sir," Capra said, not really knowing what else to say.

"I brought you here, because I need to know what you're thinking."

"Sir?" Capra said in a strained voice.

"I'm charged with defending the entirety of human space from a Bwain threat of unspecified number and location. Their concentration in the Sword Belt is, from a tactical standpoint, little threat to this planet. That would be under normal circumstances, but these aren't normal circumstances. They've joined with a human commander, a man who knows where Earth is, which is far more problematic."

"Yes sir."

"You know this man, don't you? You spent a considerable amount of time alone with him when you transported him out to his new assignment. Most of the officers who served with him while he was previously stationed on Earth have been...reassigned...and aren't accessible for comment right now. What I'd like to know from you, Falconi, is what kind of man he is."

"Sir? I'm not sure I'm qualified to answer that question," Capra said.

"You're the most qualified man I have. It's why I kept you close by when the rest of your squadrom was deployed. You have intelligence that's valuable to us. You could give insight into the war that's coming," Nico said. His voice was calm and controlled, but his presence was more like that of a venomous snake that was about to strike.

"War? Sir, this is the first I'm hearing about a war," Capra said, as a nervous sweat started dripping down into his eyes.

"A human allies with the Bwain and overthrows a colony. That is an act of war, Falconi. Now, what I'd like to know is why. What do you think Carter wants? How should we counter him?"

Capra stared straight ahead. On the holoscreens, hundreds of SSC ships circled dozens of systems, a swirl of protection so much stronger than what the Sword Belt had received.

"Speak, son. You're a grown man. Use your big boy voice," Nico urged as he stepped forward and looked him right in the eye.

"Sir, I find it hard to believe that Carter is the issue here. The man I took out there was hard, but he was a loyal SSC officer."

"Is that a fact?" Nico asked.

"Obviously there's no way to be sure, but my recommendation would be to reach out to him and gather all the information you can. Get the full facts, and then formulate what to do based on what you discover," Capra said.

Nico folded his arms across his chest and stroked his beard. His eyes flicked to Capra for a moment, and then he looked back at the feeds on the holoscreens.

"I thought you might say something along those lines. I can't really say if that's the answer I was hoping for or not, but I just want you to know Falconi, that my orders from this point forward will go a long way toward deciding the fate of our race."

"Understood, sir."

"Now, I want you to go to the Sword Belt and find Captain Carter. Go as many times as you need to. You'll have unlimited access to fuel, but do not report back to me until you find him. Is that understood?"

"Yes sir. And what are my orders when I do find him?" Capra asked.

"Tell him that I would very much like to speak with him. I want to know what his intentions are."

"Is that all?" Capra asked.

"For now, yes. You have your orders, so go and carry them out," Nico said.

"Yes sir," Capra said as he snapped him a salute, and then rigidly spun around and walked back into the elevator.

Chapter 3

The Bwainhome

"How fast are they moving, Ms. Hoff?" Captain Carter asked. He'd gathered in one of the shuttles with Hal, Granger, and Pandith, so he could communicate with the fleet normally, rather than through the Bwain. Mephista and Decival had joined on the holos, as had Danny Xiao and Julie Ford, Carter's former communications ensign. She was coordinating the fleet's communications while they wound their way through the pockets of radiation that would make normal channels of communication impossible.

"It's hard to tell," Danielle said. "All the interference, combined with the issues our sensors have even in an ideal environment..."

"My science team's best guess is that they'll reach us in three days," Mephista interjected. "I don't know if the exact hour will matter."

"We don't need that kind of fatalism right now," Carter said.

"Fatalism? Captain, I'm not being fatalistic. I'm just not sure," Mephista said defensively.

"She's right, Carter," Decival agreed. "Without any way to fight those things, quibbling over trajectories won't matter."

Carter closed his eyes for a moment and rubbed them with his fingers. He could feel the Bwainsong in his head, and the retching fear of the Bwain trying to force itself into his consciousness.

"I'm sorry, Mephista. I shouldn't have said that. What we need are options...things that have worked before," Carter clarified.

"They seemed to have had trouble interacting with purely physical objects before," Pandith noted. He grimaced slightly at the memory of his narrow escape from the reach of the First Ones as he desperately piloted the escape shuttle with survivors of the *Fate's Winds'* crew.

"But they figured it out. And if not for you, Captain...," Granger added."

"What about the radiation? Could we hide in it?" Danielle asked.

"Granger might be onto something with the *Bwainhome.* That ship of yours might be our best option," Decival added.

Carter studied the faces before him. That they'd all survived this long was a miracle, and even more so, that their confidence still showed the hope they all held onto. They were working the problem, but sometimes in life you just hit a wall that stops you cold, and Carter's biggest worry was that the First Ones would find a way to push them into that wall.

"All right everyone, we've got twenty-four hours, so unlock those caffeine cabinets. Danny, I want you to start shuttling any colonists to the forward ships. Mephista, if possible I'd like you to experiment with a purely physical shuttle, preferably one that can test out the radiation theory as well. We don't know much about what these things are capable of, other than what the Bwain have told us. It's time to learn what we can. Are there any questions?" Carter asked.

Heads shook in front of him, as no further words needed to be spoken. Their faces reflected the severity of the tasks before them, and he knew they were all more than capable of playing their roles in what was to come.

"All right then, dismissed," he said as he turned off the holoscreen.

When he turned to leave the shuttle, however, Hal, Granger, and Pandith faced him with quizzical looks.

"Gentlemen?" he asked.

"What are our orders, sir?" Pandith asked.

Behind them, a clot of Bwain crowded around the shuttle. The aliens had taken to following the humans around. Carter thought they were doing it out of fear, thinking that somehow the humans would protect them from their masters....and maybe that was the key.

"We need to understand this ship and what it can do," Carter said. He paused for a moment, considering the specialists before him, and the skills and experience each had to offer. "Hal, I need to you to get your factories set up as fast as possible. We're gonna need to be able to repair this ship if we do end up in a fight. Granger, I'd like you to do everything you can to figure out this ship's weapons systems. If it was built by the First Ones, then it has to be able to hurt 'em somehow. Pandith, that's what I want you to look into."

"Captain? I don't understand," Pandith said with a confused look.

"I'm not sure I do either, but I'd like you to look into the Bwain themselves. There's something that just doesn't feel right about them, and about this ship. Basically, I'd like you to try to understand what's been happening around here for the last few millennia," Carter instructed.

"Is that all? Any other miracles you'd like from us?" Hal asked.

Carter met the man's gaze for a moment, searching for any sign of resentment, but Hal seemed to be the kind of man who could let a fight go without too much trouble.

"If you could find a way to get rid of the smell around here, I'll name my first born after you," he said with a wry grin. "That'll be all gentlemen. Get to it."

*　*　*

At the Edge of the Gates

"I know why I'm here," Lieutenant Bryon Purcell commented as he eased the shuttle back toward the entrance to the Gates. "I just don't know why you wanted to come along."

Alistair Threed had held the dubious position and title as mayor of Judgment, the Sword Belt's penal colony that Sickyl Tannin had used as a means to get rid of anyone who spoke out against him. The former English politician had lived a hard life on the planet, and he'd helped win the fight against Decival's SSC ships with some daring EVO sabotage work, but to Purcell, Threed was no pilot.

"I've gotten to like this new direction in my life. I've gone from prisoner to commando. It's far more noble than dying on some desert planet, isn't it?"

"I'm not sure I'm following you," Bryon said as his eyes flicked back and forth between his holoscreen and the controls.

"What I mean is, when you live under the certainty of death for long enough, you no longer mind risking your life for something better."

"Now *that* I can follow," Bryon said as he glanced over at him and smiled.

The Gates was a narrow pathway through an ancient nebula bordering the Sword Belt. Through some quirk of fate, a channel with low radiation levels had developed that allowed passage through the nebula, and that was the direction the fleet was taking. While in the passageway, communications would be difficult, and it was too dangerous for one of the larger ships to slow down and wait to observe the shuttle experiment. A test shuttle had been prepared that would use no induction or nuclear power. It had been loaded with chemical rockets and propellant, stripped of any device such as its reactors or inducers that interacted with another dimension, and left in the path of the First Ones to see what would happen. Purcell's and Threed's job was to simply observe the results of the test, and return to the *Tranquility* with the information.

"Why are you here?" Threed asked. "My understanding is that they could have sent a probe."

Purcell snorted.

"I'm here because I want first crack at these things, so if there's a way to fight the First Ones, I'm gonna to find it."

On his holoscreen, the test shuttle that the *Tranquility* had sent ahead of them floated alongside the nebula's billowing orange and pink clouds.

"Are you reading me, Julie?" Bryon asked.

"Copy," she called from the *Dauntless*. She and Danielle had been tasked with keeping the fleet's navigation and communications in lockstep, and they had been transferred to Decival's flagship. "Your telemetry is spotty as we get farther away, but...should be able to...it work..."

"You're breaking up on my end as well. We're recording everything, and we'll be ready whenever."

"Do you see that?" Threed asked.

"...careful...," Julie's voice crackled in Bryon's ear.

Purcell enlarged the holoscreen feed from the experimental shuttle so that he was looking at the entrance to The Gates. At first he thought he was only seeing distortion, or some sort of interference from the radiation, but then he realized what was coming toward him.

"Those are the First Ones," he whispered.

They were disgusting, swollen things, a cross between a slug, and some sort of a strange armored creature that gave him motion sickness when he stared at them for too long. They were a diaphanous white against the blackness of space, and as he watched their approach, they seemed to grow more substantial.

"What are they doing?" Threed asked.

Bryon squinted at his screens, enlarging and rotating the computer's extrapolation of the scene. The aliens shimmered and wavered, disappearing and reappearing as the computer tried to lock on to them, just as the obelisk had done when the *Tranquility* had encountered it in the Sword Belt. It looked to him almost as if they were anemones spreading themselves open, funneling the vast colors of the nebula within themselves.

"They're feeding," he answered.

"What?"

"A nebula is gas. It's physical matter. Look, behind them. There's nothing left where they've been. No gas, no radiation, just emptiness. That's what they're doing. They're feeding, and they're getting stronger in here. Julie, are you copying this?" he called, but the only response he got back was static. "We should get back. We've gotta let the captain know what's goin' on."

"But the experiment isn't finished," Threed commented, a hint of reluctance in his voice.

Bryon eased his hand off the shuttle controls. Threed was right. They needed to know if it would be possible to hide from the creatures. He watched them swell larger and larger in the test shuttle's viewscreen. One of them was a tiger-striped thing, a creature that looked for all the world like a bloated cuttlefish with millipede legs. Bryon couldn't tell if it had eyes, but he could feel it looking at him.

"I'm firing," he said as his skin crawled with a mixture of fear and repulsion.

A salvo of six missiles lanced out toward the creature. They quickly shrank to the size of needles on their approach.

"Jesus, that thing is massive," Threed observed.

"I'm trying to get an exact distance to target," Bryon said. "They don't seem to have a hard boundary."

"It's doing something!" Threed exclaimed.

The creature was turning toward the shuttle, swimming through the gases as it left nothing but darkness in its wake.

"The missiles show impact. Firing lasers and cannon," Bryon reported, the chronology log recording every word and action as it played out.

On the screen, red bolts from the lasers arced toward the creature, while magna-cannon projectiles fired in stuttering bursts. The shuttle was small, and could muster little power without a fusion reactor, but to see the weaponry simply disappear into the creature the way it did was extremely disconcerting.

"It looks more solid than it did," Threed observed.

"Negative impact. That's our experiment," Bryon concluded.

Swelling larger before them, the First One eventually filled the shuttle's entire camera feed with a white glowing slickness, and then the holoscreen darkened.

"What happened?" Threed asked nervously.

"It didn't work," Bryon stated flatly as he throttled back toward the main fleet. "Our weapons can't hurt them, and there's no way to hide."

"So what are we gonna do?" Threed asked, somehow managing to keep his voice calm.

Bryon let the heavy acceleration press him back into the pilot's seat for a moment. This shuttle had been fitted with the test shuttle's spare inducers. He had been far enough away from the first shuttle that he had no concerns about reaching the *Tranquility* in time, but none of them would be safe in the long run. It was only a matter of time.

"I honestly have no idea. All we can do is hope that the Captain can think of something, before they catch up with us."

*　*　*

The Dauntless
The vanguard of the refugee fleet

Lieutenant Danielle Hoff pushed her pain to the back of her mind while she studied the data from Bryon's mission. Before she had been the *Fate's Winds*'s navigation officer, she'd taken both waking and hypnolearning classes on every aspect of stellar navigation. She had studied all the fundamentals, such as navigating in three-dimensional space. She had then advanced to more complicated courses that focused on using her neural implant to speed her mind's ability to assimilate the thousands of potential course corrections available to her at any given instant. Gravity had been one of the introductory courses, and now she was searching the SSC library for everything she could consume on the topic as she tried to match the information to confirm a hunch she had after observing the First Ones' movements.

"Lieutenant, did you hear me?" Captain Decival asked.

She stiffened, embarrassed at being called out by her superior. Admiral Nico had sent Commander Decival in command of a fleet of 36 SSC ships to destroy Captain Carter and the Bwain, but ultimately Decival had been forced to surrender to Carter, thanks to Carter's incredible maneuvering. When Decival had finally sat down with Carter, he'd realized that the true threat was the First Ones, and had ordered his ships to cooperate in the evacuation of the colony. He was a good officer, unlike Admiral Nico, whom Decival had shared many less than glowing stories about. She felt proud that Captain Carter had trusted her to build a relationship with the commander, while at the same time charting a course that would bring the fleet to safety.

"I'm sorry sir?" she replied.

"I asked how long we'll be in The Gates."

She tapped a control, and her course estimate flashed in front of her.

"At current course and speed, approximately twenty hours, Captain."

"Thank you, Lieutenant," Decival acknowledged. Then he leaned over the navigation station to study her work. The holodisplay shone faint gold against the captain's narrow face. He was alert, methodical, and disciplined, which was everything that she now aspired to be as an SSC officer. On the *Fate's Winds* Danielle had been much more concerned about alleviating her boredom by flirting with Aric or Bryon, but she'd learned, first from Carter, and now from Decival, what true service was.

Even though she was still in a fair amount of pain, she would never put her own needs before the needs of her crew, ever again.

"If it's the painkillers…," the commander began.

"With respect sir, it's not my leg," Danielle replied quickly.

Her left foot had been sheared off at the ankle in the Bwain's attack on the *Fate's Winds*, and she was in the middle of a painful accelerated regeneration treatment. Her leg now ended at a sterile surgical cap that housed a mix of growth accelerants and stem cells that were slowly growing into a new foot. She'd been ordered to stay off her feet as much as possible, but she had ignored the doctors. Each a time a nerve regenerated or a core of bone firmed in the limb, a fiery pain shot straight to her spine. Oddly enough, she found that the pain had helped to focus her concentration. It was a constant reminder of what would happen to her, and to everyone else if they failed.

"I was just concentrating on the data that Lieutenant Purcell brought back."

"I've got the science team poring over everything. What are you looking for?" Decival asked.

"I'm trying to figure out how the First Ones move, sir. I think there's a pattern."

"Show me."

"Yes sir," she said as she enlarged the recorded course of the First One that had attacked the test shuttle. "Our instruments use a number of methods to gauge an object's position and proximity in space, but the bulk of that information is collected from electromagnetic radiation, visible light, infrared, and those types of data points. When we look at the First Ones however, our readings break down due to an extreme gravitational lensing effect. There appears to be a distortion in space-time that surrounds them."

"That would make sense if they're multidimensional beings, wouldn't it?" Decival asked.

"It would, but it's also a clue. As we've been passing through The Gates, I've noted more and more gravitational anomalies in this region of space," she said.

"What sort of anomalies?"

"They aren't all that significant. I mean, they're nothing on the order of a black hole or anything like that. I think they're most likely leftovers from the supernova that created The Gates. They're basically areas where the heavier matter gathered together and created pockets of higher gravity."

"I'm not sure that I'm following you, Lieutenant. What does that have to do with how they move?"

Danielle winced as a bolt of pain shot through her femur and into her pelvis. She clutched at her thigh for a moment until the sensation passed, and then shook her head to try and clear it. Drops of sweat rolled from her temples, and it was clear that she was having trouble coping with the pain.

"You're pushing yourself awful hard, Lieutenant. I want you to know it's appreciated, but if you need to rest...," Decival said. He needed her on the bridge, but he also didn't want to push her beyond reasonable limits. No commander worth his salt would ever demand that of anyone who served under him. He wasn't going to order Lieutenant Hoff to go off duty, but he let the suggestion provide an option for her to do so if she needed it.

"No sir, I'm all right. Anyway, what I'm trying to say is, I think gravity affects those things. It's hard to tell for sure since the shuttle data was so spotty, but if you track the computer's best estimate of their course, they avoided each anomaly, even though there was matter there that they could have fed on."

"It's an interesting theory," Decival mused. "Why don't you turn it over to the science team for now. We've got an asteroid and a nebula in front of us that's going to affect our sensors. We need to make sure we're able to maneuver through it all right, while still maintaining the ability to see what's coming for us."

Danielle glanced up at the commander, rubbing her eyes. A cluster of Bwain crouched next to him, their heads bobbing as they glanced around at the marines that Decival had ordered to monitor the creatures at all times. Aside from Captain Carter, there were few in the fleet who actually trusted the Bwain.

"Yes sir. I'll do my best. Oh, and Commander...", she said as Decival was starting to walk away. He stopped mid-step and turned to look at her. "I'm sorry I got distracted. I'll do my best to not let it happen again."

"I've got no doubt you will Lieutenant, but even the best of us have to sleep, and I need you focused on your task. There are too many lives at stake here, so why don't you take your meds, and then get a few hours of sleep. You'll feel a whole lot better, and be a lot more focused when you wake up."

"Understood, sir," she acknowledged. She stood up, grabbed the crutch that was leaning against the side of her console, and then made her way toward the bridge's airlock. Even after she returned to her cabin however, the gravitations distortions and the patterns she'd seen in the First Ones' movements stayed with her. There was an answer that throbbed in her mind like the torn nerves in her foot, but she just couldn't quite see it. She was incredibly tired however, so perhaps after a few good, solid hours of sleep, the answer might come a bit easier.

* * *

The Bwainhome

The bowels of the *Bwainhome* dwindled from the grand, sweeping chambers of the ship's higher levels into ever-smaller corridors as Pandith followed his Bwain escort deeper into the ship. It almost felt like they were hiking down some sort of a strange, alien gullet that had long since frozen in death. The walls were a slick, violet substance that gave off a faint glow, and the deck underneath his feet hummed with an unsettling vibration. Pandith managed to put aside his claustrophobia, and kept reminding himself that Captain Carter needed him to solve the riddle of this ship if they were going to have any chance of survival.

"Captain, I don't even know what I'm supposed to be looking for," Pandith said.

A gaggle of Bwain clattered through the corridors beside Pandith, clicking their claws on the uneven floor, and fluttering in shades of pink and purple as the walls triggered their natural camouflage instincts. One of them trotted over to Pandith, squawking and fluttering to get his attention. It was strange how quickly he'd gotten used to speaking through the Bwain, as if the creatures were simply walking communicators. It really wasn't all that different from using the SSC communications implants though. In a way, Pandith preferred having a face to talk to, even if it was that of an alien.

"Neither do I," the Bwain transmitted in its best approximation of Carter's voice. "The best I can tell you is to look for something that's recent."

"I'm not sure I understand."

"When I rescued you and Granger, I was controlling the *Bwainhome* based on instinct. That came from the Bwainsong, but there was something else. The First Ones weren't able to harm this ship. If anything, they were trying to connect with it."

"Since they were the ones who built this ship in the first place, do you think they're trying to get it back?" Pandith asked.

The Bwain fell silent. Hundreds of generations of them had lived and died on this ship, and yet it seemed as if all knowledge of what the *Bwainhome* had been, or of how it could be used against the First Ones had been lost to them.

"I don't know, but that is a possibility. I just need you to explore around down there and see what you can find. They've got some secrets that they're not telling me, and ever since the First Ones have come back, they're all deathly afraid of something. I wanna know what it is they're so afraid of. More than that, I need to know whatever you can find out about this ship."

"Understood, Captain. I'll see what I can find down here, and get back to you as soon as I can," Pandith said as they continued on down the corridor.

* * *

The Bwain led Pandith past countless structures that appeared to be some combination of organic and geometrical construction. The strange shapes wove in and out of the walls as if coyly teasing about their purpose, but every one of the structures he passed seemed long inert.

When Pandith questioned the Bwain about the machinery, the aliens showed little interest in stopping, and simply wandered deeper into the ship.

On the *Fate's Winds*, Pandith had been in charge of maintaining the ship's life support and related systems. He had also served as the ship's doctor and psychologist, but there was little chance of practicing those disciplines among the Bwain since they seemed to understand nothing of themselves. Whether the aliens knew what the arcane machinery around them did and wouldn't tell him, or if they had simply never known its function at all, he couldn't tell.

"You talk to the ship. Does it talk back to you?" Pandith asked the alien guide.

"Not talk. Think," the Bwain croaked.

"Yes, I know you're telepathic. What I'm asking is, does the *Bwainhome* talk to you?"

"Bwainsong. Speak in Bwainsong."

"Yes, I know, but...," Pandith started to say, but he paused as he had to duck under a series of low ribs that looked like the roof of some stretched mouth. A dim light fell from the ridges, and it appeared as if he was walking across a floor made of pinkish ice. He couldn't shake the feeling of purpose all around him, but the Bwain weren't any help at all in explaining any of it. In fact, their absolute ignorance of a ship they'd been traveling in for eons was frustrating beyond worlds, and he had very little time to try and help Captain Carter unlock the mysteries of the ship.

"This. Here," one of the Bwain squawked.

The alien stood at the entrance to a long room. Pandith had to squat and crawl through a yellow-lit tunnel until the chamber's ceiling rose once more and he could stand. A series of small, deep blue-colored mounds pulsed in a strange rhythm. Kneeling beside one, Pandith rested his hand on its top. The texture was silky and cold, like the pearled interior of a shell. A series of veins connected each one, and for a small instant as he tried to pull his hand away, Pandith felt as if the ship did not want to let him go.

He got back to his feet and stared at the Bwain surrounding him.

"What is this?" he asked.

"Life," the Bwain responded.

"This is your life support system?"

The Bwain's heads snapped around, eying each other. He recognized this behavior in the groups of them when they were having a telepathic conversation.

"Life," another squawked.

"How does it work? Where are the oxygen interchangers? Where do you get your food?" Pandith asked.

"Food not here. This life," the creatures responded.

"Do you mean that it has come to life? Is that it?" Pandith persisted, but this way of trying to extract information was exasperating.

"Yes," the aliens replied. They whooped and squawked, fluttering around the cavern like excited children.

"Captain, can you hear me?" Pandith called.

"I'm here. Did you find something?" one of the Bwain in the corner cawed.

"The Bwain say this is new. Do you see it?"

The creatures already seemed to be losing interest, trundling toward the far side of the chamber where what looked like a ramp led down to a hazed interior.

"I do," one of the last Bwain answered with Carter's thoughts. "They keep calling it 'food.'"

"They kept saying it was life, but id doesn't look like anything I could eat, and it isn't like any life support system I've ever seen," Pandith noted.

"Keep at it. This may be something important," Carter instructed through the Bwain.

"Yes sir," he called back, and then with a sigh, he jogged to catch up to the enigmatic creatures who took their crumbling home for granted.

The slope they descended wound back on itself, until he realized that he was passing under the previous chamber. A steam rose here, and the temperature increased until he was sweating. He waved away the thick streamers of mist, following the scuttling outlines of the Bwain until he came to a startled stop at the entrance to a new chamber.

The air here was clear, almost chilly after the heat of the previous room, and as Pandith's boots splashed in a liquid that was raining from the ceiling, he stopped short and glanced wildly around the chamber. Thousands of Bwain were bending to lap at the pool that filled nearly the entirety of the chamber. A current ran through the liquid, twisting and turning it into hundreds upon thousands of variations of the form that Captain Carter had shown him in the observation room.

The ship was feeding the Bwain from itself, forming the same pattern as the Endless Knot. The creatures were bowing their necks to snap up the liquid in their beaks, and then threw their heads back to swallow. The aliens who had led him in there all waded in to join the others.

"All right Captain, this time I definitely found something," Pandith called, unable to keep the sense of awe and curiosity from his voice. The scientist in him screamed for more information, for careful studies and meticulous observation, but the voice he heard loudest, the one that called to him with a sense of urgency, was the one that reminded him that the survival of two species depended on his ability to find a solution, and unfortunately, that was something he had to accomplish without the luxury of time.

*　*　*

Hal Yellowknife surveyed the strange magenta chamber that would be his home for the next who-knew-how-long of a stretch of time. The sandy light that filtered from its roof reminded him of Gertie's sunset, but that was the lone piece of familiarity that he carried with him. Hal had been the colony's chief engineer, in charge of manufacturing everything from nuts and bolts, to prefabricated housing, to spare parts that the *Fate's Winds* had used for repairs. At the time, Hal had thought he'd had a hard job, and he had butted heads frequently with Sickyl Tannin, the colonial administrator. Tannin had been secretly skimming parts to build a ship he would have used to escape from Gertie, while at the same time leaving the colonists in the hands of the Bwain.

"I guess in a way, Tannin had the right idea," Hal chuckled to himself.

"Sorry? I'm not following you," Kilver, his apprentice, replied from the corridor where he was waiting for Hal to finish his cursory inspection.

"Oh, it's nothin'. Come on, let's keep going," Hal said as he stepped back out into the corridor.

The *Bwainhome* was a massive ship, easily the size of a small moon, and it had been an uncomplicated matter for Captain Carter to set up Hal and his apprentices in an abandoned corner of the ship and turn them loose on trying to manufacture the supplies and materials that the fleet would need. They had just begun to get the nanofactories going. It was a simple enough process, and he had been teaching Kilver along the way.

Nanofactories had been designed to be one of the first structures built on a new colony, because everything else the colony needed could flow from them. The nanobots that Hal and his apprentices had rescued from Gertie were invisible to the naked eye, although the trillions of them he'd brought to the *Bwainhome* filled up a wheelbarrow that weighed nearly 50 pounds. The tiny machines operated through electromagnetic commands that Hal would issue from his portable control station. Even if he wouldn't have been there to guide them, the nanobots were preprogrammed to carry out two orders without instruction. They would construct a factory to replicate themselves, and then build a factory large enough to manufacture anything the colony needed.

He'd had the nanobots deconstruct every factory on Gertie and reduce the facilities into their component parts. Now Hal, Kilver, and the other apprentices were trundling along with their sacks and wheelbarrows, spreading out the fine powder of what would once more become concrete, carbonite steel, and a new generation of nanobots, all in less than a day.

Hal set down the wheelbarrow he was pushing and stretched himself out as he reached around to rub his back where it was getting sore.

"Can you take over for me?" he asked Kilver, who was working just a few feet away.

"Sure thing," he said. Hal smiled and clapped him on the shoulder, and then headed back over to his monitoring station. The boy had been bored with farming on Gertie, and his desire to do something different with this life had turned him into an indispensable second hand in engineering and manufacturing. In fact, despite all the upheaval and the colonists' trepidation, everything seemed to be going better than expected.

The only real issue Hal foresaw was raw materials. The initial plan had simply been to get off Gertie before the First Ones arrived, and Hal hadn't really been thinking of the long term. Now, the reality of the situation was that no one knew how long they would be in space, and they were potentially facing a severe supply shortage.

The printing factories assembled finished components out of raw materials collected by his nanobots. The nanobots were typically used in new or terraforming colonies. They were set loose on an entire planet to search for particular elements or molecules and to bring them back to the stations in the exact quantities needed for a particular build. Once they were programmed, the nanobots operated as a silent, nearly invisible river flowing with raw materials.

That operation wasn't possible on a ship, where resources were limited and confined to what was on hand; once those were exhausted, then what? The last thing Hal wanted to happen was for his microscopic minions to strip the *Bwainhome's* hull, or some other critical piece of a ship the humans barely understood, and that the Bwain couldn't explain.

That was just one concern however. Another was food. The SSC ships carried a decade's worth of food for their crews, along with the ability to grow fresh food in their gardens, but they hadn't been stocked to support a colony of 12,000 additional people. And no one knew exactly what the Bwain ate. With a colony of farmers to lead, it was only a matter of time before Hal would have to sort out that issue as well.

His first priority however were Carter's orders to get his factories running, so they could repair any potential damage caused by the First Ones. For that to occur, he needed raw materials.

He turned to one of the Bwain that seemed to be constantly shadowing him. The creatures showed a strange mix of curiosity and fear, almost like beaten dogs who couldn't drag themselves away. They still gave Hal the heebie-jeebies, but he had to work with them, so he had to find it in himself to at least tolerate them.

"Do you understand waste? Garbage?" he asked it. He was speaking more loudly than he normally did, as if the thing were deaf.

The creature's head dipped. It had been scratching under its armpit but turned its glassed eyes to him. Then it hunched backward, shuddered, and a stream of guano splashed out behind it.

"What the hell are you doin'?" Hal asked in a strained voice as he tried to stifle his gag reflex. The ammonia smell was almost overpowering.

"Waste," the Bwain said as it turned and tilted its head toward the mess it had made.

"No, not that kind of waste. I mean trash. You know, garbage…junk. Things you guys aren't usin' any more, and stuff that can't be fixed."

This time the Bwain seemed to show more awareness. Its head swiveled to look over Hal's shoulder, and when the engineer turned around, he saw another of the aliens lifting up what looked like a damaged strut.

"Broken. Garbage," the Bwain squawked, almost seeming proud of its ability to understand Hal's wishes.

"That's right," Hal chuckled. Communicating with a telepathic species was a little uncanny, but it made for some built-in efficiencies he could appreciate as an engineer. "That's exactly what I need. Can you bring me more of that sort of stuff? I need just as much as you can find?"

The aliens nodded simultaneously, and both scuttled off into other chambers.

"What was that about?" Kilver asked as he rejoined Hal.

"We're gonna get things cleaned up around here. First things first though. Do you know how to use a shovel?"

"A shovel? Well duh, I was a farmer after all," Kilver said with a breathy laugh.

"Good. Then you should be used to shovelin' crap. So grab a shovel, and there's the crap," he said with a grin as he pointed toward the mess the Bwain had made. Kilver frowned as he turned to look at it, but when he turned back around to complain, Hal was already walking away.

"Very funny," he grumbled to himself as he wandered off to find a shovel.

* * *

His effort to understand the *Bwainhome's* weaponry had raised equal parts of both awe and frustration in Granger. The Bwain leading him had taken him along all sorts of different catwalks, and through various chambers, showing him arcane rooms and machinery that were close in appearance to something that humans might have built. The ship was a strange amalgamation of technologies that had all been glommed together over the millennia. A science officer like himself could spend lifetimes poring over every fascinating object. Much of its weaponry was similar to human weapons. There were lasers, missiles, and projectile accelerators that he was generally familiar with, even though the technology behind them was foreign in nature. Then there were other weapons that were so exotic, that he wasn't able to make any headway at all in figuring out their function, much less their operation.

Now he sat on an outcropping with his boots off, rubbing his feet while the Bwain buzzed around a set of cold, gray fins that looked like shark's gills that had grown from the walls.

The room was a blister jutting out from the *Bwainhome*'s hull. From the exterior, it would look like one of the innumerable other knobs that the Bwain had fastened onto their ship's hull over the millennia. Yet when Granger leaned his exhausted shoulders against the wall, the pink surface felt smooth. He hadn't seen any of the Bwain with any tools that indicated they might be in a constant state of construction.

"Weapon. Fight," they hissed and squawked.

"Yes, I know, but how do they work?" Granger asked the nearby aliens.

"Don't know," one of the creatures rasped.

"Of course you do," Granger answered. He was finding his scientific detachment hard to maintain in his exhaustion. It had been nearly fifteen hours since he'd slept, and he felt that he was no closer to giving Captain Carter what he needed. "The Bwainsong will tell you."

The creatures looked at each other, uncertain.

"I've seen you use your fighters, and I've seen this ship fight against humans. How can you not know how it works?"

In a particularly human gesture that the aliens had picked up, the group shrugged in unison, and then trudged on.

"Come," they said as they turned to leave. "Next."

Granger sighed, then hauled himself to his feet while the Bwain shuffled out into the corridor. He stepped around the gills, bending low to try and peer between them. There was no sign of a power coupling or controls. But then, why would there be, when the weapon was telepathic?

"Granger come," the aliens called.

They led him through another long corridor, but as he was walking his eyes fell heavy. His stomach was growling, and in spite of the urgency of his quest, he needed to turn back.

"No, I'm sorry. I can't go on any more right now. I need to get some rest," he said to the Bwain closest to him.

"Rest," it repeated.

"Captain, are you there?" Granger called as he turned around.

"Go ahead, Granger," Carter responded through the Bwain.

"I'm afraid I haven't made much progress. I'm gonna head back and get a few hours of sleep, and then I'll get back at it."

"All right, thanks for the update," Carter acknowledged.

Granger retraced his tired steps back toward the gill room. If nothing else, the survey map he'd been making of the ship would be valuable for future study. Maybe they could find interconnected patterns, or some larger schema that governed the ship. Maybe they could...

Granger suddenly came to an abrupt halt. Inside the gill room, things had changed. What looked like venous tubing had grown over the gills and pierced the hull. There were no windows that he could use to verify his hunch, but somehow Granger knew that a muzzle now jutted out into space.

The Bwain clacked and chittered behind him, poking at the walls and floors in their usual habits.

"What happened here?" Granger asked them.

One cocked its head, then shook it.

"Nothing," it answered.

"We just came through here. It looked different," Granger pressed.

Taking the alien's arm, he pulled it over to the enclosed gills. It tried to struggle out of his grip, but the creature was too diminutive. He took its hand and placed it on the tubing.

"Do you remember this? It was different before," Granger prodded. The creature's coloring flashed bone white, then black, then to purple gain. Behind him, the other aliens fell silent. Granger glanced at them as they stood huddled in a frightened cluster at the back of the chamber.

"Tell me, please! What's going on?" he begged. The Bwain just stood there trembling and shook its head.

"First Ones come! FIRST ONES COME!" it croaked as panic started to set in. With a frenzied lurch, the creature pulled away from him.

"Granger, what the hell did you just do?" Carter demanded urgently through one of the Bwain behind him.

"I didn't do anything. What are you talking about? What happened?"

"Something on this ship just fired, and it only missed the *Reichstag* by a few meters. Did you figure out the ship's weapons?"

"No, but I have a theory that we need to discuss," Granger said as he eyed the agitated Bwain in front of him.

*   *   *

The Wreckage of the Fate's Winds
In open space close to the obelisk
Drifting near the Greater Orion Nebula

Aric Keith felt his body lift from the *Fate's Winds'* frozen decking. The brittle gray of his former flesh cracked as ne moved, and his boots made no sound against the deck as the First Ones forced his body back to the ship's reactor. Aric had been Captain Carter's former engineer, and had died aboard the *Fate's Winds* after the battle with the Bwain. The First Ones rebuilt his wrecked body with the nanobots that had once protected the *Fates' Winds'* hull, and were now using him to do their bidding.

The creatures needed the *Fate's Winds'* reactor and inducers to help power the obelisk, and provide them with the matter they required to achieve physical form. It was Aric's job to keep these last vestiges of his ship running, thereby allowing the First Ones to force their way back into the physical universe through sheer compulsion of will. They were still weak and unaccustomed to physical form. The creatures could not manufacture, nor could they build. They could only consume and grow.

While they had turned him into a numb machine capable of doing their bidding and little else, they had failed to fully sieze control of his mind.

Because he still held on to a trace of his humanity, he had exulted when Captain Carter had led the last of the colony's ships out of the Sword Belt. The First Ones had felt his emotions and wracked his body with pain as a punishment, but they didn't understand that pain could be endured indefinitely when a man no longer feared its consequence. When their grasp finally relented and Aric stood upright once more, he stared out of the ship's torn hull in the direction of the distant sparkle created by the fleeing vessels, and felt the remnants of his cheek muscles pull his frozen lips into a smile.

"Aric Keith, do you mock us?" he heard one of the First Ones asking in his mind.

"Never," he thought back to them.

"Then why do you express such happiness?"

"Because my friends escaped, and you won't be in this universe for long. Captain Carter will find a way to send you back."

A screeching roar tore through Aric's mind. He collapsed once more to the frozen deck, sputtering as the white flame of the First One's anger rippled over him. Though his eyes had long ago frozen in the cold of space, the nanobots had granted him sight. Now, against his will, his eyes turned to the obelisk's brilliant white gateway in space.

"We are come, Aric Keith. We are eternal."

The First Ones swarmed around him, half-drawn creatures hundreds of kilometers long. They wore the bastardized forms of whales, squid, cephalopods, and shapes too indescribable to name. They were monstrous abominations, torn from nightmares that had driven humans mad for generations, and yet what emerged next was even worse.

The most massive creature that Aric had ever seen struggled through the gateway. This First One had the body of a narwhale crossed with a centipede. It had a seething mass of tentacles protruding out from under a skirt of white chitin, and the thing moved through space like some sort of a lumbering war galley. Its painfully white figurehead ended at a fiercely armored head that was marked in the center by a single cyclopean eye.

"The Ancient. The First of the First Ones," the other First Ones whispered around him.

Aric tried to look away from the desecration writhing above him, but the creatures' grip on him was absolute.

"BEHOLD, I AM COME," The Ancient bellowed in Aric's mind.

"The feast begins! Feed us!" the other voices called.

In the creatures' distraction, Aric felt their hold on his body lessen. In that moment, he seized his opportunity. He turned and reconnected a wire that had been shorn in the Bwain's attack, then shunted a miniscule amount of power to the ruined ship's transmitter. Before he could do more, though, he felt the cold grip of their control return.

"WHAT IS THIS CREATURE?" The Ancient asked.

"It calls itself a human," the First Ones replied.

"I'm a member of the Fate's Winds crew. I serve Atlas Carter," Aric projected through his thoughts.

"THE OTHERS HAVE TOLD ME OF CARTER."

The Ancient's chimerical head swiveled in the direction of the vanished fleet. Around him, the other First Ones flickered into greater definition. Several drifted toward the system's outer rocky and gaseous outer planets that had been uninhabitable and useless to the colony.

"WATCH, ARIC KEITH, AND UNDERSTAND WHAT IS COME," The Ancient intoned.

In his mind he could dee the gauzed First Ones dipping their tentacles into the planets. They squeezed the very matter from them, leaving gaping holes where they dug into the rock and through the crust.

The First Ones were consuming the system, and the more they consumed, the stronger they became.

"THERE IS ONLY US, AND THERE WILL ONLY EVER BE US. ARIC KEITH, ALL OF YOUR FRIENDS WILL BE CONSUMED," The Ancient roared through his mind.

Chapter 4

"You'll have to excuse me. I didn't mean to scare you, but it wouldn't do for me to be seen talking to reporters. I really can't be too careful these days."

Lana Delgato turned to face the man sitting on a disused loveseat in the center of the living room of Agricourt's house. He was Asian, with deep-brown skin and black hair topped with a set of expensive hologoggles. The communicator on his wrist looked to have cost more than Lana made in a month, and he smiled with a brightness that seemed to die in his eyes.

The men who had captured her set her on her feet. One of them held her while the other frisked her and removed her communicator.

"Ella es limpia. She's clean," he said Lana shook him away angrily, and to her surprise the man backed off.

"Señor, would you like us to stay?" the other asked, waiting for the man's instructions.

She made a note of the pair's accented Spanish. She had heard its kind somewhere before, but for now she needed to stay focused.

"No. Just watch the door," the man replied dismissively.

"Who are you? What do you want?" Lana asked her captor when the door had clicked shut behind her.

Standing, the man was no taller than five feet five, and he was plump around the middle.

"My name is Phuri Vongsa. I brought you here because I believe we can work together."

"What did you do with Captain Agricourt?" Lana demanded.

The house was clearly a setup. A layer of dust coated the tables and chairs, and the only signs of life were the unfaded sections of wall where pictures had once hung long ago.

"Nothing. He's been sent on vacation to South Africa, where he'll enjoy a safari, perhaps some hiking, and remain until he is needed."

"Needed for what?"

"To perform his duty as an officer loyal to the people of Earth and its colonies."

"You mean overthrowing President Kidewange," Lana said, her voice indicating that she was merely confirming her suspicions, rather than asking a question.

Even here, in front of a man she knew would have no qualms about killing her, Lana's curiosity rose to the surface. She'd been on the trail too long, and she needed to understand the truth in spite of the risks.

"Conspiracy theorists will always see what they want, Ms. Delgato. That's why it's so important to make sure that our theories are carefully researched before making accusations. As someone who has spent much time with Mr. Kidewange during this crisis, I can assure you that any threats against our president in these times are simply false."

"Then why have you been watching me?" she asked. "You're holding me hostage right now!"

"You're free to leave," Phuri replied smoothly as he gestured toward the closed door. "Alejandro, please...get the door for Miss Delgato."

Behind her, the door unlatched. She heard cars rolling down the waking street, felt a humid breeze stir the dead air around her.

"I've spent a lot of time researching the president's aides. Your name never came up."

Lana tore her gaze from the open door to study the man who was clearly the one responsible for this elaborate scheme. She considered his offer of freedom, then found her feet wouldn't propel her through the doorway. She had to know more, and this might be her only opportunity.

Phuri smiled once more, as if reading her thoughts. He was certain before he ever made the offer that her curiosity would win out, and he was right.

"Yes, you're quite correct. Technically, Admiral Nico is my employer, but my loyalty is to humanity, and to this planet. So, when I find that a reporter has been asking sensitive questions during a dark hour, it's my duty to follow up with that individual and ascertain where her loyalties lie. What do *you* want, Ms. Delgato?"

"I want to know what's happening. I want to know where the protests have come from, and why what's goin' on in out there in the Sword Belt is such a secret," Lana replied.

"Very well then. I'll be happy to oblige," Phuri said as he resumed his seat on the worn piece of furniture. Once again he surprised her with his openness. From every rumor she'd ever heard about Nico and his cabal, especially from Agricourt, Phuri seemed to be the opposite. Though, again, a dim bell rang in her mind, she was willing to at least listen to him, if for no other reason than he would finally give her information she so desperately needed. He didn't seem in the least concerned about talking with her openly.

"President Kidewange is weak. I'm sure you know this, as it's been reported for years that the outer colonies do not feel they receive the proper investment. But his true weakness comes from fear. The Bwain attacks have hit the outer colonies disproportionately hard, and now we have word that humans have allied themselves with the Bwain. Humans who know the location of Earth."

"Captain Carter. But how can you be sure?" Lana asked.

"Because I was there when he overthrew the colonial administration on Gertie," Phuri said. "I saw him and the aliens butcher the colonists who resisted, and I escaped only thanks to a brave messenger who rescued me. I will not allow that slaughter to reach this system."

A brave messenger. It had to be Capra, but she couldn't tell Phuri that she knew him. She didn't yet know what side this man was on.

"But you sent Agricourt's battle group out to intercept 'em. What happened?" she asked, trying to contain the eagerness she was beginning to feel now that she was finally getting the information she had been looking for.

"Yes, we did. As for what happened…Agricourt encountered them, and then tucked his tail between his legs and ran away. After that, another battle group was sent that was made up of thirty-six of our strongest ships. They haven't been heard from in over four days now, ever since they first reported engaging Captain Carter."

"But everything I've researched about him…," Lana said as she mentally flashed through what she had learned about Captain Atlas Carter.

"Yes, I'm well aware of his difficult childhood, his rise up through the SSC's ranks, and the tragedy of Belize City…if you could consider it that.

All of those things conspired to burn a hatred for humanity into him, the likes of which has not been seen before. Carter has bested two of our fleets, Ms. Delgato, and Kidewange talks only of peace and negotiations."

"But shouldn't we negotiate if we can't stop him? Aren't we at least gonna try to find out what he wants?"

"I was there, Ms. Delgato. I know what Carter wants, as does Admiral Nico, and in his way, our president as well."

"That's what you want. You want Nico in power."

"Nico is a tool, capable only of intimidation. What the planet needs is someone of vision. Someone who understands the new reality of humanity among the stars."

"You mean yourself, I'm sure," she commented.

"No, Ms. Delgato," he said. "What the planet needs is new leadership, and a whole new structure. The people are letting their voices be heard. They want security, and they want trust, both of which this government has not been able to provide."

"So why did you bring me here? Why tell me all this?" she asked.

Phuri smiled slyly as he got to his feet, took her by the arm, and led her toward the door.

"Because, I'd like your assistance in convincing the people that help is coming."

"Even if you get what you want, how's that going to stop what's coming?" she asked.

"It will definitely come if we don't act, Ms. Delgato. Now, if you'll excuse me, I have other matters to attend to. Can I assume that we've reached an understanding?" he asked as the door opened to allow them through. She stared at him for a moment, but didn't answer. She simply turned and walked out the door, with her two abductors following along behind. Phuri smiled to himself as he watched her go, and then he stepped out and closed the door behind him.

* * *

Admiral Nico watched through his holoscreens as President Kidewange's private shuttle swung onto Cape Canaveral's landing pad. It was a windy day, and the president's robes billowed out from his sides as he walked toward the elevator that would lead deep below the ocean.

"We should have made him drive. He'd see the protests," Nico sneered.

"I can assure you that he's quite aware of them," Phuri replied as Nico turned to look at him curiously.

"It is interesting how much you know,"

"I'm simply doing what you ask," Phuri said humbly.

"As you did with Falconi and Delgato?" Nico asked.

"It's one thing to force someone to do what you want. It's another to convert them to your point of view. Imagine what happens when a reporter like Delgato confirms your story of Kidewange's weakness?"

"And what if Falconi finds nothing?"

"He won't," Phuri assured him.

"It's a possibility."

"You sent Decival with 36 ships to the Sword Belt. None of them returned, not a single messenger. If Carter converted them, why would they stay silent? No, there was a battle. There will be carnage beyond description, and when Falconi finds it, we'll turn that discovery into more fuel for the people."

"The last time we had fuel, Agricourt turned it against me. He spoke out, talked to other officers. He's the one who put Delgato onto us."

"Yes, and he's been dealt with appropriately," Phuri said.

"I don't like all this plotting. It's dishonorable. We should act now," Nico grumbled. Phuri's wine glass scraped on the table when he set it down.

"Is there anyone with a clearer vision of how the Bwain threat can be addressed than you?" he asked, phrasing his question in a way he knew would require the admiral to agree with him.

"No."

"Is there anyone who commands more loyalty among the military?" Phuri asked.

"Of course not."

"And when the time comes...when the SSC receives orders that will leave Earth materially unsafe...will those loyal to you act in an appropriate fashion? Will they recognize your understanding of the problem and follow you as the only one able to solve it?"

"If they know what's good for them, they will," Nico responded with a growl.

"Then leave the reporters and messengers to me. Your job is to rein in your famous temper, and to tell Kidewange that he's doing the right thing."

Nico considered the smaller man before him. There was something about Phuri he didn't quite trust. The man had surrounded himself with aides from the Latin American senators, and Nico's own intelligence service had had a difficult time piercing that veil. In a way, the admiral hoped that being honest with Capra Falconi would give him another perspective on Phuri's intelligence. He disliked putting so much trust in one man, especially one who seemed to prefer his own brand of power.

"One way or another, we'll bring Atlas Carter's head back to Earth on a pike," Phuri said with a mirthless smile of triumph.

Nico narrowed his eyes as he noticed the expression. Was Phuri gloating because he had successfully manipulated the SCC's most powerful military man into trusting him? Phuri gave him the impression of a coiled snake, awaiting its opportunity to strike. He would definitely need to be cautious with the man, even though, at least for the moment, they seemed to share the same objectives.

Just then, the entrance chimes sounded. Nico stiffened to attention as Kidewange entered. The president stopped short, seemingly surprised by Nico's sign of deference. He returned the gesture stiffly, and a smile tugged at his exhausted face when he shook the admiral's hand.

"I'd hoped we could work out our differences. We've been sparring with each other for far too long. If we're all gonna get through this crisis, we need to be united," he said.

"I feel the same, Mr. President. And I can assure you that, while I have assembled a second fleet and am ready to personally command any further expedition against hostile aliens, I will not act without giving you a chance to make peace," Nico assured him, forcing a note of sincerity into his voice.

Kidewange glanced at Phuri. The president seemed guarded, not believing the sudden change in Nico's tone, but for their plan to work, Nico had to convince him thoroughly that he was on the side of peace.

"So, the protestors haven't swayed your mind?" Kidewange asked, figuring that it was best to get right down to the business at hand.

"What are the concerns of the sheep to the wolves?" Nico answered.

"And when you speak with those senators who would support new leadership, which do you consider me?" Kidewange asked him bluntly.

"I consider you our president, sir. And, like myself, someone committed to the safety and security of all humanity. Just to bring you up to date, I'm currently gathering more information about the events in the Sword Belt. As soon as it becomes available, I will release it to you and the public so that we can all make the most informed decision."

"I knew you'd make the right decision," the president said as he smile returned. "Now, if you'll excuse me, I have business to attend to while my quarters are being arranged. I'll be speaking to the planet this afternoon, and I'd appreciate it if you were at my side when I do so."

"Of course," the Admiral replied with a tight nod.

The president nodded back, and then turned and left the room. After the door slid closed behind him, Nico held himself rigid for a moment longer, then turned and slammed his fist against the wall.

"How much longer will you have me licking his boots?" he bellowed.

"It all rests on Falconi now. Maybe another week at the most, and all this will be yours," Phuri said. His lips curled into a strained smile, but his eyes remained cold and emotionless. Nico eyed him for a moment, and then slammed the wall once again with his fist.

* * *

The Sword Belt

The Sword Belt was a scene of horrors.

Capra had purposely set his Alcubierre jump destination point behind the system's sun, hoping that the star's radiation would shield him from any craft hunting for intruders. As he had passed the hours in his faster-than-light bubble, he'd grown more and more nervous about what he might find upon his arrival. He entered in dozens of evasive navigation solutions, charged his craft's meager weaponry, and shunted additional power toward the antimatter containment field so that it would recharge his Alcubierre drive more quickly.

He thought he had been prepared for anything. But when he arrived, the entire Sword Belt had disappeared.

His holoscreen showed a faint outline of the system's sun and its six planets, but his instruments showed nothing but blackness. He checked the star charts, which triangulated his location based on three stars in neighboring systems. The location came back as confirmed. His jump had taken him exactly where he had programmed it to, but what had happened to the Sword Belt?

Capra plotted a cautious course toward where Gertie used to be. There was no sign of Decival's flotilla, and no evidence of any Bwain activity. He scanned every frequency, but there was no trace of the colony's distress beacon. There was also no sign of debris, and no life pods containing survivors.

Could the Bwain have done this? Did they have the power to destroy worlds? If so, maybe Carter had little choice but to join them.

Despite his better judgment, Capra tapped his deep scan button, and then triggered the *Mosquito* to broadcast.

"This is SSC messenger vessel *Mosquito* to any SSC or human-crewed ship in the Sword Belt. Do you copy? Over," Capra called.

He set the broadcast to repeat while he coasted toward the blankness that had once been a green planet of rolling hills. Then he leaned forward, studying a signature on his holoscreen just as the first results from his deep scan pinged.

What looked like streaks of white appeared in front of his vessel. He enlarged the magnification one hundred times, then five hundred. And what he saw was terrifying.

Gertie had not entirely disappeared. The planet's glowing core seethed and writhed with giant creatures that appeared to be feeding on the planet like maggots gnawing on flesh. The scavengers were huge, easily double or triple the size of the largest SSC capital ship. As he watched, one drilled a glowing white spike into Gertie's magma, slurping up the steaming lava into its body.

He set his instruments to record all frequencies and spectra. Whatever was happening here, Earth needed to know that Atlas Carter and the Bwain were the least of its problems right now.

The deep scan results chimed for his attention. His instruments showed a single signature near where The Gates used to be. And when he turned his telescopes toward the target, Capra nearly lost control of his bowels.

Thousands of the scavenger things were arrayed around what appeared to be a fissure in space. The seam was connected by what looked like lightning bolts to a giant creature that towered over the others. As Capra took note of the readings, he noticed the thing's head turn toward him, as if it were suddenly aware of his presence.

The transmission! He had been broadcasting this entire time!

He slapped his broadcast signal off, and then began preparation for his return jump to Earth. On his holoscreen, the strange beings shuddered toward him. He couldn't tell if they were ships, or some kind of alien. When he tried to focus on one, its exact shape blurred, and shifted out of his vision.

His heart was pounding. His throat was dry. He wanted to scream and run, but he had thirty more seconds until he could make his next jump.

Suddenly the cabin speakers groaned with static. The sound was like the elemental scream of space burrowing into his mind. It grew louder and louder, until Capra felt its cold blackness in the depths of his heart.

"Capra," a voice hissed. It sounded mechanical, strangely muffled. His blood chilled.

"Who is this?" Capra asked.

"They can be stopped. You must close the obelisk. Use the dimensions."

Falconi's hand rose to the holocontrol that would trigger the Alcubierre jump. It glowed under his finger, waiting for his touch while the horrible things undulated toward him.

"I don't understand. What are you?" Capra stammered, but the haunting voice didn't respond.

* * *

The Fate's Winds

Flame enveloped Aric Keith, lifting him away from the radio and hurling him against the frozen metal of the far hull.

"WHAT DID YOU TELL IT?" The Ancient demanded.

He no longer had the ability to smile, but even in his torture Aric watched the *Mosquito* disappear from the system with a sense of satisfaction.

No matter how much pain they gave him, the First Ones could not defeat Aric's mind, and every time they exposed more of themselves to him, he understood the weakness behind their hunger.

"I told him to run. I won't let you consume my friends," Aric groaned through his tormented mind.

* * *

Earth

The hot sun blistered the highway. While her erstwhile bodyguards drove her back to her hotel, Lana Delgato sat sweating in the backseat, trying to sort out all the things that Phuri had told her. If Kidewange's weakness and Nico's warmongering were really dangers, what was the solution? Phuri had been coy about his own role in what was coming, asking her only to judge what would happen based on the facts that revealed themselves, or that he chose to reveal to her in any case. He wanted her to write about the missing fleet. If she did, that would likely lead to an outbreak of mass panic and rioting, but the people had a right to know.

The longer she thought about the encounter, the more she realized how deftly he'd manipulated her. He had told her little of substance at all, and yet she couldn't say he was wrong in thinking that the threat from the Sword Belt was far greater than anyone on Earth seemed to realize.

Without Agricourt or Falconi, she was on her own, and the truth seemed farther away than ever before. She would not let herself be intimidated however. If there was one thing she was good at, it was standing on her own.

She leaned forward, putting her head between her watchmen in the front seat.

"Your accents, where are you guys from? I knew in Madrid that you weren't Spanish."

The squat one in the passenger seat glanced at the driver, but neither answered.

"I don't suppose you guys would know what's really goin' on anyway. Your whole job is probably just to walk around looking intimidating," Lana said, prodding at their egos a bit. She leaned back in her seat, as if not wanting to waste her time talking to these know-nothing lackeys.

Again, the squat one's eyes flicked to her. A Latin man's machismo was always his weak spot. They were so predictable that way.

"We know enough," the man replied defensively. There was the accent again, the bubbling, almost Caribbean rhythms that could have been from anywhere in the old Spanish colonies.

"Then what do you think of Carter?" she asked.

"This Carter, we don't know," the man answered.

"So you trust what Phuri says."

A deep snort burst from the driver. His eyes rose to meet hers in the rearview mirror. They were firm, almost arrogant, with the entitlement she recognized in so many who clung to the powerful.

"We trust no one," he said flatly.

"But he hired you. You work for him."

"Do we? I had no idea," the passenger said, and then he smiled at the driver as they both started chuckling.

A few moments later, both men fell silent again as her hotel's sign rose from the horizon's palm trees. She was running out of time, but she needed to keep them talking.

"You both seemed out of place in Madrid. Your clothes weren't right. You didn't fit in," she tried again.

The driver clicked his turn signal and slowed to make the turn into the hotel's parking lot.

"So did Phuri just hire you off the street? You're nothing but a couple of thugs, aren't you?" she sneered.

The eyes in the rearview narrowed at her insult.

The passenger twisted to face her. He was smiling again, but a coldness hung in his face.

"Where we come from, the reporters were all executed. We'd hate to see that happen to you," he said acidly.

Her stomach clenched as the SUV screeched to a halt, but at least she was outside her hotel. The passenger exited and opened the door for her, bowing in feigned politeness.

"Cockroach nu go da fowl dance," the man said to Lana as he stared intently into her eyes, reinforcing the threat that his voice held. He resumed his position in the front passenger seat, slammed the vehicles door, and jerked his head in Lana's direction as the SUV sped away.

She recognized the saying, and the hint of Creole in it. He'd been warning her not to go where she didn't belong. It was an old wives' tale she'd heard as a girl on vacation with her family.

Lana searched through long-forgotten memories. There had been white beaches, a town on the water, and a sea as blue as the sky that stretched endlessly along the coast.

Belize! The men were from. They were from Belize City, the capital of the *Narcos*. What were they doing all the way up here though, and working for Phuri no less? Something just wasn't right, and despite the warmth of the sun on her skin, she felt a shiver of fear crawl down her spine as she hurried into her hotel room.

Chapter 5

The Bwainhome

Captain Carter climbed upward through the core of the *Bwainhome*. Here and there he passed small bands of colonists touring the alien ship, or hurrying around on some mission for Hal. They seemed half in awe, and half terrified of what they were seeing, so he stopped to offer a few words of encouragement to each group he passed.

"Don't worry, they're harmless," he assured a group of families shying away from the flocks of Bwain that were scuttling in camouflage through the shadows.

"Harmless! Harmless!" the Bwain squawked in unison.

"You'll get used to the light," Carter told a group of farmers who were pointing flashlights toward the ceiling.

"When are we going home, Captain?" one of the men asked.

"You're taking us to Earth, right?"

"Soon. If we stay together, we'll get through this," Carter replied, but the words were mechanical. Though the people he passed stood a little straighter, and even managed a smile or two, Carter himself felt the heavy strain of responsibility pulling ever tighter. What would happen if he needed to sacrifice the people on this ship? What would happen if they realized there was no escape?

He climbed the purple ramps in a fog of thought. He was tired, and his own anxiety combined with the agitation he felt in the Bwainsong had made it difficult for him to sleep. The creatures were terrified of their masters, but not scared enough of him. The strain of long weeks against terrible odds was catching up with him, and he was tired of dealing with their secrets.

Even before Granger's discovery of the weaponry, Carter had been convinced that the Bwain knew more than they were sharing. Several times now when the *Bwainhome* had reacted to his emotions, the Bwain themselves had acted as if nothing had happened. Even when he reactivated the ship's dimensional drive and put the *Bwainhome* in between the First Ones and the fleet, and the ship had taken little damage from the First Ones attacks, they still held tightly to their secrets.

The Bwain had to know something. Either they had a mental block put in place by their former masters, or there was some deeper issue with the creatures. He studied the aliens trotting through the corridors with him. What if he had to sacrifice them as well as the humans after they'd begged him to save them, and he had promised he would? Could he bring himself to do it?

"Bwainslayer ask question?" one of the creatures squawked. This one was slightly taller than the others, its feathers rippling purple, pink, and green as it trundled beside him.

Carter looked at the alien, startled. Even after so many days with the Bwainsong in his head, it surprised him.

"No, just thinking." Carter had long since realized that the moments of quiet or the rare occasions when he was physically alone, there was always the presence of the telepathic creatures through the Bwainsong. Even his own thoughts were no longer his alone.

His legs were growing tired as he climbed the winding passages. Cazador would have laughed to see him in this kind of shape. Atlas recalled those many times when he had been in training, with Cazador pedaling beside him on a squeaking bicycle, cursing and taunting him, pushing him relentlessly as the young fighter jogged through the tropical heat in his sweat suit. Carter was preparing for a different fight now, though, and for this one, he needed to train his mind.

Granger and Pandith were on their way to give him the results of their investigations, but he wanted to pursue his own theories first. He needed to ask the aliens some questions that he would prefer the humans didn't hear the answers to just yet.

After several more turns, the ramp opened onto a wide path that climbed over a large hold toward a sweeping entrance. A group of columns rose up on either side, disappearing into the space where the ship's deck should have been. Rather than the gray-blue flooring so prevalent on the ship, the roof here in this chamber was a turning vortex, as if a holoscreen were rendering the galaxy's churning in almost real time. Carter stepped through the entrance, squinting at what lay beyond while he tried to keep the whispers out of his mind.

Writhing before him, directly underneath the vortex, was the Endless Knot. A slinking, glistening confluence of energy, the Knot's exact form defied his perception as it blurred between the twelve dimensions of the universe. The Knot was the ship's power source, its nerve center, the source of sustenance and intelligence for the Bwain. When Carter had first arrived on the ship, he had thrust his hand into its cold brilliance of golden light and had somehow taken control of the aliens and their ship. For most of the past few days, he'd been operating on a combination of his fighter's instinct and whispers from what might have been the Bwainsong, but it might have been something deeper as well. Now the time had come to understand exactly what had happened when he'd arrived in this chamber prepared to slaughter every Bwain on board to protect his crew.

A few dozen Bwain were gathered around the room's walls, rippling in gold and white as they bathed in the Knot's messages. Their heads swiveled toward him as one. Some portion of his thoughts must have been leaking through their mental connection with him, though he could never understand exactly how much. They seemed tense as he Carter strode toward the light and thrust his hand deep into the ship's essence.

Immediately, the sensation of his body fell away. Carter felt an instant union with a greater consciousness, the sensation of millions of synapses firing in total synchronization. Each flash was a Bwain, a single creature united by the Knot in a massive, unified wave of thought, and yet, there was a shadow among them. There was something hidden.

"Bwainslayer," the creatures called. *"Bwainslayer, help us. First Ones come."*

"Yes, I'll help you, but first you must help me," Carter thought.

"Ask."

"Where did the Bwainhome come from?"

"Bwainhome always. Never not here."

"Who made it?" he asked.

"We do not know."

"But you remember before," Carter thought as he showed them the vision of the aliens' former home they'd shared with him previously. It

was a place of dense woodlands where they'd spent their days flitting through the heavy trees, and sunning themselves near the streams where they found their food.

"*Yes. Yes, our planet. We want to find our planet.*"

"*You didn't always live on the Bwainhome. How did you come here?*"

This was the question he believed they had answered before, but its exact manner was what he needed.

"*First Ones came. First Ones took us.*"

"*Yes, but how?*" he persisted.

"*First Ones come again!*"

Sour, jittery fear washed through the Bwainsong. The creatures were panicking, losing the thin hold they had on the courage that Carter had been able to build for them.

"*But they never left, did they?*" Carter asked.

"*We cannot answer. We do not know. Please.*"

"*You remember everything,*" Carter insisted firmly. He shared the creatures' visits to other planets, including ancient Earth, where they had left Stone Age peoples with the concept of the endless knot that showed up in so many cultures around the globe. "*If you remember these things, then why do you remember nothing of how you came on board the ship?*"

"*We are slaves. Carter will free us. Carter will save.*"

"*When I came here, when I came on your ship, what happened?*"

"*Bwainslayer came. Bwainslayer freed us.*"

"*And who guided you before? Who told you what to do?*" Carter asked.

"*We do not know.*"

"*But you do, you do know. You were starving, and you attacked the humans. Why?*"

"*Masters will come. Masters will take us again.*"

"*Yes, they most certainly will, unless you help me,*" Carter thought. He could feel their agitation, but he pressed on.

"*No, we are not strong. We are weak. We are nothing.*"

"*You are whatever you choose to be. You make yourselves who you are,"* Carter thought. To them.

"What does Bwainslayer want? Please, tell us," the creatures begged him.

"I want to know how to fight them. I want to know how to kill them."

Suddenly, Carter felt something he'd never experienced within the Bwainsong before. It was the sensation of a great current surging against him, and the voices around him flickered.

"Where are you going? What are you doing?" Carter called to them.

"Surviving," the Bwain replied.

When Carter's eyes opened in the Knot's chamber and he sucked in a shocked breath, he suddenly realized that he was now quite alone. The Bwain had fled from his mind.

* * *

"It's evolving, Captain," Granger reported.

His voice echoed in the strange quiet of the Knot's chamber. It had been so long since he'd been away from the constant squawking and chittering of the Bwain, that Carter himself felt disoriented. Despite the fact that both Granger and Pandith had spent hours with him in the chamber, they still seemed uneasy in the Knot's cold light. At least they were finally able to communicate face to face.

"What do you mean?" Carter asked.

"This ship. It's alive, and it's evolving."

"He's right, sir," Pandith added. "You remember what the Bwain told you before? They said they were starving, and that they needed a home. Well, things have changed. The ship's feeding 'em again."

"Granger, if what you're saying is true, then..."

"Captain, I trekked across half this ship looking for a weapon. Then, all of a sudden when I really needed one and started getting emotional, one just magically appeared," Granger said.

"Our theory is that emotions modulate the Majorana particle emissions in some way. It must be how the Bwain communicate with the ship," Pandith explained.

"That's how you were able to start the interdimensional drive. It had nothing to do with anything I did to it. You just told the ship what to do," Granger said.

"And it listened," Carter said slowly, as he considered the implications of what he was hearing. Their theories were beginning to make a whole lot of sense, and they would certainly answer some of the questions that had been nagging at him.

"I think we should operate under the assumption that it's always listening, Captain," Pandith said.

Carter squinted into the Knot, studying the strange half-shapes and geometries that frothed in front of him.

"How do we know which side the ship's on?" he asked. Granger and Pandith looked at each other questioningly. "All right, you guys both had plenty of time to discuss your theories on the way here, so now I'd like to hear 'em."

As was his custom, Carter got straight to the point. His officers appreciated his forthrightness, as it was an unspoken permission to move forward with their thoughts and ideas without need for time-consuming formality. They were also able to speak their minds and present their suggestions and solutions without reservation, knowing their captain would not dismiss them offhandedly, or retaliate if they presented him with information he didn't want to hear.

"I think that our assumptions regarding what exactly the Bwain are and their relationship with the ship need to change. If the *Bwainhome* in essence *is* a First One, it's completely different from the those that came from the obelisk," Pandith said.

"The Bwain weren't allowed to push the ship into growing weaponry that would harm the First Ones. Or at least, not until we came along," Granger continued.

"But they had plenty of weapons to attack humans," Carter noted. An image of the swarm of attacking Bwain flashed through his mind, the alien ships forcing their way through The Gates, headed for the colony on Gertie.

"Yes, they did. And think about what they were trying to do," Pandith added.

Carter ran his hand across his scalp, as if somehow the reflexive motion would erase the recent attacks by the Bwain from his memory.

"They were trying to make us like them. It's what they did to Kaylee's ship...the crew of the *Ichikari*."

"They thought they were all alone. But where would that have come from?" Pandith asked, although it was apparent he felt he already knew the answer to his own question. He had clearly asked himself and Granger the same questions, and Carter could see his officer's methodical, scientific mind at work as he detailed the discoveries they had gleaned over the past several hours.

"From the First Ones?" Carter asked.

"Exactly. It was like a reflex, a muscle memory of the combined species. Millions of years ago, when they'd last existed in the physical universe, the First Ones must have been desperate to find other creatures like themselves. The only ones they ever found, the Bwain, had been barely intelligent, and the Bwain themselves never really got any smarter, or learned what they were doing."

"That's the way it is with slaves. You can't let 'em get too smart," Carter said. "So anyway, that explains a part of it, but how is the ship evolving now? Humans have been interacting with the Bwain for decades. What's making 'em change now all of a sudden?"

"Acually...we think it's you," Pandith said.

"Me?"

"You're the first non-hostile interaction the Bwain have ever had, and somehow the Knot gave you the ability to interact with their telepathy in ways that only you really understand," Granger explained.

"So you're saying that I can use this ship to fight the First Ones?" Carter asked.

"I don't know. They seem to respond to what you want. If you can stay focused, if you can let yourself go and be comfortable with that, then you may be able to control this ship," Granger said.

"All right, keep this to yourselves for now," Carter said.

"Captain, are you gonna be all right?" Pandith asked with a concerned look. "I mean, we've seen the strain you've been under with all this."

Carter studied the two officers for a brief moment. Apparently they hadn't confined their conversation to just scientific theories about the Bwain and the alien ship. Their carefully worded concern for his mental and emotional stamina and physical well-being was something that would make any captain proud of his crew.

"I'll be fine," he said stoically.

"Just...please be careful," Pandith said, and then he and Granger both snapped him a salute. Carter returned the gesture, and then watched them as they left the chamber.

Once they were gone, he turned his attention back to the Knot. He couldn't be sure, but it seemed to have shifted somewhat. The light seemed slightly more pale and wan than before, though he didn't understand what would have caused such a change.

*　*　*

For a long time after Granger and Pandith left, Carter simply sat on one of the low benches that ringed the chamber, staring at the Endless Knot. It pulsed before him like some infinitely complex anemone, waving in and out of currents he couldn't understand. The light was constant, but it wasn't giving off heat, and it was bright enough that when he looked away, it left afterimages against his retinas.

"Would you fight your own kind? Are you actually one of them?" he asked. There was no answer. The galaxy swung above him, silent and awesome.

Was that where his reluctance came from? He'd had everything in life within his grasp back on Earth, and he had let it all fall apart. There were times when he still saw Aida struggling on the rooftop, and still felt the numb fury that coursed through him after she died.

He'd sacrificed her, just like he'd sacrificed so many others. Aric, the colonists, Threed's men, Mephista's crew... How many more would have to die in order for a few of them to survive?

The time would come when he would have to make a choice. If he pushed the *Bwainhome* into something – else, something different – what would happen to the people on board? And if there was no other choice to save the rest of the fleet, would he do it? Would he leave those he cared about behind once more?

He turned at a rustling behind him. The Bwain were coming back, rippling from the black shades they used to try and hide when they were nervous, back to their shades of gray and purple. From the Bwainsong he knew that once they had been deep green and brown, mottled like the forests that were once their home. Would they remember what they had been? When the time came to fight for themselves rather than to survive as an echo of their masters, what path would they choose?

"Bwainslayer?" one of the aliens hissed. "Talk."

Carter roused from his thoughts, somewhat startled by the sudden communication.

"You want me to talk to you? Why not just..."

"Atlas, it's Elise," one of the other creatures relayed in its best imitation of Captain Mephista's voice. For the first time in a long while, he actually smiled.

"It's good to hear from you. How are you doin' back there?" Carter asked. He'd come to appreciate having someone with whom he could share his true thoughts. Someone who wouldn't judge him, or misunderstand his intentions. She was easy to talk to, and because of that, as well as for many other reasons, she held a special place in his heart.

"We're just out here following the flight plan, hoping that we don't suddenly get torn down into our component parts."

"I won't let that happen."

"Yeah, we'd appreciate that," she said. Even though he was listening to the Bwain croak its best approximation of English, he could still detect her humor.

"It's good having you with me," Carter said.

"I'm here for whatever you need," the Bwain said, flushing a deep shade of pink as it tried to convey whatever emotion it was picking up from her.

"How's the rest of the fleet?" she asked.

"Commander Decival's at the front, and Danielle's been assigned to assist him. Hopefully she'll be able to make sure that we don't run into any more surprises. I've got Danny and Julie on the *Reichstag* running as escort for the *Bwainhome*, because I figured having them centrally located would help 'em to coordinate things. Most of the SSC ships need a dry dock, but they're functional. As for the colonists, they're having a tough time adjusting to everything."

"Tell that to Threed. He's having the time of his life playing soldier at the moment," Mephista said, then waited expectantly for his reaction.

She was trying another joke, testing him to try and lighten his mood. They'd grown to care about each other, two rogue captains drawn together by the Sword Belt's events. But Carter couldn't release the knot of uncertainty in his stomach.

"I'm sorry, I know you're just trying to help," he replied after a slight pause.

"Come on Atlas, don't worry. We'll figure it out. We have up to this point anyway, haven't we?" she asked.

"So far, but I just have a bad feeling that our luck's gonna run out at some point. If you can call what we've had up to this point luck," he said wryly as he gazed up at the chamber's ceiling, studying the swirl of stars and galaxies that spun in arcane patterns. It was like a pinwheel of life and matter moving, infinitesimally across the emptiness of space.

Suddenly, the Bwain flashed a deep reddish color then faded to black. All around him, the bird creatures began flapping and squawking.

"Mephista? Mephista, what's happening?" Carter demanded as he suddenly felt the weight of their desperate situation settle heavily once more upon him.

"They're coming Atlas!" she cried. "Oh God...they're coming!"

Chapter 6

The Tranquility

Mephista hurtled through the sound of screaming klaxons to the bridge. The airlock doors opened and she burst onto the bridge, prepared to call out orders. If the First Ones were indeed coming, maybe there was some way that her battered rear guard could throw the creatures off the scent of the rest of the fleet.

For a moment, she simply floated, stunned into silence at the images she was seeing on the holoscreen.

Where before The Gates had glowed with the fading gases of long-ago nova, there was now only blackness. Blackness, and a school of amorphous white shapes growing ever larger, as if they were swimming up from the depths of the ocean toward her ship. Each undulation brought them thousands of kilometers closer in a single effort. Clusters of arms and teeth reached toward her ship like eels, hungry to consume whatever they could secure. They flickered in and out of sight, blurring at the edges, as if they were some kind of warped jellyfish.

A hideous shrieking rang out from behind her. Mephista pushed against a railing and turned, finding that the Bwain gone stark white, and were screaming in fear. As she watched, a gray trickle leaked out of the bird-lizard thing and rang down its leg. The Bwain was so scared that it had actually soiled itself. It would be useless to her now.

The First Ones were still gaining in impossible bursts of speed and distance. She had to act.

"Comms, get me the rear guard ships," she called.

There was no answer.

"Comms!" Mephista snapped.

"Yes ma'am. The rear guard. Go ahead, ma'am," her officer finally replied.

"We all know what's behind us," Mephista said. Her implant carried her orders to the three other ships that flanked the *Tranquility*. Their battered engines were all pushed to maximum, and their crews were no doubt barely holding on. Even Mephista couldn't remove the tremor from her voice. "We've been training for this. We're the fleet's rear guard, and it's our job to buy the colonists enough time to get away. Stand by for further instructions."

"I'm having trouble with the firing solution, ma'am," her weapons officer called. "The targeting computer can't seem to find those things."

"Try targeting the coordinates where the cameras are focused," Bryon suggested.

"No!" the Bwain squawked. It was cringing terribly, and shuddering with fear, but then it stilled as Atlas' control clamped down on it.

"Mephista, the First Ones feed off matter. Anything you throw at 'em will just make 'em stronger," Carter said through the Bwain.

"Then we'll have to lose 'em in the nebula," Mephista replied. "Nav, give me course solutions for..."

"Ma'am, they..."

"Spit it out! We haven't got time for hesitation now," Mephista practically shouted.

"They're eating the nebula, ma'am!" the nav officer called back.

Mephista's head jerked back to the holoscreens, and she tapped her haptics, zooming in to confirm what her ensign was telling her. There on the screen, where a green outline marked where her star charts had once marked the location of The Gates, there was only blackness behind the First Ones. When she zoomed her view further, she could see what looked like a hideous series of gaping maws on the creatures, with what was left of the nebula's gasses and particiles pouring into them.

"They're getting stronger...faster," she whispered.

Static, screaming, and conflicting orders poured through Mephista's earpiece, but she needed to think. She was in combat now; there was no time for distractions. Pushing toward her captain's chair, Mephista simultaneously tapped her haptics to bring up a computer diagram of the battle. The *Tranquility* was the second-to-last ship in the fleet, trailed only by the *Serengeti*. Mephista saw the passenger manifest floating above the ship. There were 2,500 crew and colonists on that ship, compared to her 1,800, and the *Archer's* 1,636. The bulk of the fleet was another few thousand kilometers ahead, which was no more than a few hours' difference if the First Ones maintained their current speed, but she would have something to say about that.

The Bwain was trying to cover its face with its wings, but Carter's influence kept lowering them, forcing it to remain in place as the telepathic interpreter. The creature vacillated between a deep black and gray, and when she floated nearer to it, it would not meet her gaze.

"Atlas, I'm sorry, but I have to do this," she said to it.

The Bwain's head twisted toward her, and the waddle underneath its beak shuddered as it swallowed.

"Live! Save!" the alien croaked in terror.

The creature was speaking for itself, not Atlas. They had lived longer than they would have if Atlas hadn't saved them, and so had she. Now, she felt honor and sacrifice calling her to her to do her duty once more.

"Mephista, what are you doing?" the Bwain squawked as Carter regained control. "I missed what you said. This Bwain is fighting me."

"Comms, do you copy me?" Mephista said, ignoring the Bwain in front of her.

"Yes, ma'am," the officer acknowledged.

"Record and transmit the following message to Captain Carter and the rest of the fleet: *We are aware of the First Ones pursuit. We will engage, and attempt to delay them for as long as possible. Good luck, and Godspeed.* Transmit."

"Yes, ma'am," her communications officer replied.

"Ma'am, weapons are up," Purcell reported from his weapons station. "We're at 73 percent missile capacity, laser array fully charged. Projectiles are armed and ready."

"Countermeasures?" she asked.

The weapons officer spared her a quick glance over his shoulder.

"Depleted, ma'am. But hey, on the bright side, I don't think they'd be effective anyway."

The writhing creatures bucked and rose in a wave of white fury across the bridge's holoscreens, like frenzied sharks ready to rip apart and devour anything in their path.

"The best reading I can get puts them at about two million kilometers, ma'am," her helmsman called.

"Plot an evasive course that takes us away from the fleet," the captain ordered. "And get me a count on those things if you can. Comms, open a channel to the rear guard."

"Channel open," the comms officer called back.

"This is Mephista to *Archer* and *Serengeti*. I will engage first. My plan is to draw them away from the fleet. Transmitting our nav solution to you now," she said as she tapped a holocontrol. "Good luck."

"It's not going to matter," Captain Stringer on the *Serengeti* said through her implant. "With our engine damage, we can't even run."

"We just need to give the rest of the fleet some time. That's all," Mephista responded, and then she terminated the connection. There was no need to discuss it further, because there were no other options left open to them.

* * *

The Dauntless

Danielle listened to the broadcasts from the rear guard with a sick feeling in the pit of her stomach. On her nav screen, she watched the three battered ships of the fleet's rear guard slow and turn toward the onrushing First Ones.

"What in the hell do they think they're doing?" Captain Decival exclaimed. "They have to know they can't fight those things."

"I don't think Captain Mephista is trying to fight 'em, sir. I think she's trying to delay 'em to give the rest of us some time," Danielle said.

"Sol-blast it!" Decival muttered. "Ms. Hoff, get me nav solutions if we need to break the fleet into smaller groups. At least some of us might be able to survive this. I'm gonna consult with Carter and see if we can come up with some sort of an answer."

"Yes sir," she acknowledged. Behind her, Decival rose from his station and knelt next to the Bwain that shadowed him. Part of Danielle wanted to listen in on the conversation and hear how Captain Carter would come to the fleet's rescue again, but her task right now took priority over everything else. She needed to assist her current captain to the best of her abilities, which meant finding him a solution he could use to save as many lives as possible. If they were to have any chance of survival at all, it was going to take the efforts of everyone in the fleet. She reached down to massage her aching shin above her still-forming foot, and then set about her task.

The fleet had nearly made it through The Gates. It had been close to an entire day's flight, but they were emerging onto the other side. As they did, Danielle's sensor view of the unexplored space before them widened with each passing minute.

A few billion kilometers from the fleet's vanguard was an asteroid field, no doubt the remains of what had once been a planet. If the fleet headed for the planetoids, maybe the First Ones would grow distracted and consume the asteroids. The question would be how much time that distraction would get them, and how much distance the fleet could manage to put between themselves and the destruction that was sure to follow.

She started plotting different solutions for different groups of ships, putting the fastest in one category, and the slowest in another, searching for a combination that would be capable of outrunning the First Ones. If one existed, then maybe they could transfer all the colonists to those ships, so that at least some of them could survive.

Each solution that appeared on her monitor, was dismissed in a quarter of a second. The First Ones were too fast, they'd overtake every ship except the *Bwainhome*. If they could use its dimensional drive, somehow flee the system completely...

She looked back at Captain Decival, who was murmuring to the Bwain.

Captain Carter had vowed not to lead the First Ones to Earth, but the *Bwainhome* could run anywhere else, could it not?

She turned back to her screens, studying the asteroids once more. If she led the fleet to the far end of the field, the First Ones would have to stop and slow down. They had slowed slightly to consume the nebula's gasses. Whole planetoids would no doubt take them longer.

Pulling up the best telemetry she had of the First One's passage through the nebula, she asked the computer to estimate their speed variations. It was then that she noticed something. The variations were erratic, the creatures moving side to side or speeding up and down based on no change in the gas density that her instruments could have observed. It was almost as if they were avoiding something.

Her eyes widened. She thought back to her earlier calculations of the gravitational effects on the creatures' movements. When she overlaid those results with the First Ones' speed changes, they were nearly a perfect match.

Something about gravity affected the creatures. They didn't like it. The planetoids that remained would have been ordered and sorted by gravity. She started scanning for further anomalies, extending her search across all of space that lay before her, and her pulse quickened.

Danielle spun in her chair and called out to Decival. "Captain! I think I've found a solution!"

*　*　*

The Tranquility

Mephista grasped the handrail by her captain's station as her battered ship lurched upward and outward above the predicted course of the First Ones. On her holodisplay, the *Archer* broke right, while the *Serengeti* limped away to the left of her ship's relative position.

The First Ones bore on like a wave of malignancy, leaving nothing but empty blackness in their wake.

"Evasive maneuver package alpha initiated," her navigation officer called.

"Weapons are standing by," Purcell added from his nearby station.

"Remember, they get strong by consuming matter. We can't use our weapons until the last possible instant. Only danger close," Mephista reminded her crew.

"Ma'am, with all due respect..."

"We're decoys now to protect the rest of the fleet. That's all we are," she added without emotion.

"Ma'am, the *Serengeti!*" her science officer called. Mephista spun aound to focus on the new images.

On the holoscreens, Captain Stringer's ship was trailing a mix of gas and debris.

"Depressurization?" someone asked.

"Ma'am, I have Captain Stringer on comms," a voice called.

"Put him through," Mephista ordered.

"...had a malfunction. Our induction repairs didn't hold," Stringer was saying.

The *Serengeti* had not even made it halfway to the nebula, and as Mephista watched, the First Ones veered toward it.

"Captain, you have to abandon ship!" she insisted.

"It won't matter. You know that as well as anyone," Captain Stringer said, his voice strangely calm.

"Ma'am, they're powering up their weapons!" Purcell called.

The First Ones knifed through the nebula and blackness as if they had been born to it, heading straight for the crippled ship.

"Stringer, what are you doing?" Mephista demanded.

"I show no life pods or shuttles launched," her science officer said.

"They're firing!" Purcell cried.

"*Serengeti*, cease fire!" Mephista nearly screamed. "You're going to strengthen them!" she yelled.

"Ma'am, we're receiving a message from the *Dauntless*," her comms officer called.

"The First Ones have deviated course, Captain," her nav officer called.

"How long?" Mephista asked.

"It's difficult to tell with our imprecise readings."

"I SAID HOW LONG GOD DAMN IT?" she barked.

"My best estimate is that they'll reach the *Serengeti* within forty-five seconds, Captain."

A small hand gripped her arm. Startled, Mephista snapped her head around to see the terrified Bwain kneading her uniform sleeve.

"Mephista, please...listen to Decival," the Bwain croaked.

"Jesus and everything that's holy!" Purcell yelped.

Brilliant blue laser fire streaked from the *Serengeti*'s dozen cannons toward the seething creatures. A continuous stream of magna-cannon projectiles followed, then a volley of hundreds of missiles.

When the weapons hit, the First Ones' bodies closed around the impact immediately.

"They're getting bigger," her navigation officer gasped, and it was true. Where the lasers struck a First One, the concentrated energy only bubbled on the surface and left a blister that was quickly smoothed over the creature's new, larger skin.

"Stringer, please! You have to stop!" Mephista shouted into her communications implant, but it was too late. The creatures closed the distance toward the *Serengeti* in several blinks, leaping forward so quickly that it almost seemed as though she was watching their progress in the flashes of a strobe light.

"They're firing with everything they have," Purcell said.

It was no use. The First Ones extended their sucking arms toward the ship, and for the first time since they'd first discovered the First Ones, Mephista got a sense of their true size. They were each half as large as the *Serengeti*, a large cruiser that could hold up to five-thousand people. When the First Ones seized the hull, their tentacles bulged and rippled, melting their way through the carbyne steel, as though it were nothing more than air.

"They're eating the ship!" her science officer gasped, unable to tear his eyes away from the images before him.

"Stringer, get your people out of there!" Mephista cried.

Hundreds of life pods did fire, filling the holoscreens with amber SOS icons that disappeared as quickly as they'd blossomed. The First Ones' grasping arms swept through the space around the *Serengeti*, absorbing the pods one after another.

"I'm transmitting this data to the fleet. Maybe it will help," Captain Stringer called. His voice was eerily calm. He knew that his fate, and that of the *Serengeti's* crew had already been decided. His final act reflected his desperate hope of survival for the remainder of the fleet.

"Ma'am, the First Ones have all stopped," her nav officer reported. "Should I comply with the *Dauntless'* instructions?"

On the holoscreen, the First Ones had hacked their way through two-thirds of the ship, splitting it like piano keys. A cluster of them drifted toward the ship's rear generator to feast on the radiation.

"Captain?" Mephista called into the silence, the communication channel still open.

"We never had much hope, Mephista," the captain said, his voice dull and emotionless. "I just wish..."

The transmission ended. On the holoscreen, one of the First Ones had slithered inside the ship and suddenly burst through the *Serengeti*'s bow. In a matter of moments, the ship was gone.

"Ma'am...the *Dauntless*?" her comms officer reminded her.

Mephista stared at the sickening creatures. They were like death itself, rolling through whatever remnants of Captain Stringer and his crew they could find. She was responsible for protecting the fleet. Despite the horror of the loss of so many lives, she knew that Stringer had bought the rest of the colonists, and Atlas, some valuable time.

"Mephista, what are you thinking?" the Bwain's voice asked. The small creature tugged weakly on her sleeve once more. It was terrified, but forced to talk to her through Atlas' will.

"What does Decival want?" Mephista asked the communications officer, again ignoring Carter's question through the Bwain.

"They want us to change course."

"To where?" she asked.

"Toward a gravity anomaly, a singularity six million kilometers from our position."

"They want us to steer toward a black hole?" she asked.

"Yes, ma'am."

Finished with their meal, the hellish creatures on her holoscreens stilled. They drifted here and there as if searching, then slowly swung to face her ship.

"Can we make it to the anomaly in time?" Mephista asked.

"I don't know ma'am."

She turned to the Bwain. Her reflection was just visible in the creature's glassed eyes. She had hoped she'd see Atlas' face again, but if this was the best she could manage, then it would have to do.

"I'm sorry, Atlas. I'm going to buy you more time," she whispered.

Then she turned to face her crew. Every one of them was grim, each considering the inevitable fate they were about to meet in a matter of mere moments. They knew the crippled state of disrepair of the *Tranquility*, just as she did, and they had just seen what would happen to them. Yet, despite the hopelessness of their situation, they remained at their stations, awaiting one final order from their captain. They would not give up; they would stay with her to the very end.

On the holoscreen, Mephista watched the First Ones slip toward her ship. At least she could buy Atlas more time.

"Mr. Purcell, fire everything we've got at those things," she ordered. "We're going to lead them away from the fleet."

* * *

The Bwainhome

The Bwainsong grew sick with terror. Standing in the Knot's great chamber, Captain Carter fought the creature's paralyzing visions of torture and pain as the First Ones' attack took the *Serengeti*. The Bwain he had sent to the destroyed cruiser wailed their last, and a part of Carter felt their minds as the creatures were torn apart.

A deeper part of him, that which was connected to the ship, stirred in a way he could not yet grasp. Too much was happening at once for his mind to track everything.

"They come! They come!" the Bwain screamed. *"Flee, hide, fly, live!"*

The creatures' collective will rose up, trying to initiate the dimensional drive so they could run, and leave the rest of the fleet behind. As battered as he was by their fear, Carter clamped down on them. In his mind, it felt as though he'd gripped an infinite number of squirming snakes. He gritted his teeth and pushed back the Bwain's sour fear.

"No! We can't run and leave the rest to die!" Carter urged through the Bwainsong.

"They are not us," the Bwain said.

"We are the same. We will fight," Carter reassured them.

The Bwain responded with a vision of the First Ones reaching toward the *Tranquility* as Mephista unloaded her weaponry at the things and spun away from the fleet.

"Mephista! Don't do this. I'm coming!" Carter said through the Bwain floating on the *Tranquility's* bridge.

Here the Bwain tried a new tactic, showing him visions of Earth that were constructed from his memories.

"Bwainslayer want this. Bwainslayer save us," they urged.

Carter saw Belize City's cracked streets, smelled the ocean brine in the air, felt the joy of his limbs swinging and feet pounding as he ran alongside the faded rainbow of storefronts and homes, kicking a ball, or chasing his friends. He felt the sea air on his face during his first trip on a fishing boat, the coarse line in his hands scraping his palms. He felt Aida's hands on his shoulders, running down his stomach as her lips pressed gently against his neck.

"If we don't stop them, they'll just keep coming, and they'll never stop," he said to the Bwain.

"How stop?" the Bwain asked.

With some semblance of calm restored, Carter pivoted his viewpoint to see the first of the fleet reach the gravitational distortion Danielle had discovered. Then he pushed deeper than he'd ever gone before into the mental currents that flowed through the ship and turned toward where Mephista was slipping away from him into the nebula.

He wouldn't lose anyone else – he couldn't bear it.

*   *   *

The Reichstag

Danielle was both terrified and hopeful at the same time. Three-quarters of the fleet had reached the anomaly, and Decival was passing orders to situate them in case her gamble didn't pay off. As she watched the maneuverings of the ships, the *Bwainhome* slowed and reversed itself.

"Oh, my God. Captain, look!" she said as she directed his attention to what she was seeing on her screen.

"Captain Carter, what are you doing?" Decival demanded anxiously through his Bwain.

The bridge quieted as the alien ship turned toward the First Ones.

"He's going after the *Tranquility* and the *Archer*, sir. He's gonna try to save 'em," Danielle said.

"Captain Carter, listen to me," Decival said to the Bwain huddled beside him. "You've got nearly all of our equipment and food on that ship. You're putting all of us in danger by doing this."

The alien mumbled to itself, but there was still no reply. Danielle watched the *Archer* and the *Tranquility* loop away from each other toward the nebula, leading the First Ones away from the fleet as if they were bait rather than ships carrying thousands of lives.

Danielle had plotted hundreds of courses to escape the First Ones. She knew that if it hadn't been for Mephista's actions, the fleet never would have had enough time to get to an anomaly. Then her heart rose as the *Bwainhome* hurtled toward the First Ones. Captain Carter had always known what to do. He always had a plan for how to get through even the most impossible and overwhelming situations. When they'd encountered the Bwain, she never thought a single scout ship would have been able to take on an entire fleet. When he had rescued the colonists from the SSC attack, she'd never imagined his plan could work, but Carter had earned her trust, and she would do anything for him.

Something happened then that Danielle had never seen. She sucked in a breath and held it, as if doing so could also pause the horror unfolding before her.

One of the First Ones gathered itself and shot out a glowing orb. The shimmering projectile streaked toward the *Archer*, glistening like a comet until it struck the ship at middeck. The force of the attack overrode the *Archer*'s navigation system, spinning it around its central axis until the ship's computers could compensate. When the craft came to rest, Danielle saw a gaping hole in the vessel's hull.

"Captain Vereen, status report!" Decival called.

"I don't know what that was," the *Archer*'s captain responded. We're showing a hull rupture on decks 3 through 20. Still battle worthy, continuing to execute. Wait..."

The Archer's running lights flickered, dimming to a weak halo of pale yellow. "It looks like it's draining our power. We're losing our reactors. Switching to chemical thrust," Captain Vereen reported.

The *Bwainhome* was a few thousand kilometers from the *Archer*, but the First Ones were closer. Chemical thrust was too slow to allow any kind of escape.

"Captain, I'm showing multiple life boat signatures," Danielle called.

"They're abandoning ship," Decival said to no one in particular. The captain gripped the railing around his command chair and locked his eyes on the holoscreen. "Come on, Atlas, do something."

"Is he going to fight them?" one of the bridge crew asked.

"I don't know. Jesus, I don't know!" Danielle snapped impatiently as she suddenly realized that she'd been wondering the same thing herself.

A clot of swollen First Ones reached the *Archer* simultaneously, clamping their ghost-white tendons down on the ship's hull. Where they chewed into its metal, only a deep blackness remained. Danielle could only watch helplessly as one by one, the SOS beacons faded to nothing.

"Captain Carter, whatever you're doin' out there, you gotta hurry," she whispered.

Less than a third of what had been the *Archer* remained, but the First Ones were turning toward the *Bwainhome* rather than finishing their meal.

"New signatures from the *Bwainhome*, sir. They look like the dimensional fighters," the science officer called.

"He's going to *attack* them?" Decival asked, unable to wrap his military mind around such a bold and foolhardy strategy. Was Carter a selfless hero or a battle-crazed lunatic trying to go out in a blaze of glory? Either way, Decival suddenly had an entirely new appreciation of the man. No matter the outcome, it could never be said that Atlas Carter didn't give anything less than everything he had.

Danielle felt her heart swell. It was desperate odds against a foe that none of them had ever had any success against, but if anyone could do it, it would be Captain Carter.

The First Ones turned, pushing off the *Archer's* remains as they swayed into the darkness of space like intelligent jellyfish bent on a course of savage destruction.

She squinted at her screens, trying to interpret what was happening. The fighters weren't heading toward the First Ones at all. They were doing something else instead.

"Captain, I think we need to ask our Bwain...," she began, but then a sudden round of gasps on the bridge distracted her. She snapped her head back around, and as her eyes locked onto the display, she could hardly believe that what she was seeing was real.

"Oh, my God. The *Bwainhome*...it's gone," someone murmured behind her.

* * *

The Tranquility

"I can handle this, Atlas," Mephista said to her Bwain. She had taken the creature into the airlock in order to avoid having the conversation in front of her bridge crew, and also because she didn't want them to see her break down if she had to say goodbye.

"No, you can't," the alien's voice rasped. Its coloring had changed to match the cool green and blue of the secured airlock. Pressed this close to the creature, she could smell the cedar-pine dryness of it above its strange musk. The thing was clearly terrified. Its head was darting back and forth, but she could almost feel Atlas' will forcing it to stay with her.

"None of us can," the thing hissed. "You need to get to the rest of the fleet."

"They aren't all safe yet."

"But you've done enough," the Bwain said. "I...aaaahhhh!" Suddenly the Bwain flapped its wings in terror, then bashed itself against the airlock door. Mephista grabbed its arm and felt the tense muscle and bone underneath.

"Atlas, stay with me!" she called through the Bwain.

"They're coming for the *Bwainhome*. I can't stay with you much longer," the Bwain panted.

"I can help."

"Mephista, no! That's what I'm trying to tell you. I have to do this."

"But why? Why can't you let the rest of us help?" Mephista asked as she desperately tried to fight off the panic that was threatening to consume her.

"You've done enough. Get to the anomaly!" Carter said through the Bwain, and then the creature that was floating before her suddenly slumped over and fell limp. Reaching out, she placed her hand gently against its chest. She could feel its heart beating within, but whatever was happening on the *Bwainhome* was apparently too much for the creatures to handle.

Triggering the airlock, she pushed back through and floated onto the bridge with the Bwain in tow. On the holoscreens, she could see the remains of the *Archer* listing just behind where the First Ones and the *Bwainhome* faced each other, and in the distance she could see the gravity anomaly where the rest of the fleet had gathered.

What if the anomaly didn't work? What if there was no hiding from the First Ones at all, no matter what they did?

Her spine roared with fire. Her numb, useless legs trembled underneath her. A part of her wanted the pain to be over, to simply move on into the blackness, but when the crew's eyes turned to her, she knew the orders she had to give.

"We're going to join the rest of the fleet," she announced. "Nav, get us there at full speed."

"But ma'am...what about the *Bwainhome*?" her science officer asked.

"What about it?"

"It's gone."

"Atlas, you shouldn't have done it. We weren't worth it," she thought to herself. "Was it the First Ones?"

"No, ma'am. I believe they used their dimensional drive," Bryon responded.

"We have our orders. Now, get us to the anomaly," Mephista ordered. They had all swiveled in their chairs to listen to her, and she could see the anxiety and fear they were all feeling, but she also knew that they trusted her to make the right decision, and she would do everything in her power to make sure they didn't regret their choice to stick with her to the very end.

As she floated into her captain's chair, she watched the Bwain shudder and flinch as its horrible dreams consumed it.

"Atlas, if you're going to order me to survive, then you'd better damn well do the same. I can't do this on my own," Mephista thought to herself as the *Tranquility* pushed forward to join up with the rest of the fleet.

Chapter 7

Shuttle Tiderian
The Gravity Anomaly

"Where are you taking us?" one of the colonists asked Danny Xiao. The woman was exhausted. Her face was pale and her hair hung in unwashed clumps, but her eyes burned with a desperation that was becoming all too common among the fleet.

The cockpit normally would have been sealed off from the hold, but with only a few hours until the First Ones reached the anomaly, Captain Decival had ordered every shuttle to take as many colonists as physically possible.

"We're gonna put you on board the fastest ships in the fleet. Hopefully, we won't need to run, but if we do, you'll have the best chance to survive," Danny said.

"Where did Carter go? I thought he was gonna fight those things?" someone else asked.

"I don't know. I wish I had an answer for you, but I don't right now," Danny said. That was the question the entire fleet was asking. It had been two hours since the *Bwainhome* had disappeared and the *Tranquility* had limped into the gravity anomaly's protection – or theoretical protection. The First Ones had returned to devouring the nebula and what remained of the *Archer*, but they had now consumed nearly everything, and were starting to turn toward the fleet again.

In that time, Decival had seen the writing on the wall. There was no way to fight the creatures, but at least they could save the colonists. It was what his fleet had originally arrived in the Sword Belt to do, and Danny approved of the plan. If only he knew what had happened to his captain.

For the first time, he wished he had a Bwain with him so he could at least try to get some information. According to Decival and the other captains, the aliens had all gone catatonic. The appearance of the First Ones seemed to have shattered their fragile psyches, and no one could talk to Atlas Carter at all.

"Are we going back to Earth?" the woman beside him asked.

The older part of Danny's past wanted to lie to the woman, to tell her that everything would be fine, but he had lied to himself about who he was and what he'd done for so long, that he knew now what the consequences would be.

"We can't risk leading the creatures back to Earth. That's why we're going in the opposite direction," Danny replied.

"But what good's that gonna do?" another farmer called. "This is all unexplored territory out here. How are we gonna do anything when we don't know where the hell we're goin'?"

"The plan is to keep you safe for as long as we can," Danny said.

"You're gonna get us all killed! That's what you're gonna do," someone yelled.

Danny eyed the First Ones undulating through the blackness toward the fleet's position. He had to admit it was a possibility, but Danielle's plan was the best option they had at the moment.

"Based on all available data that we have on the First Ones, the science teams believe that they won't be able to penetrate the anomaly," he explained.

"Danny, what's your status?" Julie called. She was coordinating the communications for the second evacuation, and it buoyed him to hear a familiar voice over the radio.

"ETA to the *Panther* is eight minutes. Passenger load is 220. I should be offloaded and back en route to the *Dauntless* in 15 minutes, tops," he reported as he expertly maneuvered the small craft.

"You might not have that much time," she cautioned.

His eyes widened. Julie's message had been transmitted through his cochlear implant, so the passengers hadn't heard, but he hadn't realized the First Ones were traveling so fast.

"Please advise," he said with a slight hesitation, trying to keep his voice even.

"You're ordered to stay with the *Panther*. They're going to leave as soon as the First Ones reach the anomaly."

"Understood," he acknowledged. The speed and ferocity with which the First Ones were advancing made the fleet's chances for survival even more bleak. This could be the end for them all. "Hey listen, Julie…"

"Yeah?"

"I just wanted to say that I'm sorry for who I was before."

"You don't need to apologize, Danny. We were all different people not so long ago," Julie said, a note of sadness in her voice.

"It sounds like you're sayin' goodbye," the colonist beside him commented anxiously. "What are they tellin' you?"

"That you're my last passengers. We're all staying on the *Panther* when we get there, and we're gonna try to get outta here."

"But where are we gonna go? Those things will just find us no matter where we end up!"

Danny chewed his lip. Of course the colonists were right, but as he put his shuttle into final approach toward the *Panther*'s cargo bay, he couldn't look away from the First Ones.

They were coming toward Decival's picket line impossibly fast, growing larger and larger before him until they nearly filled his view screen. The plan was for different ships to peel off and serve as decoys, cycling through different weapons to try and find a combination that worked, while the ships carrying the colonists sprinted away in different directions.

No one knew if it would work, and yet they all knew that they had to try. There were no other options.

The First Ones came gibbering and howling through the dark, faster and faster as if they could somehow smell the matter before them. They were ravenous banshees, the hungry gui ghosts from stories his mother used to tell him before she'd been consumed by the Bwain herself, and Danny fully expected them to consume the fleet, just as they had the *Serengeti* and the *Archer*.

Just as the First Ones reached the border of the gravity anomaly, a massive black shape appeared in front of them. Danny's shoulders stiffened with alertness, then he felt the anxiety in his stomach begin to ease.

"What is that?" the colonist next to him cried.

"It's Captain Carter! He's come back!" Danny exclaimed.

"This is Captain Decival to all fleet ships," Danny heard in his implant. "Apparently Lieutenant Hoff was correct about the First Ones' aversion to gravity. They're unable to enter the anomaly, so maintain your positions and await further orders."

"What are they saying to you?" a woman cried as she grasped his arm.

"It worked!" Danny shouted. He reached over and squeezed the woman beside him into a happy embrace. "They can't get through. We're all gonna be safe here!"

As word spread to passengers seated farther away, a wave of cheers and cries of relief washed over them all. Danny could not suppress a grin as the shuttle settled into the docking station. Even though they were all still in critical danger, for this brief moment at least, they'd found a small flicker of hope that they so desperately needed.

*   *   *

The obelisk

The First Ones were desperate to feed. As Aric Keith's enslaved body shambled through the wreckage of the *Fate's Winds*, he wondered what drove their hunger. His frozen fingers worked at the ship's reactor, feeding its radiation to the obelisk so that the portal could allow more and more of the First Ones to enter into the physical dimension. His tongue and jaw were frozen shut, and knives of pain struck him whenever he slowed in his duties for even the briefest moment. The obelisk and the First Ones were his only light now that the Sword Belt had been consumed, but the creatures could still not control his mind. It was all that remained to remind him that he was once human, and it was the only asset he had in his fight to free himself.

The First Ones were a collective, much in the same way that the Bwain were. Thoughts and memories were not unique to individuals. They had existed in such a state for countless eons, with all the parts of the collective making up the larger whole. They were bound to each other through their interdimensional fabric, so when one of them strengthened, they all did. He had the sense that they hadn't always been this way, that at some point they had been individuals, but The Ancient had changed all that.

Their leader's form, if it could be called that, pulsed like a misshapen heart at the center of thousands of threads spread throughout the system. A flickering cord joined its bulbous body near where its navel would have been, tying it to the obelisk, which was still open, but was slowly closing. Once the First Ones had consumed enough matter in this dimension, they would be able to sustain themselves permanently, and when the last of the hideous scavengers managed to ooze through the interdimensional port made possible by the obelisk, they would be absolutely unstoppable. That is, unless Aric could do something to help Carter and the others. Something more than than the feeble message he'd managed to send to Capra Falconi in any case.

When the First Ones had consumed the first human ship, Aric almost missed the momentary slackening of their maddening hunger. The electric burning that arced across his skin dimmed for the briefest of moments as he adjusted the reactor's venting, and a strange quietness came over him. For the first time in days, since The Ancient's last punishment, he regained enough freedom of movement to turn his head and glance at where the lesser First Ones circled their master, begging for permission to consume the scraps of matter that lay farther and farther from the portal.

"ARIC KEITH, WE WILL CONSUME YOUR CARTER," The Ancient roared.

He felt the creatures sink their talons into the second ship, drawing its molecular essence into themselves, taking the massive energies from the ship's weapons as they grew and expanded in the blackness of space. The feeling that flowed from The Ancient wasn't the satiety one feels after a full meal, or a quenched thirst. It was something different...more primal in nature. Aric thudded toward a malfunctioning fuel conduit, tools gripped in his numb hands. As he knelt to execute his task, he felt a cooling relief flood him.

It was desperation that drove the creatures' hunger, but why? What more could they possibly need?

"YOU WILL WATCH, ARIC KEITH, AS WE TAKE YOUR FOOLISH

HOPE FROM YOU."

His mind's eye filled with a blurred image of the *Bwainhome* streaking toward the First Ones. Their tentacles lashed out toward the ship, but they seemed to have no effect on the massive alien craft. He thought that Carter's intention was to fight the First Ones, and he felt an indignant reaction ripple through their consciousness. This slave craft should not have been able to resist them, and yet it somehow held them back while its fighters rescues as many of the human escape pods as possible.

"WHAT IS IT DOING?" The Ancient roared.

"He's outsmarting you. I told you he would beat you," Aric replied.

Just as the gloating thoughts were transmitted, the *Bwainhome* suddenly disappeared.

"No! It can't be!" Aric thought.

The Ancient fell silent. No boastful taunts struck him, which he took to mean that the First Ones didn't know what had happened either. It was only a matter of time until they returned to their feeding. They sensed matter like a dog locked onto a scent, and once they devoured the last of the second ship, they turned toward the bulk of the fleet.

Aric's view through the creatures' eyes had always been blurry, but when they focused on the remaining human ships, he felt a strange headache fill him. Something painful to the creatures was almost blocking their senses.

The Ancient's bellow urged the creatures forward. Around the obelisk, another flock of them peeled away and headed in the direction of where the nebula had once been. Aric had seen a clue. Somehow, whatever Captain Carter or the fleet had done, had worried the First Ones considerably, and for the very first time, he felt a sense of doubt rippling through them.

As they streaked toward the last ship in the fleet that was just entering the haze before them, their trepidation grew.

The sensation of them breaking across the blurred area of space was like the slamming shut of his jaw, the bloodying of a nose. Howling and screaming, the creatures lashed themselves against the barrier before them, desperate to reach the ships within. And yet, they were powerless to push through.

Aric sagged to the deck as the unnatural motive force left him. The entire First One's consciousness had turned to the problem of reaching the human fleet and feeding on the energy concentrations they found there. Freed from his pain at last, Aric finally had time to think.

Somehow the refugee fleet had found a way to shield itself from the First Ones. The aliens had been able to consume even an entire star, so what could have stopped them? Outside The Gates was unexplored territory. He tried to remember back to his astronavigation studies. but he had never focused on that sector of space.

"MUST GET INSIDE! MUST PUSH BACK AGAINST THE PRESSURE, " The Ancient bellowed.

The pressure? Was that it?

Suddenly, the First Ones' hunger made sense. They were no longer of the three-dimensional world. They had been born, in effect, through the obelisk, and while they could consume all matter in the universe, the physical laws of existence were not consumable. It took them effort to survive and move in this environment, and the strongest force in existence was gravity.

The First Ones had to feed continually, or be crushed by the gravitational forces that pushed back against their very existence. That was their weakness, the way they could be defeated.

Dimly, Aric felt the flesh of his cheeks crack and splinter from his reflexive smile. He had learned how the First Ones could be beaten, but now he had no way to communicate this after The Ancient had forced him to destroy the radio.

Despair took him. He sagged on the deck, lamenting his condition. He was at the heart of an incredible threat to the universe's existence with the key to the First One's destruction, and he had no means to tell anyone.

If he would still have been human, he would have wept. With the little motive power that had been returned to him, he started beating the wrench against the deck. Of course there was no sound, with no air to carry it, but the feeling alone was enough to soothe his anger.

It was a long time until he realized that another voice was calling to him.

"*Aric...,*" the voice said through his thoughts. "*Aric, can you hear me?*"

* * *

The Bwainhome

"Well that's a hell of a thing," Hal Yellowknife said. His voice would have echoed in the massive hold when he'd first arrived on the *Bwainhome*, but now that his nanofactories were set up and running, the low hum of their welds and fusings filled the gargantuan chamber.

He had the vague impression that something had been happening outside of the hold where he'd been working, but he hadn't paid it much attention. His charge was to figure out a way to support and supply the fleet if they had to spend an extended amount of time in space, and he was hard at work trying to figure out exactly how to do that without a steady supply of resources.

He had set the Bwain Carter had given him to collecting the ship's waste and manufacturing what he could from it. A constant stream of the creatures had been lugging all manner of garbage and detritus from all corners of the ship into the cordoned off area where he had programmed his nanobots to receive the waste. The Bwain had been living on the ship for thousands of years, and they brought all manner of strange components, bedding and feathers that could have been the bodies of their ancestors, mysterious chunks of metal, miles and miles of wiring and many other components that he couldn't even begin to comprehend.

"Yes, waste," they'd hiss as they scurried forward and tossed the garbage into the nanopit. The creatures seemed to enjoy watching it slowly dissolve as the nanobots reduced the components to individual molecules and transported them across the purple hull. The nanobots then marched the materials to the ten factories his apprentices had set up so far. It had been hard work, but Hal's team had finally begun producing components for the human ships. They'd managed to produce some carbyne steel, and he had a crude holopanel for Captain Carter on the bridge. Next, he planned to work on a water recycler for Pandith's environmental engineering project, and more Majorana probes for Granger.

Hal felt alive and worth something for the first time since before he'd started drinking back on Earth. He was building a legacy for generations, and that was a good feeling, or it was anyway, until all around him the Bwain suddenly collapsed and turned into a bunch of gibbering idiots.

A few seconds later, his apprentice Kilver came running over with a concerned look on his face. The beefy teenager pulled up beside him, holding what looked for all the world like a stalk of gray seaweed. Kilver had been orphaned in the farmer's uprising against Tannin on Gertie, and he'd become Hal's most trusted apprentice. He was so focused on what he wanted to show Hal that he hadn't even noticed the Bwain.

"This is exactly what happened on Gertie when the obelisk first opened," Kilver said as he handed over the strange assembly. Hal rubbed the faux leaves between his finger and thumb. They had a waxy consistency, and felt strangely cool in his hand.

"No, those weren't fully formed shapes," Hal said. On Gertie, the First Ones had tried to take control of his factories, and had incorporated elements unknown to humanity into the strange experiments that had superseded Hal's programs. "These are something else."

"It almost looks like pieces of something," Kilver said.

"Agreed, but we've got bigger issues right now. Take a look..."

"What do you...oh! What the hell happened to them?"

The Bwain were rolling around on the floor, their coloration striating between the purples and pinks of the chamber, and a dull, gray-black color. They seemed to be locked in the throes of a shared nightmare.

"I have no idea, but I think we need to find the captain. Come on," Hal said.

The pair headed toward the distant entryway that would lead up to the center of the ship. The *Bwainhome* was massive, and he sighed at having to make the kilometer trek upward, but at least he was keeping his wind up and losing his gut.

"Do you think the captain's all right?" Kilver asked.

"That's what we're gonna find out," Hal said, but then suddenly he stopped short as a panting Granger stumbled into the chamber. Squinting, the science officer called out to them.

"Hal! I need you to…hey, how did you get that?" he asked. Hal looked down at the rope-like object he still held in his hand.

"I dunno. I think it was a malfunction in one of the printing stations. What's goin' on with our feathered friends?" he asked.

"There's too much to explain right now. You need to come with me," Granger replied as he motioned for them to hurry.

"Why? What's goin' on?" Kilver asked eagerly as he puffed along up the ascending corridor with the others.

"We've figured out how to fight 'em," Granger said as his legs propelled him effortlessly upwards.

* * *

The Gravity Anomaly
Shuttle en route to the Dauntless

"That's all they've been doing for the last twenty-four hours, Captain," Danny said. The supply officer was piloting his shuttle toward Captain Decival's ship for a strategy meeting, and Captain Carter was studying both the holoscreen and the First Ones' glimmering shapes a few hundred thousand kilometers outside of his fleet's perimeter.

Their mercurial shapes bulged and seethed against gravity's invisible barrier. The First Ones had formed a furious, shifting sphere of tentacles and gnashing mouths. They were so much larger now, three-quarters the size of most of his ships. Seeing them like this terrified Pandith, and he worried about how the captain's plan was going to affect morale among the colonists and officers.

"So they can't push through gravity?" Hal asked from behind Danny.

"We need to do more analysis, but Lieutenant Hoff's theory that they were avoiding gravity anomalies was dead on the mark," Granger noted.

"She saved the fleet," Captain Carter added.

"Sir, with all due respect, *you* saved the fleet by taking the *Bwainhome* toward the first ones," Pandith added. "You bought them the time they needed to get to the anomaly, and you helped all those people in the life pods."

The environmental engineer was worried about Captain Carter. Ever since the strange lapse in the Bwain's consciousness and the encounter with the First Ones, the captain had seemed more distant. In fact, he seemed downright exhausted. A gray frost had settled over his temples, and he was constantly thumbing at the corners of his eyes. The proud, strong man he had been when he first boarded the *Fates' Winds* now looked battered and stressed. It had been Pandith's job to look after the psychological well-being of his crew, and what he was seeing in Carter disturbed him. There was an anger to him, mixed with a certain level of hope and despair that seemed to put him in constant conflict.

"Captain, when was the last time that you slept?" Pandith asked using his soft-spoken voice a beacon of calm to anchor the captain as he pulled himself away from the collective thought of the Bwainsong.

"Oh, I dunno. It was probably at some point before I was stupid enough to stick my hand in the Endless Knot," Carter said with a wry grin playing at the corners of his mouth.

"Sir, if you wouldn't mind my asking, what exactly happened to the Bwain?" Danny asked.

"They tried to make me run away. They were scared of the First Ones, so I took control of 'em the same way that they tried to take control of Kaylee and her ship."

"You put 'em into a coma? What would you have done if that didn't work?" Hal asked, surprised by the captain's admission.

"I would have killed 'em," Carter said without even the slightest bit of hesitation.

Pandith studied the faces around him in the shuttle. Hal and Kilver both seemed rather startled to hear for the first time just how brutal the captain could be. Something seemed to be weighing on him, but he needed to wait for a private moment to speak with him about it.

"Captain, what about the *Bwainhome* itself?" Granger asked.

Atlas studied Granger's face for a moment, and tensed a bit.

"The *Bwainhome* can resist the First Ones, but it can't attack them. There's some kind of barrier there that's preventing it."

"Can it evolve?" Pandith asked.

"It might, but I'd have to go along with it," Carter said after a slight pause. Pandith wondered if the captain really wasn't sure, or if he was deliberately being vague and holding back whatever he had discovered.

"We're coming up on the *Dauntless*. Docking in five minutes," Danny reported.

"I need to ask you all something," Carter said as he glanced around at them all. "If there comes a time where we need to either sacrifice ourselves or someone else, are you going to support whatever decision I have to make?"

Pandith glanced at Granger as the science officer frowned for a moment, and then nodded.

"I think we've all shown that already," he responded.

"So did Mephista...and Aric," Danny added solemnly.

"And how many more?" Carter whispered. The *Dauntless'* shadow fell over them, and Pandith struggled with the chill as the light from the nearest stars was suddenly hidden.

"Captain, do you think we've got a chance? I mean, Hal and Granger are figuring out the weapons, but maybe Danielle can plot us a course to safety. There are lots of these anomalies out here, we could maybe hopscotch from one to the next...," Danny commented, but then his voice trailed off as he was reminded they had considered every possible solution, and still had nothing even close to a solid plan.

"It's possible we could sustain ourselves, Captain. I've been doing some calculations in my spare time," Hal offered, trying to sound positive, though he had his doubts about their survival without new resources.

"The alternative is that we aren't ever able to leave this space," Carter announced as he rested his elbows on his knees, then leaned his forehead into the palms of his hands. The others glanced at each other in stunned silence, as if mutely agreeing the captain was entitled to a least a few moments of respite before they all had to muster enough energy to keep on going. All too soon, the shuttle settled into the docking bay aboard the *Dauntless*, and the silence gave way once more to the urgency of determining the next step in their desperate struggle to survive.

* * *

The Dauntless

For Carter, being on a human ship once more felt strangely disorienting. It was as if each step brought him back to a part of himself that was no longer the same. He had grown used to the constant mental chittering from the Bwainsong at the back of his mind, but he had felt something shift in both the aliens and himself when he'd given them the ultimatum to either stop fighting him or die. There were few other alternatives, and he was a harder man now than he had ever been.

There was an anger in him now, and even when he was separated from the Endless Knot he felt like that anger was steadily consuming him. It was the same emotion he'd felt above Belize City so long ago, but this time around, he wouldn't let it control him.

A group of marines had met him in the shuttle bay and were escorting him and the rest of his human crew to the bridge. He could have had the conversation he was about to have through the Bwain now that he'd roused them back to consciousness, but he felt like he needed to reconnect with humanity. The truth was that he'd gone too far into the Knot, and he was worried that he was changing. He was worried that the path he saw open, the one that Aric had confirmed, would sacrifice them all to save the fleet.

They paused outside the airlock that led to the *Dauntless'* bridge, and then cycled through into a large room nearly twenty meters wide that was studded with tactical stations. Decival stood at the captain's rise, a hump that let him look down on any station, and gave him a clear view of the main holos. Behind him, Carter could see the First Ones writhing and skittering with the same nightmarish jerks that he had felt when they had lashed out against the *Bwainhome.* The Bwain who had been assigned to the *Dauntless* rushed toward Carter, clutching at his legs and making a guttural purr to try and curry his favor. They had seen what could happen when he grew truly angry and were more afraid of him now than ever before.

"Captain on deck!" a familiar voice called.

Decival's bridge crew stiffened to attention, and Carter paused for a moment to study them. The glimmering light from the large holoscreens flickered and twitches across their faces. Most of them were crews and captains he didn't know, and to a man, they seemed too young...too idealistic for what he was about to tell them. He hated himself for the disappointment and shock that he was about to deliver, but he had no other choice.

"If I need to leave you all, how will you feel? How will you react?" he wondered to himself.

Mephista sat on her hoverchair before him, along with Ensign Julie Ford and Lieutenant Bryon Purcell. Decival and his thirty remaining captains held a tight salute, while even the Bwain tried to stiffen and puff out their thin chests.

A part of him was so proud of them, and he wanted to appear strong in their presence, and yet he felt himself withdrawing from them at the same time.

"At ease," Carter said. As the men and women on the bridge fell into alert attention, he continued on with what he wanted to say. "Now, my first order of business is to thank Lieutenant Danielle Hoff for her quick thinking and research into the anomaly. Without your brilliant analysis, things would have gone much worse for all of us."

Danielle flashed him an exhausted smile. She still wore a re-gen cast on her ankle, and she winced in pain as she snapped another salute.

"Thank you, sir. It means a lot to me," Danielle said.

"And thanks go to Captain Decival as well, but I'd rather spend the time commemorating the crews of the *Serengeti* and the *Archer* for their actions. They, along with the help of Captain Mephista, made our escape possible," he said. Mephista couldn't help but to look away as he spoke. Heads nodded before him, but she refused to return his gaze.

"And, Captain Carter...if I may say so myself, you displayed extreme courage in executing your rescue mission. Many more lives would have been lost if not for your actions. I still hate the fact that I was forced to surrender to you, but it's been a pleasure serving with you," Decival added as he strode down toward Carter and shook his hand.

"Thank you, Captain," Carter replied. There was something familiar and comforting about the ages-old tradition of military formality, and yet it all seemed so surreal given the reason for their meeting in the first place.

"I asked you all to come in person because we're facing a threat that's unlike anything we've experienced before. Because of that, I want to give you all permission to speak freely. This might be the last...well, let's just say that we might find it difficult to meet again like this in the coming days."

Brows furrowed in front of him, and he could see the nervousness in some of the younger officers especially.

"What do you mean, Atlas?" Mephista asked. Her voice was taut with emotion, and radiating the same closed-off hostility she had when he'd first met her. She had chosen not to address him as "Captain," but that he would deal with later.

Carter's eyes wandered toward where the First Ones battered themselves against the anomaly. He watched for a moment as the creatures' edges smudged and lost focus, then snapped into clear view once more.

"We've been fortunate to encounter this anomaly, and it's given us a clue to how we can resist them. On the *Bwainhome*, we've found another," Carter said.

Hal stepped forward, showing the strange vine-like object that his factories had produced.

"What's that?" one of the captains asked.

"That is a weapon that we can use to fight the First Ones," Carter said.

Smiles broke across the group before him. He hated to have to do this, but it was important to give them all at least some semblance of hope. "The *Bwainhome* isn't a ship. It's a living creature, and it's evolving."

"Evolving?" Decival asked.

"Yes. Just like any organism would respond to a threat and environmental stimulus, the ship is evolving defense mechanisms," Granger explained.

"It *made* that thing?" Hal asked. I thought it was just some sort of a malfunction. I know I sure as heck didn't program it."

"Not only that, but it's making other weapons throughout the ship," Pandith added.

"We haven't tested them yet, but while we're safe here we'd like to arrange a resupply and retrofit for the fleet," Carter said, and then he paused to study their reaction.

"How many of these weapons do you have?" Mephista asked.

For a moment, Carter wondered if he was that transparent to her. He was trying not to show the fear he felt over what Aric had told him about the hundreds of First Ones that had emerged from the obelisk.

"A few dozen or so, but we can make more," Hal answered.

"And we think we can harvest some from the *Bwainhome*," Pandith noted.

"They have to be fired by a Bwain. There's some kind of safety mechanism, I guess you'd call it," Granger added.

"So the plan is to put these on our ships?" Julie asked.

"Once they're properly tested, that's exactly what we're gonna do," Carter said.

"So we'll fight our way through the First Ones, and then what? We go skipping happily ever after through space?" Mephista asked, her voice taking on a bitter edge.

"That's the other thing this group needs to decide. Gravity is still one of the most poorly understood of the forces that govern the universe. We can see that it clearly affects the First Ones, but we don't know how, or for how long," Carter said to the group, ignoring her remarks.

"The fleet's science teams have been working overtime, Captain. We're trying to find more anomalies, and plot a course to each of them." Decival informed him.

"That's a good start," Carter said.

"And who's to say they won't catch us before we get there? My ship is the slowest in the fleet. It's why we were...," Mephista said, but then she stopped abruptly. Carter glanced briefly in her direction, and he noticed the muscles in her jaw working as she clenched her teeth and struggled with an inner turmoil that he was all too familiar with.

"We'll take the next few days to make repairs, ma'am. We'll get the propulsion units all fixed up, and leave at full thrust," Danny assured her. He hoped his voice didn't reveal his uncertainty about their chances for success.

"What comes after the anomalies?" Danielle asked. "How are we getting home?"

"I'm sorry Danielle, but I don't know if we can," Carter said.

Many of the captains must have come to the same conclusion. They had been the ones who had vented their antimatter and disabled their Alcubierre drives after all, but Decival had clearly been thinking ahead.

"Sir, our duty is to protect the colonists. What about the dimensional drive on the *Bwainhome*? The ship is so large that you could take all of them back to Earth."

Carter sighed. This was exactly what he'd been afraid of.

"You could take us all to Earth, couldn't you, sir? The antimatter wouldn't matter at all. You could just *think* it, couldn't you?" Danielle asked. He could see a confidence in her that had been in short supply back when he'd first met her.

"We've been leading these monsters *away* from Earth. We all made the decision to sacrifice ourselves for the good of our race. It wasn't easy, but that's what we did. And now...," he said, trailing off as he studied their faces for a moment. "Well, Granger, go ahead..."

"Lieutenant Purcell asked why we didn't fight the creatures. If Lieutenant Hoff is correct, gravity may be our only chance. There is an alternative to the Alcubierre drive that's currently being tested. It's a gravity drive. It works by distorting gravity and pulling itself along."

"Unfortunately, it's currently back home, in orbit around the moon," Carter finished for him.

"So the only thing that might be able to fight these things is useless to us. We'd never get there."

"I still don't understand," Decival interrupted. "Why not just use the dimensional drive?"

"We're at war with the SSC, remember? If the *Bwainhome* shows up in Earth space, they won't think twice about blowing us out of the sky," Carter said solemnly.

The bridge was silent as the reality sank in.

"Does that mean that you're going alone?" Julie asked.

"It's the only way I can guarantee your survival," Carter said.

"With all due respect Captain, with us on the ship broadcasting, they'd have to believe us," Decival stated.

"Would they? Did you believe Captain Agricourt after he returned to Earth? With the lies that Phuri's telling, and that Nico believes, it's a miracle that they haven't sent another fleet already," Carter said flatly.

"It's only because Nico has so many messengers crisscrossing space. He's probably rebuilding the antimatter stockpiles," Decival said.

"I've asked you all for a lot, but now I'm asking you for the hardest thing of all. I'm asking you for your trust, and your patience," Carter said, and then he paused for a moment to allow them time to think about what they'd just heard. This was a lot for them to take in; they needed time to process the reality and to react to it. He wanted to make sure they all had an opportunity to ask the questions he was sure they would have.

"And what'll you do after you've returned to Earth?" Mephista asked. She'd tilted her hoverchair so that she was facing the holomonitors, because she just couldn't bear to look him in the eye at the moment.

"I'd like to take a few of the fleet's shuttlecraft. My plan is to distract Sol's defenses with the *Bwainhome* while the shuttles sneak in and steal the gravity drive. As soon as they secure it, we'll return here for you."

"And then what?" Danielle asked.

"We finish off the First Ones for good, and then we go home," Carter said.

The captains and gathered officers stared at each other for a moment. No one was really sure how to feel about Carter's plan, but it was the only plan on the table at the moment that gave them at least some semblance of a chance of getting home.

"Captain, what if the gravity drive doesn't work?" Bryon asked.

"I'll be bringing back antimatter for the fleet as well, so if the gravity drive thing doesn't work out, then you can all leave while I stay behind to fight them."

"With all due respect, Captain...," Julie started to say, but he cut her off in mid-sentence.

"Those are my orders," Carter said.

"We're all captains here ya know," Mephista commented over her shoulder.

"What's that supposed to mean?" he asked.

"It means we put it to a vote."

"This isn't a democracy," Carter replied.

"Carter, you're about to leave with the only protection we've got from those things. I think she has a valid point," Decival added. Carter felt his anger rising, but these were the people who counted on him…who looked up to him. He owed them at least some say when their lives were at stake.

"Very well," he said with a calmness he didn't feel. "How many of you are comfortable with the plan as I described?"

A smattering of hands rose. Less than a third, led by Granger, Purcell, and Danielle.

"And how many of you would like to explore alternatives?" Carter asked.

Slowly, then with more force, hands rose all around him. Mephista's shot up first, then Danny Xiao's, Julie's, and many of the captains of the more damaged ships. Decival's hand rose last. The man was punctilious in all things.

"I'm sorry, Captain, but it seems that we need time to think of alternatives," Decival said.

"You won't find them," Carter replied.

"But you'd be leaving us to die!" one of the other captains objected, and several others nodded in agreement.

"No, I'd be coming back for you," Carter corrected. Decival stared at him hard for a moment before he responded.

"You know, you've proven your bravery out here more times over than I can count. Just yesterday you put yourself in harm's way to save the crew of one of my ships, but with all due respect, *sir*, you can't use us as bait. It's just too much to ask right now."

* * *

When Atlas found Mephista after the meeting, she was in a small observation lounge two decks below the bridge. She'd positioned her hoverchair so that she was facing the porthole, and she was quietly staring out into the darkness of space. It must have taken her some time to find the only view on the ship that didn't show the First Ones or the fleet.

"You know this is the only chance that any of us have to survive. Why were you so vocal against it?" he asked from the doorway.

"I can't believe you'd propose something like that," Mephista replied.

"Because it's the only way, Elise. You know that."

"And so you expect the rest of us to just sit around here and wait for you so you can run off and play the hero? You'd abandon the rest of us," she retorted acidly.

"Like you did when you tried to fight the First Ones?" he countered.

"I did the only thing I could. I didn't turn away. I wasn't scared."

"Is that what you think I'm doing?" Carter asked.

"Yes. I know what you did back on Earth. I know how you ran here. And now you're trying to do the same thing again. You're leaving us all, because you're afraid, Atlas. Because it's easier to be alone than face all of our expectations."

"I'm not the one who's so desperate to get killed that I put the entire fleet at risk! You tried to fight them, Mephista. You made them stronger! What were you thinking?" Carter said accusingly.

"I command my own ship, *Captain*. Don't think you suddenly outrank me," Mephista said, her voice trembling with anger.

"I am in charge of this entire fleet, *Captain*," Carter said. His voice was rising. He could feel the anger coursing through him that he had restrained for so long. The feeling that he was powerless, and was simply delaying the inevitable. It was the same feeling that had trapped him in Belize, and had sent him to the Sword Belt in the first place.

"Then you should start thinking like that. I deployed my ships in order to buy you time. That was the plan. That's what a rear guard does. But how many of the rest of us do you want to lose?" Mephista demanded.

"Is that what you think? You think I want to lose you?" he asked, narrowing his eyes at her in disbelief.

"I've watched a lot of people die who depended on me to keep them alive, Atlas. It would be nice to not have to see their faces when I close my eyes," she said as she turned to face him and folded her arms across her chest. Whether in defiance, or just simple defensiveness, it was hard to tell.

"That's why you have to give me this chance. Those men and women, the ones on the *Serengeti* and the *Archer* will have all died for nothing if he don't fight back," Carter argued.

"But you want to leave us here as bait."

He walked over to join her, and saw the porthole's reflection glistening in her eyes for just a moment before she turned away from him once again.

"You know that I have to go with the *Bwainhome*."

"I was ready, Atlas. If I had to go down, I was going to do it. Not just for you, but for everyone else as well. Now you're saying we have weapons to fight 'em, but..."

"Weapons that we need to test," he said, not wanting to foster any false expectations about their effectiveness.

"And the only thing that's given us any semblance of hope, the *Bwainhome*...you wanna just run off with it while you leave us back here to duke it out with those things using weapons that we don't even know will work against 'em."

"Is that what this is about? You were willing to sacrifice yourself, but you're not willing to let me go, even if it means condemning the whole fleet and the lives of everyone in it?" Carter asked.

"I was more than willing to sacrifice myself and my crew for the rest of the fleet!" she yelled, but then she fell silent for a moment as she raised a shaking hand to wipe away the wetness in her eyes. "Maybe it would have been better in the long run. But you ordered me back to the fleet, and I followed your orders."

"I would have done the same for any ship."

"Listen to me...I can't lose you, Atlas. There's no one else who understands."

"Elise, we have to stop these things, and you know that I'm the only one that can do this."

"You know, I've gone rogue before. I'm not even remotely worried about a court martial."

"But what about your crew? What about those men and women who are depending on you?" Carter asked. The anger that seethed within him was threatening to bubble up to the surface, but he was doing his best to prevent that from happening.

"They've died depending on me, and they'll keep on dying. I just want it to stop," Mephista nearly shouted as she turned to face him. The amount of pain and agony she saw in his eyes sent a sudden wave of regret washing through her. He'd seen those very same things, and if anyone understood what she was feeling, it was him.

She took a deep breath and expelled it slowly, as if purging the emotions from her body.

"I just want it to stop," she repeated in what barely amounted to a whisper.

She turned her hoverchair toward the doorway and banged out into the corridor.

"Mephista...Elise, please...," Carter called after her.

"What if you're wrong, Atlas?" she asked over her shoulder. "Have you ever thought of that?"

"Every single minute," he murmured as she floated off down the corridor.

Chapter 8

Shuttle Tiderian

"Do you know what these things look like?" Danny asked as he stood in the shuttle bay of the *Bwainhome* examining one of the weapons that Hal's machines had produced. The two-meter-long tube looked like a thick cluster of vines wrapped around a pair of hollow shafts. The vines twisted and pulsed in time to a light that flared at the swollen tip of the weapon. Its cold, glassy material weighed next to nothing, and the weapon itself seemed both incredibly fragile and impossibly dense at the same time. It had the vague appearance of a bioengineered shotgun in reverse, or what Bryon Purcell would call a *schnoz*.

"It's better if you don't think about it," Hal answered. The engineer lifted the device out of Danny's grasp and handed it to the Bwain that fluttered around him. The creatures had recovered from their loss of consciousness, and now seemed to have returned to normal...more or less. The alien that took the weapon from Hal and handed it to one of the other creatures that was flapping overhead. That Bwain took the weapon in its talons and rested the construction on the nose of Danny's shuttle. Then, as Danny watched, the weapon's base flashed and fused to the carbyne steel.

"How does it know what to do?" Threed asked from beside Danny.

"Probably better not to think about that either," Hal suggested with a slight smile. "According to the captain, the *Bwainhome* is a living thing. It's evolving, and the weapons it's producing for us are intelligent in some way."

Danny thought back to when he was aboard the *Fate's Winds* and saw the bulging monstrosity that was the *Bwainhome's* hull for the first time. He had assumed that the creatures had been scavengers, collecting pieces of whatever ships they had conquered to add on to their ship. As it turned out, the *Bwainhome* had simply been protecting its passengers by evolving weapons for them to fight humanity.

The more he thought about it, the more he realized Hal was right. It was enough to know that Carter was in communication with the ship itself. The implication that the ship could read and react to their thoughts was more alien than anything the Bwain had done.

"So how are they supposed to work?" Threed asked.

"You'll need to have a Bwain with you. The creatures need to be close to the thing. Then just tell the Bwain that you want to use the weapon. Carter will be able to hear you and arrange it through the Bwainsong," Hal explained.

Threed glanced at Hal for a moment, and then he shot a look over at Danny. His shaved head was finally growing in hair again, but the scars on his face had grown more prominent as his tan had faded.

"So, that's it? We're just supposed to *think* at the bastards that ate my home planet, and hope by some miracle that this thingamabob works?"

"I didn't know you'd grown so fond of Judgment," Danny commented.

"Now, that's true enough," Threed said with a wry grin as he watched two of the Bwain step into the shuttle. He wore a rough-made combat EVO suit that was a pale but functional imitation of the more evolved suit Danny had on, and he looked almost heroic with his helmet clutched at his hip.

"Has Captain Carter ever been wrong before?" Danny asked. Threed gave him a serious look, and then slipped on his helmet as Danny did the same.

"Not so far, but I don't wanna be there to see what happens if he ever is," Threed said over the suit's intercom.

* * *

"Danny, you don't have to do this," Julie's voice whispered in his cochlear implant. He'd turned the volume far down so he wouldn't be distracted by anything that came from the fleet.

"You know I have to. I don't have any choice. None of us do," he said.

The edge of the gravity anomaly pulsed in a green line on his holoscreens as Danny piloted the shuttle away from the fleet. In front of him, the First Ones plastered themselves against the invisible barrier like so many octopi pressing themselves against the plexiglass walls of an aquarium.

"Just...please be careful out there."

"You know me, I'm a sucker for the calm, quiet life," he said with a breathy laugh. It was the first time he could remember joking about anything in a long time. In spite of the odds, and his lack of faith in the strange device that looked like a brittle lance mounted just a few meters in front of him, he was in good spirits. The crew, and in fact, the fleet as a whole, were all working well together. Thanks to Danielle, they all had a chance now at survival, and he was proud that Captain Carter had selected him for such an important mission. Ever since he'd thrown off Tannin's shackles, he'd found a quiet confidence in both himself, and his abilities.

"Sometimes I really wish I would have gone into banking," Julie joked back. "Sitting on my butt all day shuffling numbers around from one account to another doesn't sound half bad right now. Anyway, we're recording everything. Good luck Danny."

"What's so funny?" Threed asked from beside him in the copilot's chair. It was hard to read body language in an EVO suit, but there were certain emotions, like laughter or panic, that were easy to see.

"Hmmm? Oh, nothing. I was just talking to Julie. Was just picturing her sitting on her butt in a bank somewhere," Danny said.

"A bank? Where'd that come from?" Threed asked.

"Never mind. It's that, plus I can't help but to laugh about how stupid this whole thing is. We're headed out to do battle with the First Ones with a giant whatsit welded to our hull, and we don't even know if it works or not, but we're cruisin' on out there anyway like a couple of idiots," Danny responded through the intercom.

"I don't like having to rely on the Bwain to make these damn things work, but as long as they do their part, I guess we'll be ok," Threed said as he cast a quick glance over at the Bwain beside him and shook his head, still not able to believe that one of the alien creatures, so recently a threat to all of humanity, was now sitting here next to him, ready to man the only weapon that might be able to save both of their species.

Danny twisted his head so that he could see the two Bwain crouching behind the pilots' chairs. Their heads snapped back and forth, tensely scanning the space visible through the electroglass viewshield. At this distance, the First Ones were maggot-sized masses of writhing light, but they were growing rapidly. Danny had expected the Bwain to fear what would come, but an uneasy acceptance seemed to have gripped the creatures. The creatures seemed tense, their coloration drifting from a deep black to the gray of the seats on which they sat, with their beaks chattering. One of the bird-thing's small hands plucked at nodules on the reptilian skin of its belly.

Danny tapped the side of his helmet, and his faceshield slid up.

"Captain, are you with us?" he asked.

"Always, Mr. Xiao," the bird-thing squawked.

"We're entering our approach," he reported. Smiling again, Danny increased his thrust. It was good to know that his captain, a man whom he looked up to, was right there with him.

The cabin fell silent as Danny turned his attention back to the path that laid before them. The shuttle was not even as large as the end of one of their enemy's grasping tendrils, and as they closed the distance, more and more of the First Ones' features came into view.

None of them looked the same as any of the others. They flickered at the edges like lungs expanding and contracting or ghosts about to withdraw into the emptiness at any moment. Their bodies were generally shaped like long, slick tubes, or massively bloated bladders, and each seemed to have dozens of eyes peering out from different joins and crotches within them.

"They're watching us," Threed commented as the shuttle approached.

"Of course they are," Danny answered. He'd kept his eye on the holoscreen that showed a top-down view of his shuttle in relation to the anomaly's edge, and he watched the shuttle's nose inch into the edge of the green-tinted barrier. The First Ones scratched and clawed toward him like insects around a bright light, but they came no closer.

"I think we're probably the only people to have ever seen them this close," Threed said, his voice tinged with a mix of awe and nervousness.

"The only ones who saw them this close and survived so far," Danny added. "We're in position, Captain."

The Bwain behind him was visibly distressed. Its hands kept combing its feathers in reflexive jabs, and when it shuffled out of its seat Danny swore he saw it swallow nervously.

"Standby...," Carter said through the alien.

Its small stature allowed the Bwain to easily slip in beside Danny and Threed. The creature's nictitating membrane slipped shut, and then it shuddered quietly, its feathers turning a mix of colors that eventually settled on a yellow that pulsed in time to the weapon on the shuttle's nose. The color rose from its feet to the comb atop its head, and then seemed to spread through the weapon. Bobbing back and forth, the Bwain let out a low keen, and then suddenly sat down with its head drooped against its chest.

"What happened?" Threed asked, not quite sure of what he had just witnessed.

"Captain?" Danny asked as he reached over and grasped the Bwain's shoulder. "Captain?"

Suddenly, a golden light flashed on the other side of the electroglass.

For a moment, Danny's vision broke apart into a dozen angles. He was seeing the shuttle from behind, above, and beneath all at the same time, and then he watched the weapon on the front of the shuttle turn in on itself. Then, just as suddenly, his vision returned to normal.

"What the hell was that?" Threed demanded as he turned to look at the Bwain.

"I think it worked," Danny answered.

A bolt of yellow-purple light was rocketing through space toward the First Ones. Between their feet, the Bwain was shivering.

"The shot is away," Danny reported to the fleet. Then he shifted the craft's inducers to full thrust away from the First Ones. "Reversing course now."

The plan was to avoid any repercussions from the First Ones if the test was successful. Hal only had a handful of the weapons; no one knew if they would work at all, or how quickly they'd fire. Judging from the Bwain's current status, they couldn't be fired very easily.

"Status?" Decival asked through Danny's implant.

"Awaiting impact," Danny responded.

In the kilometers of space between the shuttle and the First Ones, the shot was soon lost to his vision, but it was showing on his holoscreens as a yellow bolt hurtling toward the enemy. The creatures were still pressing feverishly against the anomaly as the shot crossed its threshold.

"Look at that!" Threed exclaimed, his eyes fixed on the holoscreen before him.

The holoscreens zoomed in on the estimated area of impact, and a combination of telescopic imagery showed one of the First Ones turning a furious scarlet as it reared back from the edge of the anomaly.

"It looks like an impact! We struck one of the creatures!" Danny shouted.

"Tentacle! We hit it right in the bloody tentacle," Threed cried with excitement.

Danny watched, open-mouthed, as the creature's arm flickered. A scarlet gangrene seemed to rapidly overtake its limb, until the tentacle faded from sight like a necrotic appendage that rotted away into nothing in the space of a breath.

Sound didn't transmit through a vacuum, but Danny swore he heard the First One scream. The shuttle shook as if buffeted by an atmospheric disturbance, and he forced the controls to stay on course. Beside him, the Bwain thrashed and fell limp. Its tongue rolled out of its beak, and its chest stilled.

"Jesus, I think it's dead," Threed gasped.

"Lieutenant Xiao," Danny's earpiece transmitted when he finally could hear again. It was Captain Decival, anxiously demanding a status report.

In front of him the injured First One was swaying back and forth. The creature had lost maybe a kilometer of its mass, nothing that would have stopped it for very long, but it didn't matter.

"It worked! The weapon worked! We *can* hurt them!" Danny called. He was shouting now, excited and exuberant. He frowned, though, when he looked down and saw the Bwain lying dead beside him. "I'm afraid we've got a problem though. A really bad one."

* * *

The Fate's Winds

"HOW HAS THE CARTER LEARNED TO FIGHT US?" The Ancient bellowed. Its voice was the scratch of thousands of knives against metal, and the visions that followed of slipping back into the crushing ennui of nothingness were nauseating.

"I don't know," Aric Keith answered through his thoughts as his captive body stood on the wreckage of the *Fate's Winds.*

"WHAT WILL HE DO?"

"I don't know."

"YOU LIE!"

Aric's body fell on the cold deck, writhing in pain. Frozen strips of what had been his flesh peeled off and floated into the vacuum as The Ancient took out its rage on his body. Yet, without the ability to die, the pain was little more than something to be endured. Aric could endure anything, knowing that Captain Carter still fought his torturers.

"WHAT WILL HE DO?" The Ancient asked.

"I don't know," Aric groaned. *"He's unpredictable. He does what you don't expect."*

"WHERE DID HE LEARN THE MEANS TO HARM US?"

"He's smart. He won't ever give up."

"YOU WILL NOT TELL US?" The Ancient thundered.

"I am telling you," Aric answered.

"YOUR LIFE WILL BE FILLED WITH ENDLESS TORTURE UNTIL YOU COOPERATE."

"You already have my body. You're already torturing me. There's nothing else you can do that you haven't done already," Aric thought stoically. *"I'm already dead, so you can either let me go, or continue on the way you have been, but I can't tell you anything more than I already have."*

Just as quickly as it had begun, the pain stopped, and Aric's head cleared with a startling rapidness. The strips of his rent flesh glowed white as the nanobots that the First Ones used to resurrect him returned to their duties. His respite was short-lived, though.

Suddenly, bolts of white energy from the obelisk struck Aric, dancing across his flesh. They bathed him in a cold light that flowed over his chest, up his throat, and across his cheeks.

"WERE WE MISTAKEN? IS THERE MORE TO YOU THAN FLESH?" The Ancient demanded.

Panicked, Aric tried to roll over, tried to crawl away from the lightning that now poured into his throat, through his nose, and his shriveled eye sockets.

"YOU WILL TELL US EVERYTHING. THERE WILL BE NO MORE RESISTANCE. WE HAVE YOUR WILL, AND YOU WILL HELP US," The Ancient said, it's voice tearing through Aric's thoughts.

"No!" Aric screamed as The Ancient pried at his mind. A ravenous hunger seeped into him, consuming him in the cold whiteness of everything. The First Ones had finally come to realize that humans had a consciousness, and a will that was stronger than flesh. Their collective was churning through him, trying to get him to think how Carter would think in an effort to probe the captain's weaknesses.

He could hold them off. Gravity threatened them. They did not understand free will and consciousness. He had to keep them out of his last refuge.

It felt as if every synapse within his skull was burning in a fiery plasma. He was losing consciousness, his sight narrowing. Somewhere he had a body. Once he'd been an engineer, but this, and everything else about him, all seemed so distant and foreign now.

"WE WILL GIVE YOUR CARTER A SURPRISE," The Ancient taunted as Aric lost himself in the endless whiteness of the First Ones.

* * *

The Dauntless

"The First Ones are moving!" Danielle shouted from her station.

Gasps rang throughout the ship's bridge. On the holoscreens, the blinking marker of Danny's shuttle was streaking back toward the *Dauntless*, but Danielle's focus had been locked on the edge of the gravity anomaly where the First Ones had started spinning in a kind of whirlpool pattern that reminded her of the Bwainswarm she'd fought from the bridge of the *Fates Winds* so long ago.

"Assessment – what are they doing?" Captain Decival ordered.

The creatures were crawling up and down the edges of the anomaly, spinning in larger and larger patterns that opened spaces between them for the first time.

"I count fifty of them, sir," the science officer called.

"Any sign of their projectiles?" the captain asked.

"No, sir."

"Are they coming any closer?"

"Negative."

"Then what in the hell are they doin' out there?" Decival muttered to himself.

"They're searching for a weakness in the gravitational field. They're trying to get in," Danielle called, her fingers flying across the controls in front of her.

As she gave her hypothesis, she knew in her gut that it was right. It's what she would have done.

Gravity anomalies formed when a supernova shattered the components of what would have been a super dense neutron star into smaller objects. The gravitational warping of space was much more pronounced around these extremely small, incredibly dense solar remnants, which is what she thought kept the First Ones at bay, but there were times when the spinning neutron fragments were unstable, and their gravity could be erratic.

"And is there one, Ms. Hoff? Is there a weakness in the anomaly out there somewhere?" Decival asked.

The First Ones spidered over and below and around the fleet, crawling and grasping at the invisible shield that protected them.

"No, sir. I'm showing uniform gravitational strength," Danielle gasped. Suddenly she realized that she'd been holding her breath while she scanned through her readings.

Decival turned to the pair of Bwain beside him and knelt so that he could face them eye to eye.

"Captain Carter, it looks like we have a successful test. If you haven't already, could you have Hal begin mass production of the weapons?" Decival communicated through them.

"Wait," one of the Bwain said.

"Wait? What do you mean wait?" Decival asked.

"Need to see," the Bwain answered with a croak.

"Captain Carter, are you there, or is it the Bwain speaking?"

"Wait! Something happening," the Bwain added.

Danielle consulted her holoscreens again, searching for anything she might have missed. What was Captain Carter trying to tell them? Was there something she had missed?

Pain flared in her foot. She clenched her eyes shut and tried to push it away as best as she could, but in her exhaustion, she was finding it difficult.

"Captain, with respect, I need to understand what's happening. If there's some new threat we aren't aware of...," Decival said, eyeing the Bwain suspiciously as he did so.

"Sir! They're withdrawing!" Danielle reported.

Silence fell over the bridge. On the holoscreens, the First Ones fluttered and spasmed away from the edges of the anomaly at an impossible speed.

"Now where the hell are they goin' all of a sudden?" Decival asked.

"It from their trajectory, it looks like they're heading back toward the obelisk," Danielle said as she double checked her screens to confirm what the readings were telling her.

For the first time since she'd come on board, she saw a look of hope on Decival's narrow face. The captain had been laboring with wounded pride and a sense of desperation, but now he was almost smiling.

"Are there more? Give me a full scan," Decival ordered.

Danielle returned to her instruments, looking for any other contacts at the edge of the sphere's boundar...anything that could indicate that the creatures' behavior was nothing more than a calculated feint, but all she saw were the signatures of the First Ones speeding off toward the obelisk, until they finally disappeared from view.

"They're gone, sir. It worked!" she responded in a shaky voice as the bridge crew roared in celebration.

Chapter 9

The Bwainhome

Atlas Carter felt the First Ones' anger reverberating long after they had fled. He remained suspended in the Bwainsong for hours, not trusting that a small wound had scared off the creatures.

Hal's weapon had worked, but it had cost one of the Bwain its life. At the moment he had forced the creature to fire upon its former masters, Carter had felt the shiver of the First One's previous control reach through the Bwainsong and take the Bwain's life. The rest of the Bwain seemed to have not noticed. Their collective consciousness made it hard to recognize individuals within the collective. So much so, that he often wondered if they even had names.

If they were going to fight the First Ones like this, they would have to murder the Bwain to do so. Carter may have unwittingly given the First Ones a way to neutralize his only weapon. As such, whatever security the fleet had found was temporary at best.

When he withdrew from the Bwainsong, he felt weak and somewhat jittery. He'd been sitting on a low bench in the *Bwainhome's* bridge, surrounded by the creatures. The aliens had flushed various colors of greens, browns, and blues as a rainbow of their natural coloration came through at long last. They were excited, buzzing, twittering, and lifting themselves into the air on their short wings.

He'd shown them what sacrifice was, but he was worried that they'd take to it too quickly.

"Captain?" Pandith said from beside him.

Carter's neck and shoulders ached. When he tried to stand, his legs seemed almost asleep.

"You're starting to stay down for longer and longer," Granger observed from his other side.

Both men helped him to rise, and he gripped their collars to steady himself.

"It worked," Carter said weakly. His lips and his throat were dry, and in his current state, his words sounded somewhat strained.

"Hal told us. He ran back down to the workshop to start making more of those weapons," Granger said, smiling to himself as he recalled how excited Hal had been.

"Get on the radio to Danny and the rest of the shuttle crew. Fill up the rest of the shuttles with every weapon and Bwain we can spare, and get them to the other ships," Carter instructed as he breathed slowly to regain his balance.

"Yes, Captain. But for now, you may wanna lay down and rest for a bit. We've got time to...," Granger was saying, but Carter angrily cut him off and jerked himself away from them both.

"There isn't any time for that!" he growled in frustration.

"Sir?" Pandith asked.

"Those things out there have been waiting for nearly as long as the universe has existed. Do you really think they're gonna give up so easily?" Carter asked harshly.

"Sir, all I meant was that it'll take Hal time to produce the quantities we need. I didn't mean to imply that we'd all take a holiday. In fact, I was going to download the data from Danny's shuttle in the meantime. It'll be useful to look at power usage versus the damage done. I think that...," Granger started to explain, but then he stopped abruptly when he sensed the captain's impatience.

"No. Let the *Dauntless'* science team handle that," Carter said.

"Sir?"

"Captain, I think you may be pushing a bit too...," Pandith warned, but Carter ignored him as he continued to detail tasks for Granger's immediate attention.

"Granger, I'd like you to look into retrofitting one of the human shuttles with the Bwain's transdimensional technology."

"All right, I can do that, but is that our most important objective at the moment?" Granger asked cautiously.

"It will be. This is an order, Granger. That's where I need your focus," Carter said. The tone of his voice made it clear that he didn't want to hear any further hesitation or questioning.

"I'll be in the shuttle bay then if you need me," Granger said as he gave a quick salute and then headed off down the corridor.

Pandith watched Granger go, and then turned back to the captain.

"What do you intend to do, sir?" Pandith asked in a soft voice.

Atlas studied the engineer before him, seeing the psychologist hiding behind the calm demeanor.

"I don't know yet," he answered as they headed for the ramp together.

"I think you do. I saw this same certainty from you once before, back when you saved Threed's people on Judgment," Pandith said.

"Look, we can't save everyone if we waste time," Carter replied abruptly.

"Is that what's bothering you, sir? The sacrifice?" Pandith called, his voice more of a challenge than a question.

Atlas froze. He'd been wrestling with the question of what it was all worth for days now, trying to unravel the knot within his guts that told him how little hope the fleet truly had with the plan they had all agreed to.

"Do you think we should take 'em back to Earth?" Pandith asked.

"Have you thought about the consequences if the First Ones follow us there?" Carter asked dully.

"I have, which is why we couldn't risk doing that."

"Finding this anomaly was lucky. If two crews hadn't given their lives, we might not have even made it in time. The problem is, now we're stuck here. You saw how fast the First Ones moves when they turned tail and ran back to the obelisk. They don't need a transdimensional drive to keep up with us. They could follow us anywhere, which means we can't lead them back to Earth," Carter said. His breathing was ragged, as though communicating his thoughts to Pandith verbally were as physically demanding on him as his recent immersion into the golden knot of the Bwainsong.

"I think we've already covered that," Pandith replied quietly.

"But we can't *warn* Earth either, Pandith. Do you understand? We can sit here and watch, and maybe we'll be safe for as long as our food holds out. But what happens when the First Ones look for more food? They're out there getting stronger with every atom they consume, so who knows how long this anomaly will stop them?" Carter had clearly agonized over every possible option available, and nothing tangible had taken shape.

Pandith's eyes widened as the larger picture of their struggle snapped into focus.

"May I repeat my question, sir? What exactly is it that you intend to do?" Pandith asked again.

The ramp was sloping underneath his boots. Atlas' head ached from the strain of processing so much mental stimulus, and he couldn't remember the last time he had slept. The Bwain were flowing around him, some heading toward the Knot, while others went wherever their whims took them. Could he do what was necessary, to them, and to everyone else in the fleet?

"The First Ones will stay where they have food. We'll only need a day, maybe two," Carter said.

"A day to do what, sir?"

"To go to Earth. To secure the gravity drive and come back. To give ourselves a real chance against the First Ones and finish this fight before more of us lose our lives."

He felt Pandith stop behind him, so he stopped as well and turned to face him.

"Sir, if I may ask, what if something goes wrong?" Pandith asked quietly.

"Then it'll have gone wrong while we were attempting to give the whole fleet a chance at survival. If we just sit here and wait, we have no chance at all, because eventually those things out there are either gonna find a way to get to us, or we're eventually gonna starve to death. There is no end game for us that leaves us alive if we just sit here and wait," Carter explained. Pandith stared at him in silence for a moment as he considered his captain's words, and then he slowly nodded.

"Well, you've led us this far, but you should tell the fleet what you're planning," he said with a frown.

"I can't. They'd never let me do this, and this is our only window to do it. It has to be now, before the First Ones come back," Carter said, staring at the engineer with sad, tired eyes. As Pandith looked at him, he finally began to understand the depth of the man's agony.

"Whatever you need, I'll be there with you," he said. Carter nodded at him appreciatively, and then they continued on down the corridor.

* * *

The Reichstag

With the First Ones gone, Ensign Julie Ford's job had become something she looked forward to rather than something she dreaded. From her station onboard the *Reichstag*, she was coordinating with Danny on the resupply and retrofitting of each ship in the fleet, helping with the inventory levels, and coordinating repairs. Carter was also moving Hal's factories and apprentices to the human ships so that they could make their own First Ones weapons repairs. It had been two days of 'round-the-clock work, but keeping the fleet together was the most important job she could be assigned, and she felt proud that Captain Carter had trusted her with such an important task.

"Danny, it looks like that's the last shipment of the factories and weapons. Can you confirm?" Julie asked as she watched the last shuttle leave the *Bwainhome* on her holoscreen.

"Confirmed. That's seventy-two shuttles away," he answered.

"Seventy-two signatures confirmed. Thanks Danny," she acknowledged.

The line was still open but silent. She should have signed off and transmitted all the manifests to the destination ships. There was a long waiting list for repair parts, as well as weapons, and everyone wanted to feel as prepared as possible for whatever plan Captain Carter would come up with to go after the First Ones, but still, she still wanted to keep the line open with Danny for just a moment longer.

"It was brave of you to test the weapon. You might have saved us all." Julie said, her voice filling the silence.

"I was just carrying out the captain's orders. It was really Hal who did everything," he replied.

"I know. I just...I mean, you've come a long way," she said awkwardly. "I'm really proud of you."

For a moment, he didn't answer. She worried that once again she had been too forward, and that she'd been pushing too hard because of her loneliness and insecurity.

"Thanks Julie. That really means a lot," he said.

"What do you think the captain's gonna do?" she asked.

"I'm not sure. If it was me, I'd send a few shuttles out on remote pilot with the Bwain in them, just to see how well the weapons work in a real fight. And then I'd load up every inch of every ship we had with them and then go on the attack. What do you think?"

"I think it's good you're not in charge," she responded.

On the other end of the transmission, he went silent again.

"It was a joke, Danny. Come on, I didn't hurt your feelings, did I?"

"Julie have you checked the holos?" Danny called in a panicked voice.

"All hands to battle stations," Captain Van Stadt's voice boomed in her ear.

"What's going on?" she asked.

"It's the *Bwainhome*," Danny said. "It's...can you double check your instruments?"

Captain Van Stadt had stationed the *Reichstag*'s compliment of Bwain near the communications station. Julie checked her holoscreens, then turned to one of the creatures.

"Captain Carter?" she asked.

The Bwain cocked its head, blinked, and then turned to rummage in the set of blankets that someone had brought the creatures so they could nest and sleep.

"I need to speak to Captain Carter," Julie said.

"Bwainslayer gone," it hissed.

"What do you mean he's gone?"

"Gone!" it said.

Looking up, she saw the holos that showed the fleet's disposition. They had been arrayed with the *Bwainhome* at the center, but now...

"The *Bwainhome*'s disappeared, sir," the nav officer called.

"Jesus, I can see that, but what happened?" Van Stadt snapped. "Ensign Ford, are you hearing anything?"

Julie scanned every frequency of electromagnetic radiation her instruments could read. Beyond the fleet's traffic, there was nothing. She left her station and pulled at the Bwain's leathery hand.

"Please Captain…please answer," Julie begged. The creature was shimmering with a peacock mix of green, blue, and brown. It shook its head, blinked its eyes, and curled into a ball, saying nothing.

"Captain, I'm not sure, but I think Captain Carter left us," Julie said, her voice trembling as she tried to understand why he would do such a thing.

Chapter 10

The Mosquito
Alcubierre Bubble Headed Toward Earth

Capra Falconi stared at the gray nothing outside his ship. No external light could penetrate an Alcubierre bubble; he was moving much too fast for photons. The Alcubierre drive acted by using its antimatter fuel to create a sheath of negative mass around his ship. This Alcubierre bubble was sized to be larger at his ship's bow, so that when space itself rushed to fill the void, the act of doing so pulled his ship forward faster and faster, until it was traveling at many multiples of the speed of light. In essence, there was nothing for him to see outside except the future, and it was one that Capra didn't like.

An entire solar system had been consumed by a horrific new species of alien. The creatures had enslaved at least one human...a brave soul who'd no doubt risked his life to warn Capra of what was happening; but when he had asked the poor crewman how the things could be stopped, the transmission had ended. Now, it was left up to him to figure out what to do.

He stood, stretching to brush his fingertips against the tiny craft's ceiling. Atlas Carter had once stuffed himself into the copilot's couch and had shared the tiny living facilities for the week-long transit between Earth and the Sword Belt. For a time, it had been easy for Capra to believe Admiral Nico and Phuri when they claimed that Carter had been the problem. Then he'd been quarantined, Lana Delgato somehow managed to find him, and things had snowballed from there. He worried that he was heading back to a corrupt government. He feared that they would think that he'd formed some kind of alliance with Atlas Carter if he arrived back on Earth and told Nico that he needed to drop whatever plans he'd been forming and redirect his attention toward the new alien threat.

The *Mosquito*'s computers carried terabytes of data that would back up his story. He had little doubt that any rational observer would believe him. The question would be what Nico was trying to accomplish. Against a power that could consume a star, Earth would have to put aside its divisive factions and come together, united and strong against this alien threat. There was no other choice.

Capra rubbed his eyes, fighting the lethargy that the dim grayness brought upon him. He brightened the cabin interior until the lights were almost painful and tried to think through what he would tell the admiral.

"Find Carter," the strange transmission from the Sword Belt had begged him, but when Capra had asked how, the voice hadn't known or couldn't answer. Capra still remembered Carter's transmission to Decival's fleet. The captain had claimed to not want to harm anyone, but Decival hadn't listened. Would Nico?

Sighing, Capra felt himself slipping into the drowsiness that a week's voyage through a dull mist instilled in him, but he couldn't seem to fall asleep. Whatever happened, however Nico took the information, Capra knew that he would be on the front lines once again with the rest of the messengers, scouting the new threat that appeared in his mind's vision whenever he tried to close his eyes. If Earth couldn't bring itself to unite again this threat now, then all would be lost.

*   *   *

Cape Canaveral

As was often the case these days, Admiral Nico was furious.

"I told you that I was committed. I can't undo a coup that's already in motion, but now you're asking me to wait so you can see what happens?" Nico raged at Phuri.

"Waiting for Falconi is the prudent move. We still don't know what's going on in the Sword Belt. Carter could be on his way to Earth at this very moment. Whatever happens, we know the threat will still exist. Kidewange will preach caution, and you will use the data the messenger retrieves to show why the president must be replaced," Phuri explained, maintaining his calm demeanor as he studied his fingernails. Nico's eyes hardened as they bored a hole into him.

"Would you want Carter to arrive in this system, Phuri? I mean, I don't have any proof that he actually overthrew you and Tannin on Gertie, now do I?" Nico snarled.

"That's preposterous, and you know it," Phuri said as he met Nico's glare. "The minute any Bwain ship, or Carter himself arrives in this system, you have standing orders from the president to destroy him. So if he does arrive, you should thank me for paving the way for you to become a great hero to the people. My allegiance is to that goal, and nothing mor," Phuri said flatly.

Nico paced behind the desk. Though normally the ventilation system in his office performed well, today the humidity levels had risen, and he was feeling both flushed and angry.

"Those same standing orders keep my ships here in Sol, when we should be in the Sword Belt tracking down Carter and running him into the ground."

"Patience at this point. Backing a war hero is a much more palatable approach for certain senators who still have feelings for Kidewange," Phuri said evenly.

"I'm not the lapdog to a weak president. And the more you tell me to wait, the more I wonder if you want this to go through at all," Nico growled, but Phuri could tell he was beginning to slow his pacing, which was always a good sign.

"It will, when the time is right."

Nico tried to calm himself. He knew Phuri had a point, but the thought of remaining on the defensive was insulting to him. A soldier's duty was to fight, to put himself in harm's way for the safety of his people. It was the reason Kidewange had to go; the man wasn't equipped for all-out war against an alien species. He was too soft. This business of currying favor, trying to gather senators in secret meetings and the self-serving favors they asked, the promotions and trading contracts they demanded – it was downright nauseating.

"The protests are dying down. Our leverage is slipping," Nico noted as he glanced out his window.

"And so when Capra arrives we release the data to the people, show them exactly what's happened. Spur their fear, fan the flames. There will be no choice for the people but to demand more protection," Phuri advised slyly as he watched Nico resume his seat behind the desk.

"I'm gonna come back with Carter's head," Nico vowed through clenched teeth.

"I'd like that very much," Phuri answered.

"You've never told me why," Nico said. Not for the first time, he wanted to probe this man who'd come bearing the method to acquire exactly what he wanted. The SSC intelligence service had checked out every aspect of the man's story. He certainly had justification for hating Carter, especially if Carter was responsible for Phuri losing the small shred of power he had retained in the Sword Belt. Still, he wanted to hear it from Phuri's own mouth.

"Carter, at least to me, is a symbol. He is a tarnished, weak man, who's been allowed to run rampant. You know what he did here on Earth," Phuri said casually.

"I do, and my sources tell me you're quite involved in Latin America."

Did Phuri's smile stiffen for a moment? Was there a suspicious hesitation in his response? Nico couldn't be sure, but he'd struck something with that comment.

"It's no secret that the Latin delegates revile Kidewange for his treatment of the *Narco* issues. They are a valuable asset for us if needed."

"But we won't need them, will we?" Nico asked.

"No. They are merely a hobby of mine. Former business associates that I enjoy speaking with now and again."

Nico felt calmer now. Phuri and Tannin's drug smuggling past was well known. It was why they were exiled to the Sword Belt in the first place. It wasn't hard to put the pieces together. Phuri wanted a righteous officer eliminated, one who knew too much about how the *Narcos* had worked with the SSC to take power in that part of the world. It was a well thought out plan.

"Back to Capra's findings. How are we going to release the data?" Nico asked. "It can't look like it came from the SSC. Kidewange would have me court-martialed."

Phuri smiled. "You can leave that to me. I've been cultivating a media asset who I think will be quite eager to break a story."

Nico's stubble rasped under his palm. He was starting to let his imagination run further ahead.

"As soon as the information is out there, I'll speak out against further inaction. We'll have Carter's head on a stake in two weeks," Nico said, already picturing the accolades to come.

"If not sooner. I have no doubt that you'll overwhelm him."

"What position do you want in the Cabinet? We haven't talked much about that yet," Nico asked in a much calmer tone.

"I think, Admiral, those conversations are premature. It is my pleasure to serve you in the capacity I have since you so graciously took me into your service."

"What are you planning, Phuri?" he asked. He rose to his feet and began pacing once more, his boots thudding dully along the floor as he moved closer to his visitor. "You were so persuasive before. Why so noncommittal now?"

"What happened to Decival's fleet was unexpected. We have to be ready to pursue every alternative. Just tell your faction to hold off for now. It won't be too much longer until the truth is revealed," Phuri said as he rose to his feet and turned to leave without waiting for Nico to dismiss him. Nico watched him go as his mind flicked back to that small moment of discomfort that Phuri had displayed during their conversation. Anyone else might have missed it, but it was obvious that Phuri had some secrets that he wasn't willing to reveal.

*　*　*

On the elevator up to the surface from Nico's office, Phuri wiped sweat from his forehead. For all the man's churlishness and his volcanic anger, Nico was quite intelligent, and he'd come close to forcing Phuri into revealing an uncomfortable truth.

Atlas Carter was a pawn, as were Nico and Kidewange. There would be fire and ash while the three of them fought each other, making the world weak enough for a single leader to rise to the occasion. When those ashes settled, there would be no one more qualified to lead than Phuri himself, and that's when he'd make his move.

The elevator doors opened onto the shuttle pad, and bright streaming sunlight nearly blinded him. The ocean breeze poured in rich and heavy, and Phuri stopped to take a few deep breaths to calm himself. His pilot beckoned him toward the hatch, but Phuri signaled for the man to wait a moment. He had a bit of business to attend to first, and he tapped his communicator to call a number that he had triple encrypted, with codes that were unbreakable even with the help of artificial intelligence.

"*Sí?*" the husky voice on the other end answered.

"Would you believe I'm calling you from Cape Canaveral?" Phuri asked without preamble.

"I will be hanging up now," the man said. The English was heavily accented, a sign that the man had learned it as an adult.

"It's quite all right. I just wanted to let you know that we may have an issue with Nico," Phuri said.

"And what would you like me to do about this?"

"Nothing for now, but we'll need to be ready sooner than I thought."

"I will need to see you," the man stated without emotion.

"Then I'll join you for coffee this afternoon," Phuri said, and then he tapped off the connection and jogged to the waiting shuttle.

"Welcome aboard, sir. Where to?" the pilot asked as he prepared for takeoff.

Glancing out the window, Phuri watched the ocean sparkle and shine beneath him. The possibilities were sorting themselves out now, and the path he had wanted for so long was becoming more and more clear.

"Take me to Belize City. I need to pay a visit to an old friend," Phuri said, smiling to himself as he closed his eyes and settled himself into the comfortable seat of the shuttle.

* * *

"WHAT DO WE WANT?" a woman standing on an orange crate screamed into her microphone.

"SAFETY AND JUSTICE!" the crowd roared in response.

The march's leader stabbed her fist into the air as the sound wave from thousands of protestors washed over Lana Delgato. She was covering the march from a makeshift media platform erected underneath the shade of a pair of palm trees. Across the Indian River, the SSC's headquarters rose in a glistening beacon of glass and steel. The protestors were marching up and down the highway in front of the navy's headquarters, in combination of a show of support and demand for action.

Admiral Nico was vowing to exterminate Carter's threat. Kidewange was pushing for more time to understand what was happening. The gloves were coming off on both fronts, but the only one who truly knew what was happening, SSC messenger Capra Falconi, hadn't yet returned to Earth.

"WHO'S GOING TO GIVE IT TO US?" the woman roared.

"THE SSC!"

"AND WHO NEEDS TO GO?"

"KIDEWANGEEEEE!"

She wondered how many of these rallies Phuri was behind, and what his true intentions were. There had always been rumors about the SSC's connection with the *Narcos*. No doubt Captain Carter had taken the fall to provide the shroud of righteousness for those corrupt officials who had remained. Despite her best reporter's instinct, she hadn't done anything.

Ever since Phuri had asked her to wait for the footage that would show the truth, she had given up her investigative journalism, reconnected with her editor, and started going for the easy stories. The protest coverage, the pieces about what Admiral Nico might be thinking.

She didn't want to admit it, but for the first time in her life she was scared. She finally had what looked a story that would make her career, and yet there were very real consequences if she were to report it. People would lose their lives, Agricourt was gone, the protests against Kidewange's government were turning violent, thousands upon thousands of people had already been arrested, and the man she knew was responsible for it all was watching her like a hawk. Because of that, she'd decided to back off for the moment and bide her time.

"Are you getting this?" Lana asked her editor. She was recording everything from her holovisor and transmitting it to the BBC news desk in Madrid. Her editor, Eduardo, was collating her feed with dozens of others as he stitched together a story about a planet in chaos.

"I am. It's the same story in South Africa, and a dozen other places as well. We need an angle, Lana. Do you think Kidewange can survive this?" he asked.

"I'm not sure."

"Well, what if he doesn't? Who's next in line to take over? I keep hearing rumors about Nico maneuvering. You were on that angle for a while. What kind of substantiation can you give me?"

"I don't have anything good on that front," she said as feedback squealed from the protest megaphones, and group of helicopters chopped the air overhead.

"Lana, what exactly are you doing over there? You went dark for two weeks, telling me you were working on something big, and now this is the best you have? What's goin' on?"

Another call flashed on her hololens.

"I'm sorry, I have another call coming in. I'll get back to you later," Lana shouted, so that she could be heard over all the noise.

"Lana, we have a serious issue with your coverage. The expenses for what you're doing are not covering the costs. I need to talk to you about...," he said, but then she cut him off and answered the new call. There was no face

She hung up and picked up the new call. There was no face, just a black screen projected onto her eye in the middle of the sunlight.

"Ms. Delgato, I hope that you're enjoying the protests," a familiar voice said.

"Phuri..."

"Oh good, you remembered me."

"Of course," she said, keeping her tone as neutral as possible. "I wanted to ask you for an exclusive, on the record interview about your background and that sort of thing. We could...," she started to say, but Phuri quickly cut her off.

"I think I have something much more interesting for you, Ms. Delgato." Check your messages later tonight, and you'll have your exclusive."

The connection clicked off, and her hololens turned transparent once more. Thousands of sweating, screaming faces paraded under the hot Florida sun, but Lana had gone cold, suddenly aware of how much was happening all around her, and wondering what role she might be forced to play in the events that were still to come.

* * *

Capra was sweating as he walked down the echoing corridor toward Admiral Nico's office, and it had nothing to do with the humidity under the ocean. Two marines were escorting him along at a brisk pace. The soldiers had said little when they'd met him at the *Mosquito*'s landing pad. All they said was that he was to provide an immediate, in-person report to Admiral Nico.

Something was wrong. Per protocol, he had immediately transmitted his data via an encrypted feed directly to the SSC intelligence office. Typically, he would receive a confirmation, and would be debriefed before he reached Earth's orbit. So far, the only communication he had received had been a single line of text ordering him to land immediately at Cape Canaveral. He had just delivered what was quite possibly the most sensitive information in the history of mankind, so maybe Nico just needed time to sort it all out, and maybe...just maybe, it would finally be the catalyst to get people to work together for the good of humanity.

He allowed himself this flimsy hope as the steel security doors slid open to allow his entry into Nico's inner office. Yet the man who stood within wasn't the bearish man he'd expected to see.

"Surprised to see me?" Phuri asked as he noted Capra's startled look.

The marines behind him smashed their heels against the concrete floor, turned, and then exited. Capra was alone with a man who worried him much more than Nico ever did.

"No, sir," Capra answered. Not knowing what to do or what would happen next, Capra simply stood at attention and waited.

"There's no need for that," Phuri said casually. "I'm not in your chain of command. Please, have a seat and make yourself comfortable. Would you like a drink?"

"With all due respect, I think I'll stand. And I'm on duty, so...thanks, but I can't at the moment."

Capra was trying to size up what had happened. His trip hadn't taken long enough for Nico to be deposed, had it? If Nico was still in power, where was he, and what was Phuri doing here? Was that subtle reference to the chain of command as innocuous as it sounded?

Phuri glanced at Capra for a moment, seeming a bit disappointed, and then he poured himself two fingers of whiskey over a steel cube.

"One of the things I missed the most on Gertie was alcohol. We had a gin made from the local berries, but it was vile stuff. More than a few of the colonists gave in to it and had to be shipped to the penal planet," Phuri commented absently.

"So I've heard. I was told Admiral Nico wanted to see me," Capra said. He was growing more uncomfortable by the second, and just wanted to get the whole thing over with.

"He does, and he will. He's currently at a security meeting related to all these protests that are going on. You're aware of the protests, aren't you?" Phuri asked casually.

"Unfortunately," Capra said flatly.

"And which side would you fall on, if a situation were to arise where one would have to make a decision about such things?" he asked. Capra swallowed nervously. This was what it had come to. Loyalty before truth.

"I'm on the side of this planet. There's a threat out there, and this navy is the only force capable of acting on it. I'm not sure if...," he continued, but Phuri interrupted him, clearly not interested in the answer.

"Yes, the threat. Tell me, you saw nothing of the Bwain? No sign of Atlas Carter, or any of Decival's fleet?"

"No sir. I only know what I reported. Those ships, or creatures, or whatever they are...they're the real threat."

"And you think they devoured the Bwain and our ships, just as they were consuming the planets?"

"I don't know what happened to our ships or the Bwain," Capra answered. The questioning was making him uncomfortable.

"That's correct Mr. Falconi. You don't know, and yet you fled back to Earth. If these creatures could somehow follow your course, somehow travel faster than light, what then?" Phuri asked.

"I don't know. I only had enough antimatter for one jump. I thought you needed to be warned."

"Yes, you acted on your own initiative with the best information you had at the time, but we don't know if Carter's threat has been extinguished, and he knows exactly how to get back here to Earth."

"So what's the admiral planning on doing?" Capra asked. Phuri set down his drink and smiled.

"The admiral is planning on acting in a manner befitting the leader of the strongest military that mankind has ever known. He will provision a fleet that will leave the Earth, ready to deal with any threat that may present itself. If there are others who would stand in his way, or who see things differently, then they will be eliminated."

"I'm sure the protestors will be pleased to hear that action is being taken," Capra said in a controlled voice. He was left little choice now but to play along with what Phuri was saying.

"Yes, the protestors," Phuri answered. Nico's aide turned to the window, studying the distant shore and the mass of people marching along it. "They're useful in their own way I suppose. I'm sure they'll be quite pleased that Admiral Nico will be leading a battle group to combat the Bwain threat."

"But the Bwain are gone," Capra said awkwardly as the magnitude of the deception began to sink in.

"No Mr. Falconi, they're not. As we speak, your findings are being edited and replaced with Bwain ships, and those altered findings will be released in the next news cycle."

"What? You can't do that!" Capra protested.

"I can and will," Phuri said casually. He was still smiling, but his eyes remained watchful, like a snake that was ready to strike.

"But that's insane! Those things out there killed a damn star!" Capra cried. "You don't understand..."

"No, I don't." Phuri said as the marines stormed back into the room and seized Capra's arms, pinning them to his sides. "The biggest threat this planet faces is from the Bwain, and I do suggest that you keep that in mind when join the admiral on his next mission

Chapter 11

The Tranquility

Atlas had left her. What hurt the most was that, in spite of everything she had said to him, she knew he was still going to do it. She couldn't decide which one of them was more of a coward. She had a death wish, and he was running around clinging to false hope, where there was no hope to be found.

After the news of the *Bwainhome's* departure had trickled through the fleet, she'd had a conversation with Captain Decival about their readiness for what would soon be upon them. At first she'd thought that Carter had been smart to distribute his manufacturing resources among the fleet, but now she knew why. Not even Hal, who was ensconced on the *Dauntless*, had known of Atlas' plan.

"You're gonna run for glory, Atlas. You're risking us all because you think you can win," she thought with a stab of anger.

Whether her bitterness came from the fact that he might be right, or from the fact that she hadn't been able to go with the only person she truly cared about, she couldn't tell, and on top of everything else, the Bwain were no longer on speaking terms with her.

Her cabin's door chime sounded. Her inclination was to just not answer it, but she was the captain. When her crew needed her, she had to be there for them.

"Come in," she called.

The door slid open, revealing Lieutenant Purcell standing behind a bashful Kaylee.

"Ma'am, may we enter?" he asked.

"Of course, Lieutenant," she answered.

Kaylee floated toward her, arms outstretched. Before Mephista realized what was happening she was locked in an embrace.

Despite the tangle of thoughts that choked through her mind, she smiled.

"We...uhhh...permission to speak freely, Captain?" Bryon said.

"Of course."

"We were wondering if you heard anything from Captain Carter before he left."

"Unfortunately, I didn't. Why would you think that?" Mephista asked, doing her best to keep her expression calm and emotionless.

"Well this isn't like him at all, and I just thought that…well…you know…"

"He cares about you," Kaylee finished for him.

The former comfort girl nuzzled into Mephista's shoulder, but the captain was taken aback.

"I'm not sure I know what you mean," she said awkwardly.

"I guess it doesn't matter really. I mean, he has his reasons for what he did," Bryon said.

"Really? You think so, Lieutenant? And what reason would he have for abandoning us out here?" she asked, trying to keep her voice even.

"I can only tell you what it was like on the *Fate's Winds* back when you were still a pirate," Bryon said. "We were as low as we could be. Danny was a traitor, and all I wanted was to get done with my tour so I could rotate back to Earth. That was when Captain Carter came and took over. He made us all believe again in what we were doing. He showed us that you could do good if you just held yourself up to a higher standard, and he made us believe in ourselves. It was strange really. Who'd ever expect to find someone like that out here in the butthole of the galaxy. I was lucky to serve with him, and I know that a man like that wouldn't just abandon us out here."

"If that's true, then why did he leave when the fleet asked him not to?" Mephista asked.

"Because he knew better," Kaylee said.

"Is that what you think?" Mephista asked, not wanting to startle the girl by responding with the harshness she struggled to control.

"Whatever he's doing, I know he's doing it for us. I never saw him make a decision any other way, so we have to believe in him, and trust that he knows what he's doing," Bryon said.

Mephista stared at him for a moment, and then let out a heavy sigh. The hardest part was admitting that he might be right. She'd had a hard time trusting anyone the way she trusted him, but the way he ran out on them left her feeling like her trust had been misplaced, and in her brooding and anger, she found a way to comfort herself over the fact that she may never see him again. Knowing that Carter had run off in an attempt to do something noble would only make it harder to deal with if she in fact never saw him again. It was easy to be angry, but much harder to hold on to a hope that could end up destroying you.

"Maybe you're right," she said. "I just don't know what we're supposed to do in the meantime."

"We're supposed to stay alive. It's all we can ever do," he said.

"That's just not enough," Mephista grumbled.

"Maybe not, but when Captain Carter gets back we'll have bigger things to deal with, so you won't have time to sit around being angry at him," Bryon said. In her eyes, he could see that her anger had softened considerably, and had been replaced by a resolve that had been missing ever since Carter left in the *Bwainhome.*

Kaylee was twirling Mephista's hair in her fingers when she suddenly got a thoughtful look on her face, and started splitting it into separate strands that she then started braiding. Bryon watched it all with a smile on his face.

"What?" Mephista asked.

"Oh, nothing really. It's just a nice look for you, that's all," he said casually.

Mephista reached out and started tickling the girl's sides until she released her hair, and then hugged her once again.

"Well, I guess we should get goin'. We just wanted to check in on you and make sure you were ok. I'll do my best to keep this one out of your hair. Pun intended," Bryon said with a grin as he took Kaylee's hand and pulled her off toward the door.

"Thank you both for coming," Mephista called after them.

"Any time, Captain. I'm looking forward to trying out those new weapons of Hal's, so if you wanna do any test firings, you just say the word."

Their moment of casual camaraderie had passed. Bryon once more assumed his role as a member of the crew, and she his superior officer.

"Of course, Lieutenant. And if you hear anything more from the Bwain…"

"Captain to the bridge, immediately," she suddenly heard through her implant.

"On my way. What is it?" Mephista asked as she left her quarters.

"The First Ones, ma'am. They're back, and there's a whole bunch of 'em this time."

* * *

The Dauntless

"They're so fast," Danielle whispered in shock. The First Ones moved more quickly than any object she had ever seen. They were like living nightmares, headed straight for the fleet.

"Time to impact with the anomaly?" Decival asked in the midst of the flurry of activity on the bridge around him.

"Thirty seconds," Danielle responded, as her fingers flashed across her holoscreen.

"Get the fleet an evasive solution. Prepare to initiate but keep us in the anomaly," Decival ordered.

"To the entire fleet, this is Captain Decival. We are uploading evasive maneuvers now. Get your new weapons ready; now might be the time to use them,"

At the front of the bridge, the Bwain were squirming and jerking, watching the holoscreens and flashing black and gray with fear, trying to blend into the deck as if they didn't exist.

Decival grabbed one by the feathered wing and pulled it to face him.

"Carter, are you there?" he asked.

A part of Danielle knew that Captain Carter would never abandon them, but the Bwain said nothing, other than to shiver and try to pull away.

On her screen, the white indicia of their best guess at the First Ones' individual positions shot toward the anomaly's boundary. There were more than fifty of them this time around.

"Ten seconds," she announced, and then she held her breath in tense anticipation.

"Carter, you son of a bitch! Are you there?" Decival shouted at the Bwain. "We need your weapons."

"We have impact!" Danielle cried.

The First Ones plowed into the anomaly's boundary. On her holoscreen, the creatures seemed to stop dead, but something didn't seem quite right.

"The anomaly appears to be holding, Captain," one of the science officers called.

"Negative," Danielle said as she studied the images on her holoscreen.

The First Ones seemed bruised, pieces of their exteriors marbled with the color of bloody flesh. They squirmed against the apparent emptiness before them, straining to writhe forward, and they were succeeding.

"Ms. Hoff?" Decival asked.

"Sir, the anomaly is holding them off, but...," she said, but then she fell silent and sent her readings to the main holoscreen.

A cheer rose from the bridge. The First Ones were backing away, using a disjointed backstroke to rapidly dwindle to small flickers in the darkness.

"No, quiet everyone! Look!" Danielle shouted over the din.

The celebration quickly faded. On the holoscreen, what had once been a spherical depiction of the gravitational effect now had a crater in it, exactly where the First Ones had struck it.

"What did they do?" someone gasped.

"No, that's not possible," the science officer said nervously as he studied the images before him.

"Will the anomaly hold, Ms. Hoff?" Decival asked as the bridge grew quiet.

"They're coming again!" the weapons officer called.

Once more, the rush of First Ones streaked toward the fleet at impossible speeds, and once more they flashed in pain as a venous bruising scarred their white surfaces. Some of the creatures phased and shook as if struggling to maintain their form.

Danielle studied the computer's representation of the anomaly.

Somehow, the First Ones' charges were affecting gravity's force. The battering rams were resulting in small shifts, but they were working.

"No sir. It'll take 'em a while, but eventually they'll be able to get to us," Danielle responded as she continued to study the rapidly changing information at it was updated.

"How long do you think we have, Ms. Hoff?" Decival asked.

"From this data, possibly a few days."

"Comms, get me Mephista and the other captains," Decival ordered. "We're gonna have to learn to fight these things on our own."

Chapter 12

SSC Kuiper Belt Research Facility
In orbit around Pluto

Declan Rowe's job was to keep the skies clear. From his monitoring station on the small space station orbiting Pluto's reddish-white surface, he ensured that every one of the trillions of rocky objects that made up the Kuiper Belt stayed out of the main shipping lanes that led from Sol out to humanity's hundreds of colonies. When a protoplanet or a comet crossed into the areas of space he was tasked with keeping clear, he dispatched his drones to intercept the mass and redirect its course to somewhere less hazardous. It was important work, but not glorious in any way. Certainly nothing to write home about to his parents back in Edinburgh.

When the anomaly proximity alarm sounded, he didn't immediately check the holos. He was more interested in why none of his models and satellites had been tracking an anomaly, and how it could have slipped past the network of sensors the facility's team had positioned.

After a few moments, it suddenly became clear. Some of the sensors had either disappeared, or had been damaged to the point where they were either non-functional, or malfunctioning to the point where they'd become useless. Frowning, he rotated his view to try and make sense of the data. A massive dead zone had appeared in the middle of sensor array B-12, which covered one of the least-used shipping lanes. There was no immediate danger, but he had never seen anything like it before, and the mystery of what had happened intrigued him.

"Lieutenant, can you come to the monitoring station?" he said into his implant.

"What is it, Declan? I'm down in maintenance," came the officer's response.

"I'm not really sure. I'm getting some very strange activity. Something's knocked out the satellites in corridor B-12."

"Well, what's on the holos?" the lieutenant asked.

"That's just it, sir," Declan said as he spun and enlarged his view with his haptic glove. "All of a sudden it's just become this huge null zone. I just thought with all the stuff goin' around about the Bwain and the rebels, that you should be aware of what's goin' on."

"You think it's the aliens?" the lieutenant asked, suddenly taking on a far more serious tone. "Hang on, I'll be right there. Open a channel to Cape Canaveral, just in case we need it."

Declan directed a portion of the station's communications array to swing toward Earth. It would take nearly five hours for the signal to reach the home planet. For true emergencies, they had an Alcubierre-capable shuttle, but Declan didn't think that would be necessary quite yet.

"SSC Prime, this is Kuiper Station Three. We are tracking an anomaly in shipping corridor B-12, and wanted to make you aware. Beginning data recording and transmittal...over."

Behind him, the door slid open and the lieutenant entered. There was only room for two men in the monitoring area, and the lieutenant smelled of grease and sweat from the repairs he'd been performing.

"Now, what is it that we've got here?" the officer asked as he studied the screen.

"It's about...my god, could it really be ten kilometers long? What the hell's causing it?" Declan asked, his eyes widening with alarm as he looked over the readings.

"Do you see that?" the lieutenant exclaimed as he stared at the images that appeared on the holoscreen before them. "Christ, tell me we're transmitting!"

"Confirmed sir, we're recording and transmitting to Earth."

There in front of them was the most massive ship that either man had ever seen. It was like some swollen planetoid that had once had a smooth hull, but was now patched with so many alien creations it was impossible to tell what the ship had originally looked like.

"Oh my God! It's the Bwain!" the lieutenant practically shouted. "They're here!"

"Sir, they're transmitting a message!" Declan said as he opened the comms channel.

* * *

SSC Vessel Ninkovich

The bridge of Admiral Nico's flagship was pin-drop silent. Every member of his crew was fit and buttoned up with their hair shaved to within a millimeter of SSC specifications, regardless of their gender. They performed their duties with a quiet efficiency. Not a one of them seemed to question their orders to lead the largest battle fleet humanity had ever assembled to the outer reaches of human-occupied space. No one dared suggest they were heading into battle based on carefully crafted manipulations set into action to usurp the power and control of Sol's entire system.

Capra Falconi stood under guard in a corner of the bridge, staring at Nico's empty chair. The seat was made from rich red leather perched on a small pedestal that would give the admiral an unfettered view of the 360-degree holoscreens that ringed his bridge. Duty stations faced outward from the admiral's chair, which Capra assumed was suitable for a man that demanded dominance.

"So it won't be long now, will it?" Capra asked. Then he closed his eyes in embarrassment. His nervous loquaciousness had always been his weakness, and no doubt he had gotten himself placed under arrest as a result of it as well. But then it could have been worse, he thought. Nico could have executed him. So from that standpoint, he had very little to lose.

"The admiral doesn't operate on your schedule," one of the marines guarding him said. The man wore a full combat EVO suit with the helmet visor left open. The entire fleet was on battle footing. Capra watched the holos as the ships gathered in their staging areas. Nico's flotilla would be made up of 30 capital ships gathering around Earth, another cluster of 25 vessels at the antimatter fueling facility outside of Saturn, and a final combination of two other 20-ship battle groups collecting above the Martian colony.

Nico would be leading close to a hundred ships out of the solar system. Only a skeleton fleet would remain. Which meant there would be no one left to resist Nico when he returned to take control of Earth.

"There weren't any Bwain in the Sword Belt," Capra said.

He had pitched his voice to reach every corner of the large bridge, but no one said a word. The officers in front of him didn't look up. They were either busy listening to the whispers of command in their cochlear implants, or their eyes were locked on the holographic deceptions in front of them.

"The Sword Belt isn't even there anymore," he continued.

A curious navigation officer flicked his eyes toward the messenger. Emboldened, Capra raised his voice.

"There's something else there, some new sort of alien creatures. They consumed the star. I saw it and recorded it! I...ooof!" Capra grunted as a rifle butt jammed into the pit of his stomach. The marine who hit him then stepped back and spun his rifle to point the muzzle at Capra's face as the messenger dropped to a knee.

"That's enough, Falconi," he said.

Capra's eyes teared as he struggled for breath, and he was still blinking to clear his vision when a massive man stepped through the bridge airlock. The bearded shape loomed larger and larger, climbing the steps up to the admiral's chair at the center of the bridge. The marines on either side of Capra snapped to attention, but Capra was finished saluting a man who wouldn't listen to reason.

Capra expected the admiral to roar at him when he saw him standing there, but instead, Nico just smiled. In that look, Capra realized that nothing he said mattered. This had always been about President Kidewange, and Nico was in on the lie.

"The Bwain are gone!" Capra croaked. His voice strengthened as his breath returned. "The Bwain are gone. This is about a coup against the president!"

Nico's smile hardened into a rictus. He stood, towering over the entire crew.

"This fleet is going to eliminate any threat to Earth and her colonies, regardless of what you think you saw, Falconi," Nico sneered. "Take him to the brig until I decide how to deal with him."

The marines seized Capra under the armpits and dragged him toward the airlock.

"Admiral," Capra heard a voice call. "Sir, I'm showing a new signature in the system. Origin unknown."

"Where?" Nico demanded as he turned to the officer.

"It's near Pluto at the moment."

"The Kuiper Belt? What assets do we have in that area?"

"None sir, it's not a human vessel. I don't recognize the elements."

"Show me," Nico growled.

Capra threw his shoulder into one of the marines, knocking the man into the airlock. Struggling with the other, he bellowed to the rest of the crew.

"You're not going to get away with this!" Capra yelled. "You're all going to die out there!"

On the holos, surrounding the crew in an endlessly replicated image, was a massive, bloated ship that looked like it had been sailing the void for millennia.

"It's broadcasting, sir...in English," the comms officer called.

"Put it through."

"To all SSC installations and vessels, this is Captain Atlas Carter..."

"Carter!" Nico bellowed. "Order all ships to the Kuiper Belt. Jam any transmission from that vessel, and get that traitor off my bridge!"

The marines regained control of Capra and shoved him into the airlock, but instead of struggling, Capra went with a smile on his face. Carter was here, so maybe there was a chance for the Earth to survive after all.

* * *

"Why aren't we hearing anything?" Carter asked. He stood in the hatchway of one of the two human shuttles that the *Bwainhome* had carried into Earth's home solar system. Granger's fingers flew over the communications array from the copilot's station, scanning for any malfunction or interference.

"I'm not sure, Captain," he said. "Perhaps you could try again?"

Carter sighed. This was his biggest gamble, a feint that would no doubt rile up Earth and the SSC to a point of no return. Drawing attention to himself now was his only choice if he was going to save the rest of the fleet trapped near the Sword Belt. He had to bring them home, even if it meant his own sacrifice.

"To all SSC installations and vessels: This is Captain Atlas Carter. I am aboard the Bwain ship and am in command of it. We mean you no harm. There is a much larger threat than the Bwain coming, another hostile alien species of much more advanced technology. The Bwain and the ships you sent to the Sword Belt have joined forces to fight this threat, but we need your help. I'll be standing by to hear from SSC command, over."

Carter's jawbone microphone picked up the vibrations in his skull and transmitted the message to the shuttle's computer, which broadcast his voice on an open channel toward every installation in the solar system: the Kuiper Belt stations, the mining facilities in orbit around Uranus, the recreation stations above Saturn, the shipyards within the asteroid belt, the antimatter manufacturing facility on Mars, and then to the hive of ships on Earth.

Granger's holoscreen showed the web of human infrastructure stretched out among the planets, along with the green arcs of hundreds of ships in three distinct clusters. A yellow wave indicating Carter's transmission spread out from the *Bwainhome* toward Earth.

"It's going to take nearly five hours for the transmission to reach SSC command on Earth," Granger noted.

"We've already waited two. Something's wrong."

Squinting, Granger enlarged the edge of the transmission just before Neptune. The SSC's deep-space communications array orbited Neptune, amplifying any signals from that region of space and sending them toward Earth. In the current solar system's orbital positioning, it should have been boosting Carter's message.

"There' interference, sir. Man-made radiation. If I had to guess, I'd say it was reactor venting from a group of ships," Granger reported. "The navy's jamming us, Captain. They've already decided we're hostile."

"The whole solar system will think we're here to fight 'em," Carter muttered to himself.

"What are your orders, sir?"

Carter closed his eyes. For a moment, the Bwainsong called to him. Hundreds of voices from the Sword Belt clamored for his attention, but he didn't have time for them now.

"Hang on and wait for me," Carter urged them before he reluctantly withdrew his thoughts. He then opened his eyes and found Granger's tense face in front of him.

"We're gonna go to Plan B. Keep transmitting. I'm gonna brief Pandith about what's going on. He'll need to be ready to go," Carter said tightly.

"Sir, permission to go with him?" Granger asked.

Carter had taken two steps away from the shuttle, but he turned back to look at Granger once more.

"Pandith's my friend, sir. I can't send him into this alone."

"Just make sure you both come back," he said. Then he turned to a cluster of Bwain who had gathered around Granger's shuttle.

"Get the ship ready," Carter instructed them. "Things are about to get interesting."

* * *

Earth

"You weren't even the first to report this, Lana," Eduardo said. Sweat shone from his forehead, and he looked as if he hadn't slept since the *Bwainhome* had first arrived in the Kuiper Belt. "I'm not paying for your trip to Florida so the auto-net can do your job."

Sighing, Lana tried to force herself to remain calm. Things were moving now, and even though Phuri thought he was using her, she had seen a path around his manipulations. She just needed Eduardo to go along with her plans for a little while longer.

As soon as the net-based reporting programs had flashed an alert across the planet's communications network about the *Bwainhome* arriving in the Kuiper Belt with a demand from Atlas Carter, she had known something was wrong. This feeling was confirmed when Phuri had delivered raw footage of Capra's messenger ship encountering a battle between the Bwain and Decival's fleet in the Sword Belt, with instructions that she should keep her ears open.

He was trying to use her as his unofficial mouthpiece, and she knew she couldn't say anything because it would be the last anyone saw of her. If the footage from Capra was real, then why hadn't she heard from him? And if Carter had been fighting the navy in the Sword Belt just a few days ago, how had he all of a sudden shown up in the Kuiper Belt? None of it made any sense. The pieces just didn't fit.

"The Bwain showing up aren't the story. I mean...their ship and Captain Carter...there's definitely a story there, but think about it Eduardo. Carter doesn't care about who the president is. The statement makes no sense! The inconsistencies in what's being given to us just don't add up. *That*'s the real story," Lana said, hoping that her editor would understand how important it was to get to the real truth of the story.

Eduardo met her with an angry frown, then he stabbed at a holo control just out of her view.

"I'm going to play this again for you, Lana. You tell me if there's anything that's not clear."

Lana closed her eyes in frustration as she, listened to Atlas Carter's voice for the umpteenth time.

"To all SSC installations and vessels. This is Captain Atlas Carter. I am aboard the Bwain ship and am in command of it. The ships you sent to the Sword Belt have been destroyed. We are a much larger threat, but we mean you no harm if you comply with my demands. President Kidewange must resign. I will negotiate only with Admiral Nico, and I will be standing by to hear from SSC command."

"This is the exact opposite of the man I've been researching, and that's not even mentioning the timeline issues," Lana protested.

"The date was scrubbed from that combat footage you sent me," Eduardo commented.

"And think about that too. I'm asking you to trust me here. My source has an agenda," Lana argued.

"You mean your shadow man in the cabinet?"

"He's not a shadow. You've seen the transportation records. He's going to Belize City."

"I have, and of course the SSC wants to keep him close. He's the only one alive who has seen the threat firsthand. To say that a former senator's aide is manipulating this entire situation just doesn't make any sense with the evidence that I'm seeing," Eduardo said.

"It makes perfect sense. If he puts Nico in power, he's given himself an iron-clad hold on being second in command, and with the Bwain threat hovering over everyone's head, no one will question Nico's orders. Not the Senate, or anyone else."

"Lana, I'm sorry, but I need you to come back to Madrid."

"What are you saying?"

"I'm saying that when you left for Florida, you said you were going to dig into some back story, and now you're running wild with conspiracy theories. I need you here covering the Eurozone reaction to the crisis of this crazy Captain Carter."

"Carter isn't a dictator damn it! If he wanted to be a dictator, he'd have joined the *Narcos* and become one in Belize. Instead, he…"

"He what, Lana?" Eduardo asked.

"Oh my God, the *Narcos*! That's what's happening here," she thought aloud, as the realization suddenly hit her. One of the final pieces of the puzzle had just fallen into place, and everything was beginning to make sense.

"You think the drug dealers are somehow behind this?" Eduardo asked, his voice containing equal part of incredulity and sarcasm.

"I'm sorry, Eduardo. I'm not coming back. There's too much here, and I have to do something to try to stop it," Lana said with sudden confidence.

"What are you saying?"

"I'm saying that whether you believe me or not there are bad people trying to seize power, and I'm gonna do whatever I can to try to stop 'em."

"You've lost your journalistic objectivity entirely," he snapped, and the image of his face became somewhat distorted as he leaned forward in his chair.

She paused, her finger hovering over the holocontrol that would close the connection. She was about to start on a new chapter, something entirely terrifying, but it was the right thing to do. She had let herself be manipulated for too long.

"No, Eduardo. I'm remembering why I took this job in the first place," Lana said, and then she smiled to herself as she closed the connection.

* * *

Lana had to give Phuri credit. The man's manipulations had been so smooth that she almost didn't believe what she now knew to be true. All it took was for Eduardo to help her jog loose the means and motive. Someone who had been exiled to the far corner of the galaxy would never come back gladly into the hands of the rulers who had tossed him aside. While she had wondered for the longest time what Phuri actually wanted, now she knew.

Nico was nothing more than a stepping stone to his ultimate goal. The Bwain had conveniently arrived, and Nico had taken his fleet to protect the Earth. Now that he was preoccupied with that, he'd be too busy to monitor any of the political intrigue that was going on back home. He would have to trust Phuri, who would stand alone as the only expert against Carter when Kidewange resigned. The president was too kind and decent of a man to stay in office; so his resignation would be inevitable.

Nico would return, only to find that the *Narcos* had taken his place. His coup would be put down by "loyalists" who spoke with the same accents as the men who had shadowed her ever since Madrid. Men who were clearly loyal to no one but those who paid them, and the *Narcos* had incredibly deep pockets.

Eduardo had abandoned her, but she still had her credentials. As her heart raced, she tapped on her communicator and started recording.

"This is Lana Delgato, reporting to you with a story so explosive that no major news network would touch it. By the time you hear this story I may or may not be dead."

She paused for a moment, swallowing back her emotions before she began to lay out every piece of evidence she'd encountered.

"And I pledge to you that I'm going to find the truth. You deserve to know what's happening, and you deserve to have an opportunity to take a stand. Until then, this is Lana Delgato, signing off."

Grabbing her bag, she raced out of her hotel room and threw herself into the auto-taxi she'd called before starting the broadcast. No doubt Phuri's men were still watching her, and she had to hope that the plan she'd hatched would get her away from them in time.

She stripped off her haptic gloves and tossed them out the auto-taxi's window as the vehicle pulled away from the curb. Then came her earrings, her necklace, her communicator apparatus in the bracelet around her wrist, and anything that could be used to track her in any way whatsoever. They all flew out of the window and disappeared.

"Please do not litter," the auto-driver's recorded voice sounded.

"Ignore," she said. Then she twisted around to watch the highway. There were few other cars on the road in the mid-afternoon, but several hulking SUV's glimmered like black diamonds a few hundred feet behind her. She had little doubt that these were the *Narcos*.

"I need you to go faster. Do you understand? *Rapido!*" Lana instructed the taxi.

"Efficiency and safety are our highest priorities," the machine answered.

"Of course you don't understand," she muttered in frustration.

Up ahead Lana could just see the arcs of several craft taking off from Canaveral's civilian space port. She had to worry about the *Narcos*, and whether the SSC would impose a civilian travel ban, and whether her insane plan would work, but at least she was doing something.

Buildings blurred on the horizon, then swelled into focus. In the rearview mirror, the SUVs flew closer.

"We will reach your destination in two minutes," the auto-taxi announced.

The wheel in front of her turned as the highway banked to the left. Barricades and lines of people flickered in the heat. The groups of protestors had grown every day, but how much of that was Phuri's influence? How many of those people would turn genuine anger against the SSC once her story went out?

If it went out. With her communicator gone and her terminal left behind, she had no way of checking if she'd been blocked. When she was safe and could slow down for a moment, she'd have to check.

Suddenly, her taxi lurched to the right. One of the SUVs had pulled parallel to her and tried to run her off the road. She just glimpsed a calm brown face, a pressed collar, and some fancy cufflinks before the taxi's collision avoidance software squirted her ahead to avoid another attempted attack.

Lana undid her seatbelt and threw herself into the driver's seat. She seized the comically small wheel marked with a red *For Emergencies Only* sticker, and jammed her foot down on the accelerator. The SUVs fell behind.

Stealing a glance at the navigation console in the middle of her windshield, Lana saw that her destination was only a mile away. She could make it. She had to make it.

More and more protestors were lining the highways. Police cars with their flashing lights were trying to control traffic and keep people from getting hurt. She could see the officers' heads turning as she flew past at what must have been close to 100 miles an hour.

"Your velocity is too high for this area," the helpful auto-taxi chimed in.

Asphalt blurred underneath her. She laid on the horn as she wove in and out of other traffic, but the more powerful SUVs were gaining on her. She'd never make it on her own. Somehow she needed to shake the *Narcos* off her trail. She wrenched her wheel hard to the right, calling out to the marchers in front of her that she wouldn't hurt them, then slammed on the brakes at the last second. Angry people called after her as she left the vehicle skewed just in front of a group of marchers and sprinted into the crowd. Brakes screeched behind her, and the heavy SUV doors cracked open. One of her pursuers called her name, but it was too late. She disappeared into a crowd of thousands, bashing through a thicket of arms and legs that would protect her even as the people around her hurled curses at her back. Ten minutes later, she broke out of the back of the crowd at a full run, sweating under the Florida sun that mimicked Madrid's in so many ways. Her feet pounded on the highway, but she was only on the tarmac for a short distance before she reached the exit. She then curled toward the concrete blockhouse that marked the entrance to her destination.

"Is everything all right, ma'am?" a curious guard asked as he leaned out of his air conditioned station.

"Yeah, everything's fine," she panted, trying to catch her breath. Then she realized how strange she must look. "I couldn't get through the protesters in my car and I didn't want to be late."

The man squinted toward the mass of people where the *Narcos* would still be searching for her.

"Oh...yeah, that wouldn't be good. If you miss your orbital shot, it can be days before you get reassigned. Head on in."

She forced her breathing to slow though careful breaths, and thanked the guard with a smile as she made her way toward the civilian space port. Her flight for the moon left in five minutes, and she had to hope the *Narcos* wouldn't catch up to her before then.

Chapter 13

Johannesburg

"This is the message Carter is transmitting?" President Kidewange asked.

On the holoscreen in front of him, Nico's face flickered and blurred. The admiral had reached Mars orbit, and the resultant time-lapsed conversation was infuriating Kidewange. He couldn't hear the protestors surrounding the government compound, but he could see them spilling through streets into the distance, and it broke his heart.

"You've only ever given this planet everything you had," a voice said from behind Kidewange. The voice was strangely altered, adjusted so that it could be spoken without being picked up by the holotransmitters. Not for the first time, Kidewange wondered if the two men he was speaking with were actually on the same side after all.

"Yes," Nico said four minutes later. "It's on repeat all throughout the outer systems communications network. We await your orders, Mr. President. We are ready to leave the staging area and deal with this threat within the hour."

Nico's staging area was Saturn's antimatter station. Here, his ships were poised to strike out into the solar system in an instant with their Alcubierre drives, and able to retreat and refuel if they met with heavy resistance. It was the best defensive strategy the SSC had for the solar system, and it would have to hold.

Kidewange blinked, staring through the glass. Then he reached forward and paused the transmitter.

"It's strange, isn't it? I mean, that Carter would come so far, have gone through so much, and come for me. I've never even met the man. I wonder who has?" he asked as he turned to face Phuri, who had come as Nico's personal representative to accept Kidewange's resignation. "I wonder what grudge he bears against me? Does he want the power for himself, or for someone else?"

"I can't say, Mr. President. He's changed so much, that I couldn't even guess at his motivations," Phuri answered smoothly.

"And your counsel, along with Nico's, which was so warlike for so long, now switches to appeasement?"

Phuri's eyes narrowed. The president had caught the man off guard. No doubt, he'd come expecting a simple resignation after weeks of stress and protests. Kidewange had always given the planet and humanity everything he could. There was no stain on his soul, and he would not give in to coercion so easily.

"Mr. President, may I remind you that Carter has already destroyed an entire fleet of our best ships, a fleet that we were sure had sufficient..."

"And you would bow to him now, as if he were all conquering? Who would you suggest to take my place? Admiral Nico perhaps? Or maybe you had someone else in mind," he said accusingly, as if voicing his thoughts aloud had suddenly revealed all that had been hidden from him over the past several weeks.

Phuri drew closer to the president and leaned against one of the windows.

"Mr. President, this isn't about power. This is about what will happen to everyone we're trying to protect."

"Are you still there?" Nico's stuttering voice called from the holoscreen. "I have not received a reply. Do we engage?"

Kidewange felt himself tense as the trap closed down on him. He still had enough strength to fight back though, and that's exactly what he was going to do. Smiling, he turned to the holoscreen and keyed it to begin his transmission.

"No, Admiral. We negotiate. I'd like to know exactly what Carter wants, and what he's up to. Send Falconi to communicate with him, and then have him report directly to me back on Earth for a debriefing immediately after he's finished."

As soon as he finished speaking, he turned off the holoscreen and turned to face Phuri. The shorter man's mask had slipped just a little, revealing just a hint of a furious scowl.

"The more time you give Carter, the more lives will be lost," Phuri said tightly, struggling to maintain his outward calm.

"That may be, Mr. Vongsa, but I am a man who believes in peace.

Now, if you'll excuse me, I have to speak to the people. I understand that they're quite upset," the president said as he squared his shoulders and stood a bit taller.

"I'll remain here and await your return," Phuri said as he tried to think of some way to maintain his desperate grasp on the plan that seemed to be slipping from his fingers.

"No, that won't be necessary," Kidewange said as he opened the door for Phuri and nodded toward the corridor. "Your services are no longer required."

"But President..."

"Goodbye Mr. Vongsa," the president said. Phuri stared at him hard for a moment, and then stormed out of the office.

* * *

The Ninkovich
Martian Orbit

Lying on his thin bunk in the brig, Capra Falconi had lost track of time. At first he had felt Nico's ship come under heavy acceleration, but that sensation had stopped long ago. The best scientists claimed that a human being couldn't perceive any difference between being inside or outside an Alcubierre bubble, and that the body's perceptions could only sense the physical universe. Somehow though, Capra knew that the *Ninkovich* was still in a warp bubble. After all, he had flown hundreds of messenger missions, and the light queasiness that always stirred within him had returned.

On the other hand, he could also be feeling sick at what was about to happen. Nico and Phuri were both lying, and Captain Carter was playing right into their hands. The only thing he couldn't figure out was why Nico hadn't had him killed. What was the point of bringing him on this voyage if he was going to stay in the brig the entire time? What did they expect to use him for?

Staring at the carbyne steel deck above him, Capra looked for some pattern in the 3-D printed metal, but there was only the dull glow of the ceiling lights that peeked out from crevices here and there. The cell was plain in every way, with no holoscreens or anything to occupy his mind other than his own thoughts.

He couldn't help wondering what it would be like to try and fight creatures that would consume entire worlds, and he wondered what Nico was thinking in all of this. Did he even know what he was getting himself into? Even if he did, what were his plans when it was all over?

Hours passed, and just as he was about to drift off to sleep, the door of his cell slid open and two marines stepped inside.

"Is it time for breakfast?" Capra asked them. As near as he could remember, he had just eaten, but it was hard to keep track of time when there was no visible reference for it. A quick second later, he suddenly realized that the "hunger" he was feeling was the result of them dropping out of faster than light travel, and the resulting easing of his stomach.

"Where are we?" Capra asked.

The marines, locked into combat EVO suits that made them seem almost robotic, said nothing. Instead, they hoisted him to his feet, and shoved him toward the doorway. A rough hand on his shoulder steered him down the right corridor, and they began walking at a brisk pace.

"Are you gonna tell me where I'm going?" Capra asked. "You don't need to keep hitting me ya know. I am cooperating."

"Maybe we like hitting you," a gruff voice said from behind as a hand tightened onto his shoulder and dragged him down another corridor to the left.

They entered an elevator, and the marines that were escorting him split to each side, and turned to face him. When Capra leaned around one of the marines to see where the elevator was going, he was rather shocked.

"We're going to the bridge?" he asked.

"You can ask the admiral your questions," the second marine said when the lift door opened. With that, they pulled him forward onto the battleship's massive bridge. Capra's eyes flew around the ring of holoscreens, as he tried to orient himself After staring at the inside of his cell for so long, suddenly being thrust into a room full of holoscreens and talking crewmen was causing a bit of a sensory overload. He'd expected to see the blank emptiness of what used to be the Sword Belt, or the white nightmares of the creatures that had devoured its planets. It was hard to make sense of the mass of ships and objects that were showing up on the displays, until he saw Pluto's familiar binary planetoid blipping behind the *Ninkovich*.

"We're in the Kuiper Belt? Why?" Capra asked himself in astonishment.

Admiral Nico stood on his pedestal and turned to him. The man's clipped walk could have been a rhino's charge, but this time Capra stood his ground. He knew Nico's secret, and he was already a prisoner, so what else could he possibly lose?

Nico's face was an expressionless mask of cold malevolence, but when he reached Capra he simply gripped the messenger's wrists, and then released him from the magna-cuffs.

Capra flexed his hands, worked his stiff wrists, trying to restore a bit of their flexibility.

"Thank you, sir," he said with a great deal of uncertainty.

"You can thank President Kidewange," Nico snarled, clearly unhappy about this newest development.

"The president? Why? How did even know I was here?" Capra asked. It was turning out to be one of the strangest days of his career.

Nico's haptic glove twitched, and the center holoscreen filled with a bloated black shape that was larger than any ship he had ever seen.

Of course he knew what it was. Every SSC cadet was drilled in alien ship recognition.

"The Bwain are here? What's going on?" he asked.

"It's not just the Bwain. It's Carter as well, and our illustrious president has asked that you serve as our negotiator."

*　*　*

The Bwainhome

"They would have responded by now," Carter muttered, deep in thought. It had been nearly a full day of staring down the gun barrels of what must have been half of the SSC fleet, and he still had not received any response. If there was one feeling Carter hated, it was powerlessness. He had vowed above Belize city that he would never let it affect him again, and yet here he sat, while his friends and the people who depended on him were in more danger than anyone in Sol's system could even begin to understand.

"If you stand still, you can fight," Granger said. The science officer was clad in his EVO suit, standing by in the shuttle along with two of the Bwain. Carter was leaning in from the floor of the *Bwainhome's* shuttle bay, barely noticing the aliens that crowded around the dimensional fighters.

"What's that?" Carter asked, as he refocused himself on Granger's comments.

"I heard you tell the crew that on the *Fate's Winds* the first time we ran into Mephista. I always thought it was sort of a fascinating strategy...waiting for the fight to come to you."

"It's an old boxer's trick that you use to tire out your opponents," Carter explained.

"I don't think this one's gonna tire out," Pandith noted from behind him. He had donned his EVO suit, and was now sitting in the hatchway of the second SSC shuttle.

"That's why we have a Plan B. I just hoped we wouldn't have to use it," Carter said as he glanced around the shuttle bay.

"Well, we're ready if we do, sir," Pandith said.

"I know," Carter replied. Staring at the two men, he felt a part of himself well up. "It's just...it shouldn't be like this."

"You taught us that nothing is ever easy, and you were right," Pandith reminded him.

"That's not what I mean, though," Carter said, and then he paused for a moment to control his racing thoughts. He'd been trying to put his finger on what was bothering him, and he finally had it. He snapped his fingers, then reached past Granger to turn on the holos.

"Sir?" Granger asked.

"The SSC had standing orders to attack the Bwain on sight, but they haven't done anything the entire time we've been sitting here. Other than the battle group, they haven't said a word," Carter explained.

"But what does that mean?"

"It means they wanna talk. It means we might finally be getting through to 'em," Carter said. A grim smile tugged at the corners of his lips, as he once again felt a small flicker of hope.

"Do you think so, sir? I couldn't imagine trying to fight our way through this," Pandith said as he shifted slightly to make a final adjustment to his EVO suit.

"Hopefully it won't come to...wait a second," Carter said as he held up his hand for silence.

His eyes dropped closed as the Bwainsong rose in him. He was seeing the empty space in front of the ship, a few hundred thousand kilometers that separated the *Bwainhome* from the SSC fleet. Only the space wasn't empty. A single shuttle was streaking through the blackness, headed right for them.

"What'd you see?" Granger asked when Carter opened his eyes.

"They're coming. Open a channel," Carter replied, his face now stern with resolve.

*　*　*

Capra couldn't stop staring at the inside of the alien ship. He also couldn't stop trembling with the strange mix of adrenaline and fear that had been burning within him ever since Nico had given him his orders. Now that he'd finally found Atlas Carter once again, he couldn't seem to stop talking.

"I mean, did you ever think after that week we spent together on the way out to the Sword Belt, that you'd end up coming back home again?"

"No, and I wish that I wouldn't have had to," Carter replied concisely. The captain had greeted him in the *Bwainhome*'s shuttle bay, and the alien creatures were scuttling all around him. They were odd, but even more interesting were the two SSC shuttles parked side by side.

"Was it because of those things in the Sword Belt?" Capra asked. Carter stared at him for a moment, surprised by what he'd just heard.

"You saw the First Ones?" he asked.

"Is that what they're called? Yeah, I saw 'em. Nico sent me out there to try and find you after Decival didn't come back, but when I got there, the whole system was gone except for those things."

"That's why Nico hasn't attacked us then. He knows," Carter said thoughtfully as he studied Capra's face.

"Sir, I'm not sure that's the reason."

"What do you mean?" Carter asked.

"I told him what's out there. He and his captains know, but they were gonna go the Sword Belt anyway. They were preparing the whole fleet to leave before you showed up."

"They wouldn't have stood a chance."

"No sir, but I think that was the plan all along," Capra said.

"They wanted to blame the casualties on us?" Granger asked.

"No, not the casualties. They needed some sort of a threat, so that Kidewange could be deposed."

"It's Phuri. They're planning a coup," Carter said more to himself than anyone else. As he processed what Capra had just told him, everything finally started to make sense.

"I'm afraid so, sir," Capra replied.

"But what could he hope to gain?" Pandith asked.

"He gains fear. Regardless of whether he's successful, or the fleet is destroyed, he wins either way. Nico proves he's the better ruler lead humanity against the threat."

"So why did Nico send *you* here exactly?" Carter asked.

"I'm supposed to deliver a message, although I don't quite understand it, and then broadcast your reply as soon as I leave the ship."

"What's the message?"

"Your demand that President Kidewange step down from his position, and that you will vacate the solar system as quickly as possible once this demand is granted."

"This is Nico playing peacemaker, is it?" Carter asked as he rubbed his tired eyes.

"I don't know what it is, Captain. I just know that whatever you've been transmitting, the SSC has been broadcasting something completely different." Capra said, shaking his head in disgust.

"Well then, we're just going to have to give them a message that they won't be able to alter," Carter said as a slight smile found its way to his tired visage.

* * *

Capra left the massive *Bwainhome* with a much worse feeling of nausea than the sensation that accompanied an Alcubierre jump. Captain Carter had confirmed every suspicion he'd had, and then some. As such, he asked the captain how he could help, without even the slightest bit of hesitation.

Now here he was, approaching a fleet full of personnel who needed to know the truth, and he'd been tasked with delivering it to them.

Capra replayed Carter's recording in his head as he tapped the *Mosquito*'s holocontrols to set him on a return course toward the *Ninkovich*, where Nico would be waiting.

What the SSC have been telling you is a lie," Carter had said. *"They are complicit in a coup against the president. I've come to the solar system to ask for help in defending against a much greater threat."* Here, recordings of the First Ones were cut into the message. *"Now is the time for every one of us to unite. I will speak with the president, but Admiral Nico is a traitor, and must be deposed."*

Finally, Capra felt that he was serving his true duty as a messenger. Rather than running orders and updates, he was bringing truth to those who needed it. The thought gave him a sense of calm purpose that overrode the anxiety he'd been feeling.

"Falconi, do you have Carter's response?" Nico asked, his voice coming through loud and clear over the comms channel.

"I have it sir," Capra replied. Adrenaline was coursing through him, and it was an effort for him to keep his voice controlled and steady.

"And?"

"Transmitting now, sir."

Capra tapped the holocontrol and waited. The message was less than a minute, but the time dragged. In front of him, the *Ninkovich* swelled in size, bigger and bigger until he could see the hangar doors in front of him.

"I'm sorry, Falconi," Nico said, his voice dripping with sarcasm.

"Sorry about what, sir?"

"That's not the message that we received."

Capra only had a few seconds to ponder Nico's words before the charges on his shuttle were triggered.

* * *

The Bwainhome

Carter watched the small cloud of debris that had once been Capra Falconi's ship spin and rise for a moment on Granger's shuttle's holoscreen.

"Your orders, sir?" Granger asked in a shaken voice.

"We go to Plan B, before that madman gets everyone killed!" Carter ordered, as the reality of their precarious situation loomed even larger before them.

Chapter 14

The Anomaly

"You're too close! Get back!" the voice from Threed's shuttle radio screamed at him, but the thrill of the kill was in him now. It was the same feeling that had coursed through him whenever he'd beaten a man into a bloody pulp with his bare hands back on Judgment. Though his Irregulars had been assigned as a picket line at the edge of the anomaly, Threed himself wasn't exactly used to listening to or taking orders.

The First Ones spread before him in an arc of tentacles and chitin, ravening mouths in the dozens that blotted out the black sky. He wasn't afraid of them. He hadn't been afraid in anything he'd done since leaving Judgment. After Atlas Carter had rescued him from certain death on the penal planet, because every moment since then had been nothing more than borrowed time. Now, with Carter gone, the fight against the First Ones seemed a bit more personal.

"I'm gonna get these bastards," he said into his radio as he pushed the throttle forward.

Captains Mephista and Decival had outfitted the majority of the fleet's shuttles with Hal's dimensional weapons and had arrayed Threed's tiny armada at the edges of the gravitational anomaly. Since the fleet didn't yet have many of the dimensional weapons, the plan was to keep the First Ones away from the larger ships while Hal and Danny and the retrofitting crews worked day and night to continue arming the fleet.

At least, that was the theory. Threed was no navigational expert, but even he could see the green dome of safety shrinking on his holoscreen. Whatever the First Ones were doing to the anomaly, it was working.

That's why they needed to be pushed back.

Threed turned to the group of aliens shuddering in the seat next to him. Ten Bwain had joined his craft, meaning he'd have ten shots before they were all consumed. The creatures were clearly terrified, alternating between a white color that looked eerily similar to the First Ones and the gray of the copilot's seat. It was as if they wanted to melt into the material and hide. The Bwain were the only way that they had found to fire the dimensional weapons, and Threed wondered if the creatures would be up to the task without Carter there to stiffen their spines.

"Are you ready? Let's go. Use that thing!" Threed commanded, without waiting for a response.

The first Bwain's head dove under one of its wings. The creature shuddered, silent.

"Hey!" Threed shouted as he leaned over, grabbed the animal's feathers and lifted. The creature tried to resist, but it wasn't nearly as strong, and he found its eyes blinking in a panicked flutter from near its navel. "Hey, listen. Wwe can fight these things. You know that, you've seen it, but you've gotta do your job."

He gestured toward the shuttle nose, where the strange amalgamation of what looked like a half-melted mortar had been bolted to the hull.

"We can hurt them. They hurt you for thousands of years, right? This is your chance to hurt them back," Threed urged the terrified Bwain.

The creature froze, its feathers flashing black for a moment, then purple, and then back to the gray color of the chair.

"Threed, what is your status?" Mephista called over the radio. "You're dangerously close to the event horizon."

"My status is that the Bwain don't want to fight," he said. His controls showed only a few thousand kilometers between him and the First Ones, but he was the tip of the spear, and his position suited him just fine.

Turning again to the first Bwain, Threed swung his fist and struck the thing in the chest. This time, there was a reaction. The alien flushed red and raised its head.

"Do you like that? You like being picked on?" Threed challenged the trembling creature.

Threed punched the alien in the shoulder. The creature's bone and muscle was more thin and gristly than a human's, and he didn't want to hurt it. He simply wanted to unlock whatever survival instinct lived in the deepest part of the creatures. Any animal, would fight if it was pressed far enough. He'd seen it on Judgment more times than he could count. He'd even felt it in himself when he first arrived as an exiled politician who'd dared to speak out against the *Narcos*.

"It doesn't matter how scared you are. You still only have two choices. You can fight, or you can let them eat you, so what's it gonna be?" Threed shouted as the Bwain cringed next to him.

A third strike to the Bwain's flank brought a screech. The alien swung back at Threed. Its fists bounced harmlessly off of his EVO suit's shoulder, but Threed smiled.

"Yeah, that's right!" he cried, and he jabbed his hand toward the First Ones. "Now, let 'em have it!"

The creature's head cocked, then turned toward its former masters. The membranes that guarded its eyes slipped closed, and a reddish glow filled the mortar mounted to the shuttle's hull.

"Firing...finally!" Threed relayed through his radio.

A scab of light lifted and flung itself away from the shuttle. For a moment, Threed thought it was headed straight for the lobster-like belly of one of the First Ones that was closest to him. But the shot dissipated and faded without reaching its target.

"It looks like I've got a bum one," Threed reported as he checked the readings on his holodisplay. Glancing over, he expected to see the Bwain lying dead beside him, but instead, the creature was still beside him, a malignant look of concentration on its wrinkled face.

"Withdraw for retrofitting," Mephista ordered.

"I can get closer, Captain," Threed responded, his voice tinged with eagerness.

"Threed...don't," the captain warned.

He glanced at the Bwain. The little alien was breathing heavily, flushed with streaks of red and purple. It looked like he imagined they always should have been...proud and happy.

"Let's get closer," he said to the alien.

*　*　*

The Tranquility

"Captain, I don't think he's turning around," Bryon called from his station.

Mephista's bridge had been pin-drop silent since Threed had disobeyed her order. Her crew was made up of a mishmash of the surviving members of the original crew that had joined her in mutiny, some of Threed's prisoners from Judgment, and replacements from Decival's fleet. Her ship was battered, repaired dozens of times over, and hardly recognizable compared to how it had looked when it first left the shipyard. The one constant on her ship since that time had been that she was in control, but now she felt that control slipping. First Atlas had left, and now Threed was disobeying her orders. The frustration she was feeling was tearing at her insides.

"Ms. Hoff, can Threed's shuttle, or its weaponry, affect the anomaly?" Mephista asked quickly.

The ship's computer broadcast her question across the fleet, and Danielle Hoff quickly replied.

"No ma'am. At least, I don't think so. But he's so close to the event horizon…"

"I know. It's only a matter of time," Mephista acknowledged.

They'd been bashing themselves against the anomaly for two days, and the creatures' brutal plan was working. Maybe that was what drove Threed, rather than the spirit of self-sacrifice that seemed to be worming its way through the fleet.

On the holoscreens, Threed's shuttle was a sliver of carbyne normalcy, streaking out toward a horrific nightmare.

"At least we'll get a good test of the weapons in action. I can't say I wouldn't do the same," Bryon said as he studied the images on his screen.

As the pain in her spine flared, Mephista twisted her hips to compensate. Floating there on her bridge, she'd never felt so powerless, and the anger that had been coursing through her ever since Carter left threatened to boil over. She glanced at the shuddering mass of Bwain that huddled in a corner, away from any sight of the First Ones.

"Are you talking yet, Atlas? Are you gonna let us in on your plan, or did you leave us out here to fend for ourselves?" Mephista said to the trembling cluster.

The creatures buried their heads in each other's wings, looking for all the world like feathered turtles trying to hide from the outside. Suddenly, one knobby face periscoped above the others, and its shuddering throat opened.

"I'm coming Mephista. Just hang on."

She went cold. It was the same message she had gotten every time she asked. It was like receiving a maddening recording, when all she wanted was to reach a live person. She glared at the holoscreens, where Threed's shuttle was just slipping into the green edge of the event horizon.

"I believe in Captain Carter, ma'am. He'll come back," Bryon said with a steady voice.

"Comms," she called to her communications officer. "Get me a private channel to Threed."

"Yes ma'am," the officer acknowledged.

Private channels were personal, unrecorded, and unheard by the rest of the crew. She stepped into a small shower-like alcove and drew the privacy screen. There were questions she needed to have answered, but she didn't want anyone else to hear.

"Threed, this is Mephista. We're on a private channel."

"Hello Captain," Threed responded cheerfully, as if he were delighted to hear from her.

"I need to know what you think you're doing," she demanded.

"I'm gonna show these damn things just what humans are capable of."

"You're aware of your position?"

"I am. I'm still showing that I'm inside the anomaly."

"And your Bwain?"

"Survived the first firing actually. I think I may be on to something. You need to make 'em angry."

"Threed, we can't make a kamikaze example for the crews. We don't have enough trained personnel to start losing 'em like that."

"Oh believe me, I don't have a death wish. Dyin' ain't one of my agenda items, but I ain't exactly afraid of 'em either. We've got the ability to fight 'em, so why not try?" Threed reasoned.

The logic made sense, and she knew there was little she could do to rein him in anyway. There was still one question she didn't want to ask, but she felt compelled to.

"Threed, do you think Carter's coming back?" she asked.

For a moment there was silence. She imagined this man that Carter had rescued, like so many others, thinking about how different his life would have been if not for the man who'd saved them all.

"I got to know him a bit on Judgment. He was a man of his word. He helped us when he didn't have to, and he didn't care if he got in trouble for doin' it. I don't have a doubt in my mind that he'll be back. The question is when, and what are we gonna do while we wait. I'm gettin' ready to fire again by the way."

"You chose to fight," Mephista said.

"Isn't that what we all chose?" Threed asked. His voice was calm, steady, and resolute.

"My job is to save lives," Mephista responded, feeling the panic rising like bile in her throat.

"Coming into range now," Threed reported.

"I understand that the woman who came with you from Judgment was on the *Archer*," Mephista commented, trying to find some way to break through Threed's wall of stubbornness.

"That's right, but we don't need to discuss that."

"I just want to make sure you understand that you have something to lose. Something you care about," Mephista said, again recalling all those who had already been lost.

"I most certainly do, Captain. We're all gonna die sooner or later, and not that I think I'll be able to or anything, but I'd kinda like to kill at least one of these damn things before I do. That is, if you don't mind. Firing now."

"Threed!" Mephista nearly shouted.

"I'm in full reverse. The Bwain's dead. The shot looks like it impacted. I see red on the First One's shell, or whatever it is, and...wait...," Threed said, but his voice no longer sounded calm.

"Threed?"

"It's coming, Mephista. It's..."

"Threed!" Mephista called urgently, straining to hear his response, but there was only silence.

"I've lost the connection, Captain," the communication officer's voice whispered in her ear.

Mephista spun, anchoring one arm to the handrail as she pulled open the privacy screen. The bridge crew didn't notice. To a man, their eyes were locked on the holoscreens, where Threed's shuttle no longer appeared. Not wanting to look, Mephista still forced herself. When she saw the true cause of her crew's attention, she gasped.

"It's smaller!" she exclaimed as she stared at the main screen.

Somehow, the wounded First One had burrowed a few thousand kilometers closer to the rest of the fleet. It was flashing a reddish pink haze, and as they watched, pieces of it seemed to implode or fade.

"I think Threed killed it," Purcell said as he turned to face the captain.

"No. It sacrificed itself," Mephista answered dully as the creature disappeared from the holoscreens. A dozen others slipped to the invisible indentation it had opened, tunneling a few meters closer to her every second.

"What are your orders, ma'am?" Bryon asked.

"I need to talk to Captain Decival. I think we're gonna need to make a run for it," Mephista said, letting out a slow breath as she eyed the humans and the Bwain around her. How much longer could both species possibly survive against these impossible odds?

* * *

The Dauntless

Hal was the only one in the entire fleet who'd been given unlimited access to the caffeine rations, and even though he drank the synthetic coffee like it was the last glass of Nightcrawler he would ever taste, he was still exhausted. Production of the strange weapons was difficult and dangerous, and he had no idea how to speed up output in the face of constant demands from the different captains. The printing factories operated on their own inscrutable schedules now. Whatever they'd learned on the *Bwainhome*, they were out of his control, and he could only stand by and wait as they churned out the strange devices.

He set down his mug and let his head sink onto his chest. If he could just rest for a moment, it would help. He was beyond exhausted.

"Hey, Mr. Yellowknife. We've got a problem!" Kilver called as he shook Hal awake.

Hal's heart fluttered, and pain flooded his eye sockets. For a moment, the face before him was just a white blur. He sputtered, remembering how the pirates on Gertie used to steal his precious supplies and food, and he took a dazed swing at Kilver before he was totally awake.

"Oh...sorry kid. Ya scared me there," Hal said apologetically.

"It's all right. Sorry about that," Kilver said as he reached out a hand to help Hal to his feet.

"So what's goin' on now?"

"There's a problem. Captain Mephista wants to talk to you."

"There's always a problem. I was sleepin' here," Hal grumbled. He looked funky as hell, and had his eyes half closed as he spoke.

"Yeah, well...this is a big one."

"All right, all right...I'm comin'," Hal said through a yawn as he stretched out his tired muscles.

When he lowered his arms, he saw Danny Xiao striding across the deck toward him. In spite of his sour mood, he gave Danny a rueful smile.

"Hey Danny, how ya doin'?" Hal said, and then he pulled the embarrassed lieutenant into a wam embrace. "So...please tell me these things are working, and that we haven't just been wasting our time."

"They're workin' ok, but that's not the problem. The captains want you on the holos," Danny said. Hal could tell by the seriousness of his tone that something was genuinely wrong.

"Why? What's goin' on?" he asked as the drowsiness suddenly left him.

"The anomaly is shrinking," Danny replied as they turned to leave the work station.

"Shrinking?" Hal asked with a confused look.

"Come on," Danny said as he turned and walked back the way he came, with Hal following along behind

They walked past the two printing stations ensconced in the bay while a group of weary Bwain and along with Hal's other apprentices were delicately pulling strands of the alien weaponry out of the production chambers. They then carried them off to the shuttle bay, where they were distributed to the waiting ships. The team had gotten no sleep for two days, and their weariness was beginning to show.

Mephista and Decival's faces floated on the holoscreen against the bay's far wall. Both of them looked worried.

"I don't know what else you want me to do. We're already workin' around the clock as it is," Hal announced before they could even get in a word.

"Hal, we need to know if you can make anything else that could help us," Mephista said, getting right to the point.

"Like maybe shielding, or a more powerful weapon," Decival added.

"Why, what are you plannin' on doin'?" Hal asked.

"We're gonna try and make a run to the next anomaly, but it's almost a day away at maximum throttle," Decival explained.

"We're gonna need something that can delay 'em, a bit. Some way to buy us some time," Mephista added.

Hal sighed. He ran his hand through his hair, thinking back to all the impossible requests that Tannin had made back on Gertie, but this was different. There were lives on the line now.

"I don't honestly know what I can do at this point. I'm having a hard time controlling the printers as it is. Something else is running 'em. Something that's not us, so I don't know how I could suddenly change what they're doin'," Hal said.

"Could the Bwain help you maybe?" Danny asked.

"Beats me. I hadn't really thought to ask 'em to be honest."

"Hal, we've got maybe a day before we need to figure something out. The First Ones are getting closer all the time," Mephista noted.

Hal studied Mephista's face. She looked exhausted as well, which reminded him how hard they were all working to find a way to survive.

"All right, I'll see what I can come up with. I'll let you know if we make any progress," Hal said, and then, without waiting for a response, he closed the connections on the holoscreen.

Turning away from the monitor, Hal let his frustration boil over.

"What the hell do they want from me Danny? They want me to build another *Bwainhome* or somethin' that we can all just waltz on back to Earth in? Jesus, even Tannin wasn't this bad!"

"No, that's not it at all. They're thinking that some of the ships are gonna have to stay behind and fight," Danny said with a strange calmness.

Hal stopped dead in his tracks, suddenly realizing what was happening. Mephista and Decival were trying to buy time, but for what? For an endless game of hopscotch across gravity anomalies that he knew would turn into a grinding battle of attrition? Without Carter and one of his incredible plans, the fleet was in serious trouble.

"We're not gonna get out of this alive, are we Danny?" Hal asked as a wave of overwhelming hopelessness suddenly washed through him.

"I don't know, Hal. I just don't know. Come on, let's see what we can do with the Bwain. Even if they can't help, at least we'll have tried," Danny said, his voice more solemn that Hal had ever heard it.

*   *   *

The Ninkovich

Staring at the massive Bwain ship that hunched on his private cabin's holoscreen, Admiral Nico felt the culmination of his purpose. He'd spent years listening to the civilians drone on about endless supply runs, settlement expansion, and scientific outposts. He was a man of war. As a child, he'd grown up during the final Chechen conflicts, and then as an adult he became a veteran of the early Bwain attacks. To him, bloodshed was a necessary thing, and it was something that Kidewange had avoided for far too long. Now he would end Carter's threat, and the people of the Earth would see his strength.

Just a few small matters remained before he could begin, and the black face marred with concern on his holographic channel was one of them.

"Admiral, I demand an update," President Kidewange voiced on the transmission, but the conversation wasn't in real time. Despite himself, Nico felt his heavy cheeks stretch into a smile. Due to the distance, there was a five-hour delay between his transmission and Earth's receipt. Nico could send a messenger, but it would be easy to make the argument that he'd needed to maintain them all within his fleet for tactical superiority. A lot could happen in five hours.

"Carter killed our messenger, Mr. President," Nico answered. "In light of this hostile act, I am engaging the Bwain ship effective immediately. I will be transmitting a message to the system that will follow," Nico said, and then he paused, uncertain of how to finish the message that would be his last communication with a man so weak that it made him nauseous even to converse with him from a distance.

"You have shown nothing but weakness, and that weakness has brought death to our door," the admiral concluded.

He tapped a finger against the air to send the transmission. Then, dragging his fingers across the holocontrols, he opened a separate private line to Phuri.

"The plan is in motion," he noted tersely before he tapped the screen again to send the message. Smiling to himself once again, he then got to his feet and and headed for the bridge.

In five hours, Phuri's coup would bring Nico to the brink of the power he had sought since he'd joined the SSC. Once he unified the naval and civilian governments, Nico would rid the planet of the *Narcos'* corruption. He'd bend the rebellious outer systems to his will, and usher in the golden age that Kidewange had promised, but never delivered.

An escort of marines fell in behind him as he strode through his ship. The pounding of their boots against the decking thrilled his heart.

"Communications," Nico called as he walked.

"Yes, Admiral," the officer's voice sounded in his ear.

"Prepare to record a general message for transmission across the common band."

"Yes, Admiral. Go ahead."

"Citizens of the solar system and Earth: This is Admiral Vladislav Nico on board the *Ninkovich*. We are under imminent threat by the Bwain in the Kuiper Belt region, and I am about to engage their battle group," he said. It was a small embellishment, but it wouldn't hurt to make his victory seem more impressive. Nico's pace increased, his eagerness to get to the bridge filling him with a near-manic energy. "The Bwain are led by a traitor to our species named Atlas Carter, who has allied with the aliens that have killed countless thousands of our sailors and colonists. Carter has murdered our emissary of peace, and I now have no choice but to engage."

Nico stepped into the ship's elevator. The doors whisked shut around the last of the marines. Under their faceshields, he could see their expectation. They were ready to fight. They'd trained for this, and now would be their chance to put that training to use.

"I take this action explicitly against the orders of President Kidewange," Nico continued. "For too long, the president has stood idly by as the Bwain have ravaged our outer systems. Now they've appeared on Earth's very doorstep, and still the president asked me not to engage. I no longer believe that President Kidewange is fit to lead, and effective immediately, the SSC will be taking control of the galactic president's office. We are in martial law under my command. Once the Bwain threat is lifted, we will reinstitute the senate and elect a new leader. Until then, please send your thoughts and prayers to the brave SSC personnel who will risk their lives in this desperate fight. A fight which would not have come to us if not for Kidewange's failed leadership."

The elevator doors opened, and the bright lights of the bridge's holoscreens filled his vision.

"Communications, you may transmit the message," he ordered.

"Yes, sir."

Elated, Nico walked to his chair in the center of the bridge. The officers arrayed before him were his best, and his most loyal. He would have expected them to be in furious preparation for the battle, and yet many of them simply stared. Sometimes Nico had to be reminded that not all men shared his drive and vision. Fear could cloud their hearts, causing them to question either themselves, or his leadership.

It had always been Nico's policy to engage a challenge head on, and he would do so here as well.

"You've all heard the message," his voice boomed across the silent bridge. "If you'd like to ask anything, now is the time. There will not be another opportunity."

For a moment, the silence continued, then his weapons officer turned and snapped to attention.

"Ah, Maximov. Speak up," Nico snapped.

"Sir, the *Bwainhome*... We didn't want to interrupt your transmission, but the ship..."

"Spit it out, Maximov!" Nico growled.

"The Bwain are gone, sir," the officer finished with a hard swallow.

Nico scoured the holoscreens. The bloated black ship was nowhere to be found. Instead of a massive target, he found only the glittering ice of the small asteroids glimmering back at him.

"Where the hell did they go???" Nico bellowed at his bridge crew.

The echoes of his fury reverberated across the bridge, followed by nervous silence. Crewmen were either carefully studying their screens, or finding some other activity that would enable them to avoid eye contact with the Admiral, as if a mere glance in his direction would draw them into the vortex of Nico's wrath. Silently, each of them applauded Maximov for speaking up, while at the same time breathing a sigh of relief that they had kept their own mouths shut.

Chapter 15

Johannesburg, South Africa

"Operation Anaconda –that's what you've been calling it?" Phuri chuckled.

The two Belizeans seated across from him smiled at their joke.

"The snake is big and slow, but if it seizes you, you will not escape," the taller man said.

They were sitting outside at the Sandown Café. The square was popular with the planetary government's workers, and every day around lunchtime, it was absolutely teaming with people. Black, white, and the lighter brown of dozens of other countries mingled together in tense conversations, discussing the latest reports and rumors. Giant holoscreens mounted to the office buildings that formed the square were usually set to advertising programs, but today the screens showed news anchors updating the crowd with the latest news from the Kuiper Belt. The entire world knew that Nico had sent a messenger to Captain Carter a little more than six hours ago, but no one on Earth knew what had happened next. At least, no one except for Phuri, and the rest of the members of Operation Anaconda.

Phuri drained his wine and then set down the empty glass.

"Did you enjoy it? It's from a highly prized vintage," the Belizean noted. His shorter companion still had not spoken.

"You have no idea how long I've waited to taste it," Phuri murmured, willing the flavor to linger on his tongue for as long as possible. Then he closed his eyes, letting the sun warm his face as he imagined what was about to come.

Kidewange would be barricaded in the galactic tower, but whatever defenses he and his loyalists erected wouldn't be enough to hold back the SSC marines who would be dispatched to maintain order in this turbulent time. Phuri had chosen this spot to watch the developments, because he wanted to know how the people would react. He'd spent weeks with the *Narcos*, carefully calibrating an element of hysteria that only an authoritative leader like Nico would be able to soothe. It was so close to happening now that he could almost taste it.

"And when this is finished, what's in it for you?" the talkative Belizean asked.

Phuri's eyes snapped open, searching for a challenge, but the men appeared to be making simple conversation. A breeze ruffled the hair on their arms, and they shifted lazily in their seats. These were men so used to tension that they could give off the appearance of ease, no matter what was happening around them.

"I've been very clear with your boss regarding my terms," Phuri answered.

"Yes, but what is in your heart?" The Belizean asked, thumping his chest with his fist for emphasis. The gold cross he wore at his throat stuck to his damp skin for a moment before it slid free.

Phuri laughed again. It felt good to finally empty a bottle of wine and celebrate. He tried to signal the waiter's attention, but the man stood transfixed by the holoscreens. After the lessons that Tannin had taught him, it had been so easy for him to manipulate an ignorant planet. He wanted to drink to his former master, but first there was a question to answer.

"What's in my heart?" Phuri repeated thoughtfully, and then his eyes narrowed as bitter memories flooded his mind. "My heart remembers that the same men that I helped build into senators, suddenly turned their backs on me and sent me into exile. I could have died out there in the Sword Belt. The Bwain would have come there sooner or later. They can take over your mind you know. Did you know that?"

"Yes, I have heard such things," the man said.

"Ironically, it was Captain Carter who saved me from such a fate," Phuri continued. The men chuckled again, but their eyes suddenly grew rather serious. Phuri had the impression that he was being measured somehow. The *Narcos* were nothing if not results-driven, and they were still waiting for his promised coup. No doubt they wondered if Phuri would betray those to whom he'd made many promises in exchange for their aid. Phuri was no fool however. He had no doubt that if he tried to pull something like that, he'd be dealt with just as brutally as the thousands who tried to protest the *Narcos* ways in Latin America.

"It would appear that you owe him quite a debt, but you didn't answer my question," the man reminded him.

"My heart? It feels anger, and it burns for the heads of those who would pretend virtue. My heart will dance on the graves of the overthrown, and I will retire someday, content in the knowledge that I was the reason for their downfall," Phuri said with a slight slur. He then turned to the waiter and snapped at him. When the man didn't respond a second time, he hurled the cork at the back of the thin man's head.

"What about you two? What will you receive for your part in our large snake?" he asked as he refocused on their conversation.

The *Narcos* looked at each other for a moment in silence. The bigger one shrugged, steadying his glass as the ruby wine swirled within.

"We have served the hunter for a long time. We will continue to do so."

"But why? You'll be incredibly rich."

For the first time, the smaller, stockier man spoke. His voice was more rough, his English less polished.

"Because the hunter is certain. The only thing you can know in this world is that the hunter will find you. Once you take your oath to the hunter, you can never leave."

"Then you're nothing but slaves really," Phuri said casually.

"You should watch your tongue," the taller man warned.

"Do you know what this square is called?" Phuri asked.

"I think you should apologize," the taller man said, his look growing more dangerous by the second.

"This square is called Mandela Square," Phuri said, ignoring the threat in the man's voice. He sipped the fresh wine, letting its dry spice coat his tongue before it slid down his throat. After so many years of Gertie's hideous Nightcrawler, he couldn't get enough of real Earth food and exotic drinks.

"Before that it was named for a Boer," he continued. "And before that it was a native gathering place. All things change. We are simply the moments between the change."

The holoscreens shifted suddenly, zooming in to an exploding shuttle in the gulf of space.

"It's started," Phuri commented without emotion. He stood, swaying, and swiped a napkin across his lips. "Just remember what you need to do."

"You don't need to tell us our jobs. We've been ready for some time now."

"That's what you said about the reporter," Phuri countered sarcastically.

The Belizean growled something in reply, but Phuri couldn't hear anything over the screams of the crowd. The SSC was on the march, and the time had come to take control.

*   *   *

En route to Luna Station

"But I've got the money!" Lana Delgato said in a pleading tone. Beside her, the shuttle pilot she had chartered to get her off the Earth was struggling to unbuckle the harness that ran under his heavy stomach.

Outside the shuttle's electroglass window, the moon hung in front of them like a glimmering half dollar, and she could just make out the white blips of ships coming and going from Luna Station. Her plan had been to book passage from Luna toward the outer solar system. Any number of merchants and messengers would have gladly offset their costs by adding a passenger. What she hadn't counted on was that whoever had been pursuing on her back on Earth had somehow frozen her credit accounts.

The pilot's buckle rang against his seat. She'd already stood and was backing away from him when he turned toward her, but there was nowhere to go. The shuttle was a cramped messenger vessel, its cabin not even five meters long, and there were no open compartments for her to take refuge.

"I knew I should have never left Earth with you," the pilot snarled as he moved stiffly toward her. "You doubled your price, and I thought I'd finally be able to get the new inducers I've been wanting for this thing. Now I come to find out that you don't even have a cent to pay me!"

"I can use another account!" Lana protested.

"No, I've seen your kind before," the pilot said as he continued to advance. "You disappear when it's time to pay for fuel, and you take things from my ship with you."

Lana backed against the bulkhead. There was nowhere else to go. The pilot neared her with a rolling stomp.

"I promise you, I'll get in touch with my bank and get it all straightened out," she said desperately. "I have the money. Really I do, it's just…"

"You have something to do with that coup that's goin' on down there, don't you? That's why you were so desperate to get off world. If I show up with you on Luna, or anywhere else for that matter, that implicates me in whatever you've done. I'll look like I'm aiding and abetting!"

His hand clamped down on her arm. She tried to fight him, but he was pulling her away from the bulkhead.

"Please!" she cried. "The Bwain are coming, but it's not what you think. Captain Carter…"

"Jesus lady, you just don't get it, do you? I don't care about your sob stories!" the man snapped impatiently. "I know the Bwain are coming. It's why antimatter is so much more expensive right now, and I can charge double to get people the hell away from Uranus station, but I ain't got no room for freeloaders."

The pilot mashed a meaty fist against an instrument panel, causing a panel to open on the wall. He then threw Lana to the floor, and attempted to shove her through the opening.

The coffin-like interior registered instantly. He was trying to shove her into an escape pod. She tried to push her way back into the ship, but the pilot was too strong. He gathered her kicking legs in one beefy arm and held her there as she writhed.

"You can't just leave me to die out here!" she cried.

"I'm not. The pod's programmed to go toward the nearest space station. It's a gravity research outpost. They'll send you home the next time a ship comes through, but you ain't gonna be my problem anymore," the pilot said without sympathy. He had been through all this many times before, and he had no intention of making any exceptions.

"I'll get you the money!" Lana cried, desperate to find a way to get him to listen. The pilot shoved her legs deeper until her head lay close to the life-pod's foam pillow. She kicked and struggled but he was surprisingly strong and fast. There was little she could do to fight him in the small space.

"The escape pod doors are designed to close in a millisecond," the pilot warned. "They'll cut your legs right off if you try to get out."

Desperate, she kicked at his face and got a leg out behind him. He wouldn't want to try and explain having a chopped off foot on his ship to the station inspectors, so he stepped back away from the opening.

"Thank you," she gasped.

"For what?" the pilot said as he drew a plasma pistol from his belt. The white-hot glow burned her retinas, forcing her to look away. "Now, you've got two choices. Get in that damn pod and shut the hell up, or I'll end your trip right here. It's up to you," he said. She knew trying to reason with him was pointless, so she pulled her legs back into the escape pod, and seconds later the hatch slammed shut in the blink of an eye.

*　*　*

The interior of the life pod contained a series of holoscreens and controls above a padded acceleration mat. There was a brief thump, a rushing force that shoved her back toward the pod's entry hatch, and then the hard arc of acceleration that tossed her against the cold carbyne hull.

Screaming and cursing, Lana beat against the display above her that had automatically opened to an entertainment feed. They were showing the news of Nico's so-called assault against Carter on the *Bwainhome*, interspersed with images of Kidewange being led away in handcuffs by SSC marines.

Right now, Phuri was orchestrating the deftest of coups, designed to put the *Narcos* in charge of the entire planet, and she was powerless to stop it. All she could do was watch as a small holodisplay showed her glide path toward LaGrange Station Alpha, where she would spend the most pivotal days of galactic history as a prisoner. That is, until the SSC came to collect her. Everyone who knew the truth had been eliminated, and she had no doubt that her time was coming as well, just as it had for Captain Agricourt and Capra Falconi. While everyone thought the real threat was the Bwain, the *Narcos* would rule earth with more brutality than any alien attack could ever visit upon them.

A counter showed that she had three hours until she arrived at her destination. There was little she could do but wait. The pilot had locked her navigation system before he'd ejected her, and gradually, her anger had begun to fade.

When she'd left her home in Madrid, she'd been chasing a story about Majorana particle radiation, and as a result, she had discovered a truth that needed to be told. Unfortunately, she'd been muzzled by an ignorant editor, and a conspiracy beyond anything she'd ever seen before. She was a reporter with a story to tell, and no way to tell it. Or perhaps...maybe there was a way.

A life pod was designed to transmit across the entirety of the electromagnetic spectrum. The craft's whole goal was to make sure that it was found by any human listening device, so when she tapped against the communications holocontrols, she cried in relief. They were unlocked, which meant that she could transmit a message.

Emotion still flushed the face that stared back at her through the holocamera's calibration. She smoothed her hair and wicked away the tears of frustration that had dribbled down the sides of her cheeks. If she'd been preparing a network feed, she'd have had a whole makeup team and a producer whispering in her ear, but her first major story would be reported from a lonely escape pod, out in the middle of space.

She drew a deep breath, and then tapped the broadcast button.

"This is Lana Delgato, independent reporter. I'm currently coming to you live from a life pod that's en route to LaGrange Station Alpha. What has happened today is a coup built on lies. Admiral Nico has perpetuated a deception of war since the Bwain threat was first mentioned. I have evidence from the member of the SSC messenger corps who was mysteriously killed earlier today that the Bwain have not arrived with warlike intentions, and that they didn't perpetrate the crimes against SSC vessels in the Sword Belt that were claimed by the SSC. Admiral Nico is lying to you in order to make you afraid, all so that he can seize power.

Please, please resist him in any way you possibly can. President Kidewange needs your help."

She held her breath for a moment, and then closed her lips and tapped the send control.

"Broadcasting," the pod's robotic voice informed her.

Lana had no idea what to expect. She'd never broken real news before. Hell, she'd never even been off the Earth. She was both terrified and elated at the same time. It felt so good to finally tell the world the secrets she'd known for so long, that for a brief moment, she allowed herself to celebrate what she considered to be a victory over Phuri.

Any moment now, a flood of questions and messages would reach the pod. She was a few hours from any number of shipping lanes, and her rescue would be assured. That's how it was supposed to be anyway, but the minutes dragged on without a reply.

"Broadcasting," the pod's voice repeated.

"I don't understand. I sent it correctly, and you said you're sending it. What's happening that it's not getting broadcast?"

An alarm squealed from the communication controls. She clamped her hands over her ears while the words *"PROXIMITY ALARM"* blared across her holoscreen. The life pod jerked and weaved, its computer taking evasive action to protect its occupant, and Lana was having a hard time focusing on the exterior view of her holoscreen until the pod finished its gut-wrenching maneuver.

Alongside her pod was a shuttle that was not even fifty meters distant. Where had it come from? It hadn't been there a second ago. Had the shuttle just arrived from an Alcubierre jump? Maybe it was her rescue? Maybe those loyal to Kidewange had heard her report and come to retrieve her. When she saw the soft brown face appear on her holoscreen, her heart fell. The man wore an SSC uniform, and his face was deadly serious.

"You shouldn't be broadcasting that message," the man said sternly. "It's put you in a lot of danger."

And then Lana felt her life pod shake as the shuttle clamped onto its hull.

* * *

The Bwainhome

For a moment as the *Bwainhome* traveled between the dimensions, Carter felt as if he were holding the entirety of Earth's solar system in his mind, lifting it up and peering at it as if he were some sort of a god. Was this a memory from the ship, or was it something within himself? It was becoming more and more difficult to separate himself from the ship and its alien crew.

"Captain?" Granger called from the pilot's station of the shuttle in the Bwainhome's cargo bay. "Are you with me?"

"I'm here, Granger," he said as he leaned through the hatch, trying to clear the strange disorientation he felt looking at what seemed now to be a primitive device for representing reality.

"I think we hit it just right," Granger said as he pointed to the holoscreens. The *Bwainhome's* location was solidly within a square of space near the Earth's moon that was just outside the main shipping lanes. There were no telescopes monitoring this area of space, despite its proximity. The SSC assumed that it had a monopoly on faster-than-light travel, and though Carter had already shown up in the Kuiper Belt, the navy hadn't yet had time to realize the implications of his ship's capabilities.

Carter thought briefly about his career as a boxer. His trainer and mentor Cazador had repeated his instructions day after day until they had become engrained in the young boxer's mind to the point of being subconscious reflexes rather than deliberate actions. He could almost hear Cazador's voice shouting at him as he sparred in the gym.

"When you find a weakness, exploit it quickly, over and over again until your opponent either corrects himself, or falls to the mat."

"Good luck, Pandith," Carter said as he pulled his mind back to the present.

"Thank you, sir," the environmental engineer called through Carter's cochlear implant.

"Listen...if this doesn't work for some reason...," Carter said, but he didn't need to finish; they all knew their very survival depended on the success of this plan.

Granger brought up Pandith's face in the holodisplay. The Malaysian's eyes were fixed in a firm stare straight ahead. He was nothing like the quiet man who'd first introduced his new captain to the crew of the *Fate's Winds*. The Pandith that was here now was a man who had saved the lives of his fellow crew, and who now had the chance to save so many more...if their plan actually worked. It was by far the riskiest plan Carter had come up with since he first set foot in the Sword Belt.

"It'll work, sir. Failure is not an option," Pandith said. His dark brown eyes flicked to the holocamera briefly, and then back to his instrument panel.

On the holoscreen, Pandith's shuttle flew alone toward the moon. In his mind, through the telepathic mystery of the Bwainsong, Carter could feel the swarm of Bwain fighters surrounding the craft. He hoped the aliens would be enough, and that they'd be able to control themselves. The whole point of the plan was to end a war, not start another one.

"You're a good man, Pandith. Good luck," Carter said just before the transmission ended.

"I guess it's my turn now," Granger said.

"That it is," Carter said as he closed his eyes and concentrated.

Hurling the *Bwainhome* between dimensions to another part of space was becoming more and more natural for him. Without knowing exactly how, whenever he called up the thought of traveling within the *Bwainhome* he suddenly knew the entirety of the galaxy in a way that no human scientist would ever have been able to comprehend. It was knowledge that must have taken billions of years to gather. The Bwain hadn't been the ones who had gathered this knowledge however. They had simply been along for the ride.

In the space of a heartbeat Atlas thought of the asteroid belt outside Martian orbit.

"*Go,*" he commanded the immense alien ship with a single thought.

The travel itself felt like water slipping between stones in a river. It took less than another heartbeat.

He could feel their questions coming through the Bwainsong.

"Where are you, Captain? When are you coming back?"

"Atlas, how you could you do this to us? How could you leave me?"

"Captain Carter, I don't know if you can hear me, but our situation is desperate!"

He thought he'd be able to block out their voices, but they were still calling to him.

"Captain, are you all right?" Granger asked with a look of concern.

"Don't worry. I'm all right," he said, flashing him what he hoped was a reassuring smile.

Carter was leaning against the shuttle hatch, feeling the cool metal against his forearm. He was sweating, and had to blink several times before he could focus on Granger inside the shuttle.

"I don't have a lot of time, sir," Granger reminded him.

"I'm sorry, you're right. Get going now, and good luck."

"Somehow, I think you'll need it more than I will," Granger said, still looking quite concerned about his captain's present condition.

Granger saluted as the hatch closed. Carter returned the salute, and then Carter jogged away from the shuttle as it lifted on the near-silent oscillation of its Casimir inducers, and headed toward the membrane that sealed off the bay from the vacuum of space. Like spiders scuttling from their lairs, another squadron of Bwain fighters trickled into the blackness beyond the ship, and quickly disappeared, hiding between the dimensions until they were needed.

A few curious Bwain remained with Carter in the shuttle bay, picking at bits of detritus, or studying the human among them with animalistic curiosity. He was alone with them once more, and his anxious thoughts were still churning.

In the boxing ring, Carter had learned to be still. It was a tactic that minimized his effort, and kept him fresh for the later rounds. Presently however, he felt himself having to fight off the desire to attack. It was one thing to be still, but it was quite another to avoid action altogether.

He had sent two of his former crew on what amounted to suicide missions, and he'd abandoned the rest of the fleet to be murdered, and it was all because of Phuri and Nico, the *Narcos*, and the corrupt who'd been blinded by their desire for power.

"Yes," the Bwainsong whispered.

He could end everything right here and now while he was back in the solar system.

"Aida, I could do it for you. I could make them remember what they did," he thought to himself.

"Yes," the Bwainsong hissed even more insistently. They had been patient for so long, but they wanted to attack...to take...to have. They'd been hungry for so long.

Carter closed his eyes. He could see Aida struggling against Cazador on the rooftop of their home as Belize City burned around them.

"Atlas, can you hear me?" he heard Mephista say as a vision of her floated into his mind's eye. She was hovering above the Bwain back on her ship. He could just see the wall of her tiny cabin, and one of the drawings he'd given her back on Gertie tacked to the bulkhead. *"Please, just answer me!"*

"Elise," he responded, tearing his thoughts back to the present.

"Atlas!" Mephista gasped as she reached up and covered her mouth with her hand. He could see the tears rolling down her cheeks, and it tore him up inside.

"Atlast, are you coming back for us?" she asked.

"I can't yet," Carter said through the Bwain. He was surprised at how relived he was to simply hear her voice. It was like a soothing balm in the midst of all the chaos.

"The First Ones are getting closer, she said rapidly, trying to relay as much information as she could while she was still in contact with him. *"The anomaly won't hold them. I'm giving you one more day before we have to leave, and even that's gonna be cutting it close with how quickly the anomaly is shrinking. I hope you can make it back in time, and I hope you're doing whatever you need to do. Just please understand that I'll have to do the same.*

"Mephista!" Carter called as he felt his contact with her through the Bwainsong fade away. She'd suddenly exited her cabin, but the Bwain she'd been speaking through didn't follow.

"Mephista, you'll never make it!"

Atlas expanded his mind, flitting from one Bwain to another on the ships of the fleet, trying to find one that could see Mephista. As he did so however, he felt the creatures' terror, their anger, and their fear of dying at the hands of their former masters.

Carter brought up the solar system in his mind. He envisioned the Kuiper Belt once more, and spoke the word of command to the ancient ship.

Nico's warmongering threatened to destroy everyone that Atlas cared about for a second time. Very well then. If that's how he wanted to play it, then he would so get the war he so desperately wanted.

* * *

The Ninkovich

"You will find him!" Nico barked at his fleet captains who were all staring back at him through his holoscreen. "You will search every inch of this entire solar system, every colony, every outlying territory, every outpost and scientific station. We will not let this threat go unpunished!"

Chest heaving, Nico scanned every face before him in the cowed silence, searching for any hint of loyalist leanings, or smugness at his failure. If there was a time for Kidewange's lambs to surface themselves, now would be it. Without Carter as a target, Nico's embarrassment at being so easily outmaneuvered had no target other than the president's pathetic loyalists. He hoped to find one of them and execute the man, whether on his own ship, or one of the other ships in the fleet, and yet their discipline was impeccable, as was that of all his officers. No one flinched or gave any appearance of anything other than their utter devotion and loyalty.

Carter's disappearance wasn't the result of disloyalty. Still, a good scapegoat and a public execution of a traitor might have reminded those who served under his command that they would pay a high price for their support of President Kidewange, or any other faction for that matter.

"Bah! Dismissed!" the admiral spat, somewhat disappointed as he fell heavily into his chair.

"Your orders, sir?" the deck officer called.

The reality was that Carter could be anywhere out there, flying around virtually unopposed. Not six hours ago, Nico had told the people of Earth that he would keep them safe, and now Carter was making a mockery of him.

"I want to know how he appeared and disappeared the way he did," Nico ordered as the crew returned to their duties. "You've had more than enough time for a simple analysis. Can we track him or not? Can we figure out where he'll appear next?"

"We're still not sure, sir," Nico's science officer replied. "We're studying every bit of data, but it's alien technology. We've never seen it before. It might take years of research to..."

"I need answers, not excuses damn it!" Nico shouted as he pounded his fist on the arm of his chair violently. "Peoples' lives are at risk!"

"I understand, sir. We're working on it," his officer assured him as his eyes went back to studying the displays in front of him.

Nico took a deep breath and then let it out in a huff as his eyes darted around to the rapidly shuffling holoscreens of the different sectors in the solar system. He'd already ordered more antimatter brought up from Mars to the fleet so that they'd have fuel for two to three Alcubierre jumps if necessary. The cost would be astronomical. It was the kind of decision that Kidewange would have equivocated over for hours, but Nico had at least this modicum of control over the situation with his new-found power.

"Admiral, we're receiving the first communiqués back from Earth. The Galactic Senate has a top secret message for you," his communications officer called.

This was the first message since his announcement to Earth. It was time to see exactly how much he could trust Phuri.

"I'll take it in my quarters. Inform me of any new developments," Nico ordered as he left the bridge.

Nico's thick legs felt restless as he stood. His chest was tight, and sweat ran down the heavy bones of his spine. He was tired of waiting. Let the senators deliver their message. He had the fleet with him, and that was answer enough to any thought of betrayal by Phuri.

"Admiral, he's back!" the weapons officer called just as Nico turned toward the airlock.

Spinning on his heel to face the screens, Nico growled. There on the screen in front of him was the *Bwainhome*. The bulky, charcoal colored ship that looked like a tumor-ridden mutant.

"Launch everything we have," Nico ordered. "He won't escape from me this time!"

Nico smiled to himself as he returned to his place of command on the bridge. At last, after all the careful planning and insufferable delays, opportunity was knocking at his door, and he didn't intend to wait timidly at the threshold.

Chapter 16

The Bwainhome

The *Bwainhome* was the key to Carter's plan. It was the only way he could give Pandith and Granger the chance to survive, and it was the only way he could get back to the Sword Belt and help Mephista and the others fight the First Ones.

If his plan was going to work, he had to put the *Bwainhome* in harm's way by drawing out every reserve ship in the entire solar system.

"Bwainslayer, is it time?" the aliens asked him through the Bwainsong.

Carter paced back and forth in front of the Endless Knot, his mind wandering back to his pre-fight routine from so many years ago. With so much energy and anticipation before each bout, he would do pushups, jumping jacks, stretches, and then simply pace back and forth in anticipation as he flexed his hands under the tight wrappings.

"Do we kill?" the Bwain asked. *"Do we kill humans now?"*

Carter felt swarms of the Bwain fighters slip from the shuttle bay far below him. The craft spread invisibly against the blackness of space like the devil's own emissaries.

"Bwainslayer, do we kill? they asked him again as a ripple of eagerness hummed through their collective minds.

* * *

Outside LaGrange Station Alpha

"What you're telling me doesn't make any sense," Lana replied with a frown.

She was watching the quiet man who had rescued her from the life pod rather intently. Her new pilot kept his eyes fixed on the holoscreens in front of him, studying LaGrange Station Alpha as if his life depended on it. The research station was a simple hub-and-spoke design, with the habitat rings tethered by a series of spider steel cables to the central spoke. It was a drab white and gray against the blackness of space, and for the life of her, she couldn't understand why Atlas Carter had sent this man here.

"If you're really here on behalf of Captain Carter, how did you get all the way here from the Sword Belt, and what's the point of coming here to scare a bunch of research students?" Lana asked. Her reporter's curiosity had already made her forget her forced confinement in the life pod, and she was back on the story once again.

"Stop asking me questions," Pandith said absently.

"Please, I'm on your side," Lana pleaded.

"Are you?" he asked, glancing over at her with eyes that were devoid of emotion. "Everyone that's come to the Sword Belt recently has tried to kill us, and the entire SSC home fleet is facing off against Captain Carter as we speak."

"I knew Capra Falconi. I talked to Captain Agricourt on Earth. I talked to Phuri!" Lana continued, trying desperately to assure her rescuer of her intentions.

"Phuri? What did Phuri tell you?" the engineer asked.

"He wanted to know how I felt about Kidewange. He asked me to broadcast a message that Carter had come to the solar system to demand Kidewange's surrender. The whole reason he's here is that he's been trying to stage a coup. Nico thinks that he'll be in power, but it's really the *Narcos*. They're behind everything, and Phuri is using Captain Carter's presence in the solar system to make it all happen."

Pandith stared at her for a long moment, and then went back to eyeing the research station.

"I'm sorry, but we've got bigger problems at the moment. I have a mission I need to complete."

"A mission!" Lana cried. "You can't be serious. Just the fact that Carter's here has put the *Narcos* in power! You have to...," she argued, but she fell silent when a message came in from the station.

"This is LaGrange Station Alpha to approaching shuttle," a young-sounding voice announced over the radio. "We're having trouble reading your identity beacon. Over."

"Copy. My shuttle took damage picking up a life pod earlier. Requesting permission to dock. I've got a wounded passenger."

"Understood. We'll have a medical team ready," the voice acknowledged.

"You have no idea what's happening on Earth. Whatever you're doing here, whatever Carter wants, you have to tell people. You won't have a choice if you wait," Lana continued, a hint of panic in her voice. How could she make Captain Carter's pilot understand how serious the situation was?

"If I wait, then no one will have a choice about anything for very much longer," Pandith stated calmly as he adjusted the shuttle's throttle.

*   *   *

A series of metallic clangs rang through the hull as the station's docking clamps sealed around the shuttle airlock. Lana had already left her seat and was standing by the hatch, considering what she'd say to whoever would be on the other side of the bulkhead. Did she go along with what Pandith asked by pretending to be injured, just so she could see what he was up to, or did she wait for her chance to broadcast her message again, so she could try to save the planet?

"What are you gonna do?" she asked, but Pandith didn't respond as he stepped past her, tapped his thumb on a locker near the door, and withdrew two plasma pistols.

"You're not planning on killing 'em, are you?" she gasped. At the same time, she leaned against another locker as surreptitiously as possible, and pressed her finger against the latch. There was always a third possibility to get leverage over this Pandith, even if his weapons lockers wouldn't open for her.

"Not if it can be avoided," he said flatly. "Those have been Captain Carter's orders from the beginning. If we should happen to survive, I want you to remember that."

"I could tell 'em who you are. If you don't cooperate, I could expose you," Lana said, but even to her own ears, her feeble threat seemed pitiful at best.

The airlock's lights flashed amber, indicating that someone on the other side had opened the external door and was cycling through. She could just make out the blurred faces of several station personnel through the electroglass.

Pandith spun to her. The plasma pistols had disappeared, but he seized her arm and pulled her close.

"Whatever you think you know…however you think you've supported us, know that we appreciate it, but now is not the time for questions. Lie down and be still."

"And if I don't?" she demanded petulantly.

The man considered this for a moment before he released her.

"Then make your own choice, as we all have."

The airlock hissed open.

Two men and a woman dressed in red medical jumpsuits rushed onboard. They were carrying armloads of gear. None of them looked like they were past their very early twenties.

"We understand you have a casualty. Where is she?" a woman asked.

The three looked around the shuttle, confused. The hatch that led to the cargo hold hissed open.

"In the cargo…" another one started to say before he noticed that Pandith was holding a plasma pistol on him.

"Now wait just a minute…," the woman started nervously, but he fell silent again when Pandith aimed his pistol at her chest.

"How many of you are there on the station?" he asked.

"There's only six of us right now. The scientists aren't really doing much testing, and…," one of the others said, but then they trailed off nervously.

"Good. The three of you will stay here under guard," Pandith informed them.

"I'm not guarding them," Lana said firmly. She still didn't have a clear picture of what was going on, and she had no desire to have any part of whatever was happening until she knew who to trust.

"I never said you would," Pandith answered.

"Jesus, Mary, and Joseph!" one of the medics cried as a series of mottled figures emerged from the cargo hold. The creatures scuttled forward on claw-like feet, their turkey vulture heads snapping back and forth as they surrounded the medics.

"Oh my god, what's happening?" Lana cried as the scientists threw up their hands and backed into a circle.

"No one needs to worry. I'm only here for the experiments. As long as I get what I want, no one's gonna get hurt," Pandith assured them.

*　*　*

Mars
SSC Antimatter Production and Refueling Station

With the cloaked Bwain fighters surrounding his shuttle, Granger was invisible to the SSC's sensors. Their dimensional technology meant that he'd have no trouble staying unseen by the half-dozen cruisers and smaller craft that guarded the antimatter refinery and refueling station used by nearly every SSC ship equipped with an Alcubierre drive. It was one of the highest-security facilities in the solar system, and he could get close enough to scrape of its paint without detection.

Mars was a massive orange and gray haze below him, and the ships around him were thousands of times larger than his shuttle. As long as he stayed invisible, his plan still had a chance.

The problem was, in order to make off with forty antimatter capsules they needed, he would somehow have to somehow dock with the facility unnoticed. He'd spent his time on the *Bwainhome* preparing a computer program that would provide him with counterfeit identification credentials and orders, which he *hoped* would be realistic enough for him to pass through to the storage area.

If the Bwain could maintain their discipline, and if no one questioned the orders for an antimatter resupply for Nico's fleet, the plan might just work.

His shuttle crept toward an empty slip far from any other ships docked at the facility. The station itself was composed of a rounded warehouse and habitation bubble that were attached to a large, curved cylinder that ran like an elongated finger for kilometers in two directions. This was the facility's particle accelerator, which used the perchlorate found in the Martian soil as fuel to power the massive atomic collisions. These reactions generated the trickle of antimatter that made interstellar travel possible.

As they made their approach, Granger initiated the shuttle's docking sequence. This was the moment of truth. Somewhere, a computer would register that a ship was docking with Airlock 227, and their internal cameras would show Granger stepping out of the shuttle. He had very little time to move, so after the docking was complete, he threw off his harness and ran to the hatch.

"Captain, I'm going in," he said to one of the Bwain who'd accompanied him from the shuttle.

The alien turned its head, but seemed distracted for some reason.

"Hurry Granger. I'm having trouble...controlling...," Carter answered through the Bwain.

Granger's heart sank. If the Bwain didn't stay disciplined, he'd be blown out of the sky before he even left the station.

A warning chime sounded, and his airlock hissed open. An instant later he was out of the shuttle, and quickly started looking around for what he needed.

* * *

LaGrange Station Alpha

"And what if we don't give the experiment to you?" the station's lead scientist asked. An older woman with her hair tied back in a severe ponytail faced Pandith with a defiant thrust of her narrow chin.

"Then I'll give your colleagues to the Bwain."

So far, Lana had simply followed Pandith through the cramped station. The air was sour with college student's hormones, and until they'd reached the control room, she hadn't seen a single window. But now, she could see the gravity drive tethered to a pylon jutting out from the station. It looked for all the world like a child's ring toy, consisting of a series of successively larger rings that were mounted onto a conical housing. The station must have been designed to test the drive's thrust while the drive itself was stationary. The clamps holding it must have been incredibly powerful, and the scientists were refusing to give Pandith the codes to free it.

"Would he really do that?" the woman asked Lana.

"I honestly don't know. I just met him," Lana said nervously.

"What's wrong with you people?" one of the students asked. All three of the scientists held their hands in the air in surrender, but the indignant expressions on their faces was palpable. "How could you help aliens that hate us?"

"And if I told you that those the aliens were the only ones keeping us alive right now, what would you say to me then?" Pandith asked the student.

"I'd say you sold out your species, just like Nico said," the other student answered.

Pandith's eyes flicked to the drive, then back to his prisoners. Lana could see he was at an impasse.

"This is what will happen everywhere unless we get the truth out. If you don't tell me what's going on, the entire solar system is gonna be your enemy," Lana said, her pleading eyes shining bright with desperation.

Pandith's pistol wavered. The four Bwain with him clicked and bobbed. Then, the engineer slipped the pistol into his jumpsuit and turned to the console. His fingers flew across the holocontrols, tapping at different access levels and password strings.

"You'll never find it, even if you torture me," the scientist stated as she stared at Pandith.

"I want to tell you about the torture I've seen," Pandith said. His face was still locked on the controls, and he spoke almost absently.

"I've seen a young girl's mind torn out and controlled by the Bwain. I've seen my entire crew nearly killed by them, and a captain who survived paralysis and explosive decompression that was caused by them, but I've seen something far worse. The Bwain have masters, and those creatures are coming back. We're already fighting them in the Sword Belt, but it's only a matter of time until they overwhelm us. And while the

Earth keeps sending ships to try and kill us, the Bwain are sacrificing themselves to help us fight."

Lana watched his face as he spoke. Was she finally getting to the truth of what had been happening?

"I need this drive, because it's the only thing that might stop what we're up against. You can write whatever story you want afterward. Hell, maybe I'll even be alive to read it," he said, glancing up at Lana for a moment before he drew his pistol once again and pointed it toward the research team. "All those people still fighting those things out in the Sword Belt are gonna die if you don't give me what I need, so I have no problem with burning through each and every one of your limbs until you do. My only goal right now is to save the lives of those people, no matter what it takes."

Lana's mouth fell open. Creatures more dangerous than the Bwain? How on Earth had Carter fought them, and why didn't anyone know?

She had so many questions that were running through her head that she almost missed the project scientist stepping past Pandith and operating the console. Outside the station, the gravity drive slipped free of its tether. A small ship materialized from nowhere instantly. The vessel was made of a deep black, and looked almost like a Sputnik satellite from hundreds of years before. The small craft, a Bwain ship no doubt, hung around the device as if desperate for it to move.

As for the engineer himself, the man was shaking, though whether it was from stress or relief, she couldn't tell.

"Thank you. You may have just saved us all," Pandith said quietly.

Chapter 17

The Tranquility

Kaylee tossed and turned, thrashing against the medical bay's sheets. The girl was only comfortable sleeping here, probably as a result of the time she had spent in the *Fate's Winds* med bay with Pandith after being rescued.

"Can you sedate her?" Mephista asked the doctor.

"I could, ma'am, but it's not really a good idea to sedate someone when they're having nightmares. It'd just keep 'em asleep and make 'em suffer more," he explained.

"What about electro-restraints? I don't want her to hurt herself," Bryon suggested.

"No," Mephista said, remembering how she had felt when she woke up from her own nightmares, disoriented and terrified. The feeling of being bound would make the shock nearly impossible. "It's breaking my heart to see her suffering like this, but I think we just need to let it run its course."

"Understood," the doctor said. Then with a slight bow, he turned and drifted away. Before the officer had even slowed his glide, his eyes had fallen shut. He woke again suddenly when he tapped against one of the empty beds. Realizing what happened, he shook his head to try to clear it, and then made his way out of the room.

They were all exhausted from monitoring the First Ones, and the only one who was sleeping was having worse nightmares than those who were awake.

Mephista spun and pulled herself toward the hatch. Just as she was nearing the entrance to the med bay, Bryon came floating up behind her.

"Permission to speak freely?" he asked.

"Of course," she said as she turned to face him.

"Have you heard from the captain?" Bryon asked hopefully. Despite her tense exhaustion, Mephista was actually able to smile.

"Yeah, I have actually," she said as she reached for a rail to steady herself in the zero gravity.

"Is he coming back?"

"I don't know, Lieutenant," she answered, replaying in her mind the brief contact she'd had with Carter through the Bwain.

"Well, what did he say?" Bryon persisted

"It's not important," she finally managed. Then she glanced back at where Kaylee shifted and moaned on her mattress. "We're gonna be facing a pretty one-sided battle here in a few hours, Mr. Purcell. I suggest you get some sleep."

"Roger, Captain," he said, trying to keep the disappointment from his voice. If she didn't want to discuss her conversation with him, that probably meant that the captain wouldn't be able to make it back, or at least not in time anyway.

She tried to force a half-hearted smile, and then she turned to pull herself through the door.

"Captain...," Purcell called after her.

"Yes, Lieutenant?"

The weapons officer had pushed himself toward Kaylee's bed. He reached out as if he wanted to hold her hand, but he didn't want to wake her, so he let his hand fall back to his side. The girl's nightmare seemed to have passed at least, as she was laying more still now.

"I'm not just gonna give up, and you shouldn't either. I'll go down kicking and screaming if I have to," he said with a grim look of determination as he gently brushed a wisp of hair from Kaylee's forehead.

"I wouldn't expect anything less, Lieutenant," she said as she turned and made her way out into the corridor.

* * *

The Dauntless

"Here they come again!" Captain Decival's weapons officer called.

On the holoscreens, the anomaly had shrunk to what looked the size of a beach ball compared to the massive horde of First Ones surrounding it. The creatures were battering themselves against the gravity well over and over again, shrinking it a few hundred kilometers at a time. They blazed painful reds and pinks, and some of them even faded from view entirel, but their maniacal efforts were paying off.

In an hour, maybe two, the anomaly would be too small to protect the edges of the fleet. Hal and Danny had worked for three days straight to arm the fleet as best they could. Each ship had at least a few of the strange weapons, along with enough Bwain to fire the devices several times over. Danielle knew that survival wasn't likely. That is, unless she could get them to the next anomaly in time.

As she watched their sanctuary dwindle, her breath caught against the dryness at the back of her throat. Her foot's regeneration process required her to stay hydrated, but she hadn't taken a break from her station for nearly twenty hours. On Decival's orders, she'd been planning for this contingency ever since Threed had been killed. The problem was that she was missing data. She had no idea how fast the First Ones could travel, so there was no telling if her solution would work or not. Until Captain Carter returned, they had to figure out some way to survive on their own, and she was going to do her best to make sure she didn't let everyone down.

"Captain Mephista, do you copy?" Decival called over the fleet's command channel.

"Copy, *Dauntless*. Is Ms. Hoff's solution ready?" Mephista asked. Danielle reviewed her navigation plans once last time once more. The two dozen fastest ships, loaded with every colonist and weapons factory they had, would embark upon a course for the next closest gravity anomaly. It was ten hours away at maximum thrust, and she was confident she had plotted the fastest course.

"It's ready, ma'am," Danielle responded with a final touch of the screen before her.

"Then good luck to you," Mephista said.

"Good luck to all of us," Danielle replied as her fingers hovered over her controls.

"All right, begin the maneuvers," Captain Decival ordered.

* * *

The Tranquility

On Mephista's holoscreens, a wave of one-hundred tiny signatures formed a picket line at the dwindling front of the anomaly just a few thousand kilometers from where the ravenous First Ones bashed against it. Each of the fleet's capital ships had left Earth with a dozen shuttles in theirs bays, which meant that they had just under three-hundred of the tiny craft armed with Bwain weapons. It might be good enough to buy them a few more hours...if they were lucky.

The first of the fleet slipped out the back of the anomaly's protection.

Mephista's rear guard were the most damaged of the ships, all of them battered and bruised. They were manned with skeleton crews who'd volunteered to stay behind. As she watched them perform their duties under the most impossible of circumstances, jobs she felt a small flush of pride. Many of her own crew had stayed, along with some of Threed's people, and even some of the colonists. Atlas had brought them all together, and she couldn't deny that he'd done more than she would have thought possible back when she'd considered vaporizing him for interfering with her plans to return to Earth.

She had to smile at the memory and the dim hope of ever seeing her home planet again.

"Maybe you'll survive to see it Atlas. I hope you will anyway. There's still more for you there than there is for me," she thought with a twinge of loneliness.

A single Bwain remained on her ship. The rest were disbursed among the shuttles and rear guard in order to ensure that the strange guns capable of injuring the First Ones could be fired as many times as possible.

"Mr. Purcell, what are you seeing?" she asked from her command on the *Tranquility's* bridge.

The weapons officer was in one of the lead shuttles, but his holofeed showed on her screen, and she could speak with him in real time through her implant.

"Targets, ma'am."

"By my count, there are plenty of 'em for you to shoot at. It's gonna be hard to choose," she noted.

"Nah, not at all. I'll just start with the ugliest one, and work my way over to the prettiest. It's sorta like pickin' up girls in a bar. You start with the ugliest one, because they're the easiest to score with, and then you work your way along the looks scale until you get to one that slaps you. The one just before that is the best you'll be able to do. Gotta know your limits after all."

"Well that's...jeez, I don't even know how to respond to that," Mephista said, a smile finding its way to her lips despite the seriousness of the situation. Bryon's cheeky brand of humor was always a bright spot for her in an otherwise dismal situation.

"Don't worry ma'am. I've been slapped plenty of times. I know my limits, so I'll do my best to avoid it this time."

"Please make sure you do. Good luck out there," she said.

"Thanks ma'am, and good luck to you as well. Whatever happens, I just want you to know that it's been an honor to serve with you."

"It has been for me too Lieutenant."

"Tell me somethin' I don't know," he said with a breathy laugh. Purcell out."

When the comms channel closed, she just stood there in silence, smiling to herself. The way he faced death with a joke and a laugh was nothing short of inspiring. She'd known men like him in the past, but they were a rare breed that were few and far between.

The creatures didn't seem to notice the fleeing ships. They were single-mindedly pressing forward in the same arc around the anomaly, continuing with the plan that had worked for them so far.

The job of those piloting the shuttles was to get close enough to hurt the First Ones, and then streak off in all directions to draw the creatures away. If the plan worked, it would take the creatures hours to sop up all the shuttles they managed to destroy before they were able to continue their pursuit of the fleet. When they did, Mephista's rear guard, and the second and third shuttle waves would fight the same battle twice more.

Of course, she was under no illusions about even the first wave's effectiveness, but the plan was sound. More accurately, it was all they had, regardless of whether it was an effective strategy or not.

"We're coming within range, or at least what I *think* is range with these things," Bryon's voice sounded in her ear.

The scene in front of Mephista shifted to a much more obtuse angle of the underbelly of one of the First Ones. Chitinous glowing armor streaked down its underside, and red streaks charred the edges of its flesh where the creature had been straining to penetrate the anomaly.

"It looks like it's burning," someone commented.

"Nah, not yet...but it will be in a minute," Bryon said. Mephista watched her screen as the strange tentacle mounted to the nose of Purcell's shuttle swelled and unleashed its projectile.

"Shot's away, and my Bwain is...hey there little buddy. My Bwain's still okay!" he said with a great deal of relief.

The projectile was a ball of deep pink that faded in and out of the picture as it flew. It struck its target dead in what could best be described as the creature's thorax, and melted into the chitin like acid dropped onto wax. Though she couldn't possibly hear a sound, Mephista and the rest of her crew covered their ears. They'd felt...*something.* It was like a scream or a howl. It sounded like something was dying.

"Woohoo! We got the bastard!" Bryon shouted excitedly.

"Oh my god, it worked! It's actually working!" Mephista said, her voice echoing his excitement.

"All right everyone, let's do this!" Bryon yelled through the comms channel.

Mephista watched as the shuttles opened fire with Hal's strange weapons. The First Ones reeled back, flashing red and shimmering as they drifted in and out of reality. Tentacles torn off by the onslaught were gobbled up by the others, and the wounded were hunching over their wounds, trying to protect themselves from not only the onslaught, but from their hungry brethren as well.

"Keep it going!" Mephista cried, a savage elation filling her voice. "Kill every last one of those sons of bitches, because we may not get another chance!"

* * *

The Fates Winds

The Ancient had rarely needed Aric's presence, and only rarely woke him now. For the moment at least, the creature had grown tired of playing games with the human's weak mind.

With what little was left of the man he once was, Aric dreamed of going back to Earth. He'd have given anything just to see the blue sky one last time, and to feel the warmth of the sun on his face. He dreamed of swimming in a crystal pool on a summer's day, and of having a lover's arms wrapped around him in an emotional embrace.

When the pain woke him, Aric doubled over onto the deck and tried to vomit. White-gold slurry spilled out of his frozen lips as the nanobots came spewing out of him. Seconds later, they crawled their way back up his body and into his mouth as he lay there feeling half eaten and diminished.

When he finally had strength to lift his head, Aric saw the First Ones filling the space around the obelisk for as far as the eye could see. Wave upon wave of them filled the space like some sort of a swollen, misshapen army.

They had consumed so much already. How could they possibly be stopped?

The pain struck him again, combined with the burrowing mental worms that chewed at his thoughts.

"ARIC KEITH, WHAT IS THIS?" The Ancient bellowed.

In a flash, he saw First Ones wounded and dying at the hands of what appeared to be SSC shuttles using some sort of a weapon he'd never seen before. The hope that filled his heart brought about a new wave of pain, but this time it was different. It had a new quality to it, like a cold grip that seemed to flame up the rear of his skull.

"SPEAK!"

"I don't know, but to me it looks like they've found a way to fight you."

"SLAVES ARE NOT CAPABLE."

"Humans aren't slaves. Haven't you figured that out by now?" Aric asked.

"ALL EXIST TO SERVE US."

"They don't believe that. They'll never believe that."

"THEY ARE LIKE YOU?"

"You'll never understand humanity. It's beyond you," Aric said.

A new sensation wracked him then. It was something that he hadn't felt before. The pain emanated from the center of his head now. Before, Aric had been able to shut out the feelings as simple manipulations of his nerve endings, but now he felt heartsick and emotionally spent. A crushing loneliness and despair burned through him, much like the fleet's weapons were burning through the First Ones.

"I HAVE LET YOU LIVE, ARIC KEITH. I HAVE LET YOU BELIEVE THERE WAS HOPE, AND NOW YOU GIVE ME THE GIFT OF YOUR THOUGHTS."

The pain slipped away from him. Aric lifted his head from the deck, and staring out through the shredded hull, he saw hundreds of First Ones gather themselves together, and then streak off in a single direction. Though it was impossible to have any navigational sense without a star to guide him, somehow he knew their destination.

"WE WILL DESTROY YOUR FRIENDS, ARIC KEITH, AND THEN WE WILL GO TO YOUR EARTH AND CONSUME THAT AS WELL," The Ancient intoned.

"No!" Aric screamed, but his lips were numbed and useless, and his tongue had long since frozen. The First Ones all disappeared, until only The Ancient still remained. The hideous thing's head leered at him on top of its stalk.

"I WILL CONSUME YOUR CARTER MYSELF, AND I WILL TELL YOU HOW HE TASTES IN GREAT DETAIL," The Ancient boasted.

Aric suddenly felt completely alone. He collapsed back onto the deck, sobbing tears that would not come in the unrelenting darkness.

* * *

The Refugee Fleet

"I got three so far. Someone better be keepin' score out there," Bryon said excitedly over the comms channel.

Mephista was hardly able to believe her good fortune. Hal's weapons, augmented by the Bwain, were working better than she could have expected. At least twenty of the First Ones had been killed so far, their white brilliance battered relentlessly by volley after volley. The others had started milling about in confusion, unsure of how to handle an enemy that was capable of fighting back.

Up on her holoscreen, another of the creatures shuddered, and then collapsed back in on itself.

"It actually imploded! Decival, are you seeing this?" Mephista called.

"Copy that, Captain. Suggest you make haste to join us, ASAP. We're eight hours from the second anomaly," Decival responded.

"This one looks much larger than the one we were in. I think it'll buy us some extra time," Mephista heard Danielle add in the background.

Mephista's adrenaline mixed with an incredible sense of relief. A dozen shuttles had been lost already, but they'd been so much more effective than she'd ever dared to hope.

"Copy," Mephista acknowledged as she switched over to communicate with the other ships around her.

"This is Captain Mephista to the rear guard. Transmitting navigation solutions to join the rest of the fleet. We'll depart in five. Lieutenant Purcell, get your shuttles back into formation. We'll maintain the umbrella formation as we withdraw."

On her holoscreens, the shuttle signatures tightened into an arc formation that would serve to protect the larger ships.

"Initiate," Mephista ordered, and though she knew they'd been successful, and could now at least have a chance in a fight against the First Ones, she still felt a pang of fear as her ship slipped out of the anomaly.

"We're in open space, ma'am. Estimated arrival with the rest of the fleet is in approximately 10.4 four hours," her navigation officer called.

"Copy," Mephista acknowledged.

"Ma'am the First Ones...they're not following us," the science officer reported.

Mephista zoomed out her holos, frowning at what she saw.

"Mr. Purcell, what are you seeing?" she asked.

"I'm not sure. They've just sorta stopped. They have to know they can go around the anomaly, so I'm not sure what they're doin'."

"I don't like it. Something's wrong," Mephista muttered under her breath.

"Jesus Christ!" someone cried over the fleet's broadcast network.

"What was that? Who's on this frequency?" Mephista's communications officer asked.

"Give me maximum speed, now! Push it until the engines are damn near ready to give out!" Decival ordered.

Mephista zoomed out her holos, and her heart sank.

"No, Decival...don't! You have to come *toward* me! It's your only chance!" Mephista shouted.

A flickering mass of untold numbers of First Ones had just appeared in front of Decival's portion of the fleet. They had spread out like a net, and were locking tentacles as if they meant to trawl the emptiness of space and consume the entire fleet.

Decival was trying to arrange his contingent of shuttles like a shield, but there was no possible way it would be enough.

"Captain! Answer me!" Mephista shouted.

"Mephista, we won't make it to you in time," Decival shouted over the comms channel. She could hear a flurry of activity and voices behind him on the bridge of the *Dauntless*.

"Come back *toward* me Captain! It's the only safe way," Mephista said urgently as she felt the bile of fear and panic rise in her throat.

"Oh my god!" Decival whispered, and suddenly there was a loud noise. Mephista and her crew aboard the *Tranquility* strained to hear his next words, but there was nothing but deadly silence as the transmission abruptly terminated.

Chapter 18

Martian Antimatter Facility

Granger stepped outside of his shuttle's airlock and nearly bumped into a stocky, bearded man who was backed by two marines.

"How did you get in here?" the man demanded.

"I passed through the docking protocol. How else would I do it?" Granger asked, forcing his voice to remain steady.

"That's a lie. We don't have any record of...here, give me your orders."

Granger held out the tablet with his hacked credentials. The man held the machine up to the wall scanner, then grunted as it flashed green.

"How the hell do you think I would have been able to sneak past all the ships you have here if I didn't have the right creds? Maybe it's a malfunction or something," Granger said in an annoyed tone, as if the man's suspicions were utterly ridiculous.

"Check him," the dock master ordered.

One of the marines took out a small wand, swept it up and down over Granger's body, and then nodded.

"No weaponry," the soldier confirmed.

The dock master frowned. Granger did his best to appear casual, but his guts were churning with nervousness.

"All right then, come with me," the station master said reluctantly.

Granger followed the dock master through the station's sparse corridors. The station itself was clearly little more than a warehouse, optimized to produce, store and ship antimatter as efficiently as possible.

"You're cleared for pickup. There's only one issue. Your requisition called for forty pellets. I can only give you ten."

"I don't understand," Granger replied.

"We're on a war footing with the Bwain in the outer system. I need to maintain a steady reserve."

"But this fuel is for the war effort! Why the hell else would I have a requisition for forty pellets? You think I'm gonna stuff 'em up my ass so I can fart myself a warp bubble?" he asked irritably, but the dock master more or less ignored his ramblings.

Eventually, they stopped at a gleaming wall that was lined with touch panels. The dock master tapped a holocontrol, and a container detached itself from the wall and opened to allow them access. Inside the container was more antimatter than Granger had seen in the whole of his life. Antimatter was stored in a bullet-sized module called a Penning capsule. Inside the super-strong container was an electromagnetic cage that held the fuel, so that it was prevented from coming into contact with any regular matter. This was the most precious substance in the universe. It was what allowed man to conquer the stars, and what brought him back home when he was done.

It was all Granger could do to keep his scientific mind from salivating.

"You said this was for the war effort, but that's not what your orders said. Your orders say that this is for a rotation of ships coming back from Saturn," the dock master said with a frown.

"Those ships are on alert right now since there's no telling where the Bwain are gonna strike next," Granger explained stubbornly. The dock master studied him for a moment, remembering some of his earlier suspicions.

"I'll just confirm this with your captain. It won't take but a sec...oof!" the man grunted as Granger threw an elbow into his stomach. He quickly grabbed the container from its docking station, and raced fove steps before one of the marines stunned him with a blow to the spine. Granger stumbled, collapsing on the deck. When he rolled over, a plasma rifle filled his vision.

"Now that wasn't very smart, was it?" the marine sneered.

"What were you trying to do? Don't you know this is the most heavily guarded facility in the solar system?" the station master asked incredulously. He could't believe a single man would take such an incredibly senseless risk.

"I do, but I'll have to explain what I'm about to do later," Granger answered into the muzzle of the plasma rifle.

The Marines glanced at each other and grinned, as if they were sharing some sort of a private joke about how stupid their prisoner was.

"This is unit 3-12. We have a prisoner…," one of the marines began to transmit, but he stopped in mid-sentence as he choked on his own words.

The walls in the corridor suddenly shimmered and resolved into a dozen Bwain who'd been using their camouflage ability to stay carefully hidden until they were needed. The creatures launched themselves toward the Marines and the station master. A plasma bolt rang out, vaporizing one of the aliens in a cloud of burnt feathers. The others charged ahead, swarming the two marines. Granger swung his leg and tripped the dock master as the man tried to run, and then climbed onto his back to hold him down. The smaller Bwain had the benefit of numbers, and were able to overwhelm the two marines in no time at all, pinning them down in the same way that Granger had the dock master pinned.

"You won't get away with this!" the dock master yelled as Granger allowed a couple of Bwain to replace him, while he took the magna-cuffs from the marines and bound the men's hands and feet. "You and Carter are traitors to your race!"

"No, we're not actually. We're trying to save it," Granger called over his shoulder as he reclaimed the container of antimatter and sprinted back to his shuttle with the Bwain following along behind.

* * *

Granger locked the antimatter in the cargo hold of his shuttle as quickly as he could, and then he hurried to undock the shuttle and leave the station. The Bwain squawked and flapped around him, elated by their recent activity. They were like sleepy children because they'd been inactive for so very long, but they were now reveling in their new awakening.

"Return! Fight First Ones!" one squawked.

"We will be soon enough," Granger responded as he closed and secured the cargo hold. "You all did a great job. Please tell Captain Carter that I've secured the antimatter."

One of the Bwain closed its eyes, but just as quickly, they reopened once more.

"First Ones come!" it cried.

"What do you mean? They're here?" Granger asked, as a rush of dread washed over him.

"No, not here. In other place. Sword Belt. First Ones come!"

"The fleet? They're attacking the fleet?"

"Yes, fleet! Hurry!"

"Did you tell Carter?"

"Yes," the Bwain hissed.

"Then there's nothing else we can do. We have to wait for...," he started to say, but a voice suddenly sounded over comms channel.

"Unidentified shuttle. You have ten seconds to power down and await boarding. You will not escape with the antimatter," a voice sounded.

Granger's head snapped around, scanning the space outside his electroglass.

"Where are the fighters?" he asked the Bwain, dumbfounded.

"Five seconds," the intercom announced.

Granger was sick. He had no choice. He couldn't fail the fleet.

"Three, two...," the voice continued the countdown.

"I need to explain something to you! The Bwain..."

"There will be no explanation. Stand down and prepare to be boarded," the officer said firmly.

Granger closed his eyes. He'd failed. The plan had always been a long shot, but he'd thought he would finally be able to take action rather than hiding behind his instruments and experiments. Now look where it had gotten him. Another step closer to the edge of turning humans against each other, and against a species that was just doing what they could to survive.

A clawed hand siddenly gripped Granger's shoulder.

"We help," the Bwain hissed.

* * *

Twenty Bwain dimensional fighters uncloaked themselves outside the Martian Antimatter Facility for just long enough to register on the human guard ships' holoscanners. Then, just as suddenly, they disappeared.

"Run," one of the Bwain in the shuttle rasped.

"But you'll never survive," Granger protested as he turned to face the creature behind him.

"Can hide. Carter taught," the alien said as its head bobbed, and its feathers flashed a quick blackish-purple.

They were learning, Granger realized. They understood the larger goal.

Granger rammed his shuttle's inducers to full power, heading for the rendezvous point on the far side of Mars where he would await the arrival of the *Bwainhome*.

"Captain, I'm almost in position with the fuel," Granger said to one of the Bwain.

On the holoscreens, he saw flashes of the Bwain fighters engaging with the capital ships that were moving to intercept him. The human ships paused, began evasive maneuvers, and then the Bwain vanished once more, appearing here and there to harass them as Granger's shuttle zoomed off toward the red planet.

"No casualties," Granger instructed, as he watched the swift craft swooping and twisting on his holoscreen.

"No one hurt," the Bwain confirmed with a flutter of its wings.

"Whoever the hell is in that shuttle, we're gonna hunt your ass down! You and those alien bastards!" a voice said over the comms channel.

"You don't understand. Admiral Nico is lying to you. Carter doesn't want to attack the Earth, and he definitely doesn't want to hurt anyone. There's something else out there that's...," Granger tried to explain, but he was interrupted when his holoscreens suddenly flared with danger warnings. One of the ships was sweeping the space around it with magna-cannons. First one, and then two more of the Bwain fighters sprang back into normal space, suffering damage that made them unable to sustain their dimensional cloaking.

"We're coming for you, and we're gonna put an end to your lies," the dock master growled in Granger's ear.

* * *

"You can't just leave me here!" Lana protested. Pandith had magna-cuffed the doctoral students together before using their small robotic shuttles to tow the gravity drive to his own shuttle so he could mount the experiment to its hull. He'd kept Lana free and let her watch, only because she'd asked so many questions about what was going on. It felt good to finally be able to explain everything that'd happened to another human being.

"Tell Captain Carter that I'm ready," he said to the last of the Bwain. The creature nodded, then scuttled off.

"And just like that it can talk to Carter?" Lana asked curiously.

"The Bwain communicate telepathically. It'll let Carter know," Pandith replied.

She followed him as he jogged down the corridor, but when they finally reached the airlock he turned suddenly and clamped the last pair of magna-cuffs down on Lana's wrists. Then he drew a coil of spider steel through them and locked her to a hand rail.

"No! I'm coming with you!" she exclaimed.

"We may all die where I'm going," Pandith said.

"That's why you need someone to tell your story!"

"I've told you enough. The rest is up to you now, and you won't be able to tell anyone our story if you're dead."

"It doesn't matter. No one's gonna believe Carter in all this! Nico and Phuri have been lying to and manipulating everyone. People wouldn't believe the truth now even if it walked up and slapped 'em right in the face!" Lana argued.

"What do you mean?" Pandith asked.

"Everyone heard what he said. Everyone saw him blow up the shuttle."

"What who said? Captain Carter? He just wanted to negotiate," Pandith said with a confused look.

"Look in the logs here. Look everywhere. That's not what the people were told," Lana said as her eyes met his.

Pandith considered her for a moment, then tapped the holoscreen beside him and searched for recent news about Captain Carter. His eyes flashed at the video lies that poured over him. He ground his teeth, then he undid the spider steel, grabbed Lana's hand and marched her toward the waiting shuttle. He brought her inside, and then tapped a holocontrol. An instant later, Carter's original message played for her.

"So I was right," Lana murmured breathlessly, as if she were having trouble taking it all in.

"Yes, you were. Now please inform as many people as you possibly can. I'll upload this to the station's mainframe, and tou can take it from there," he said as he led her back to the station.

* * *

The Kuiper Belt

Carter appeared in the middle of Nico's fleet, unleashing a barrage of weaponry, and then in the next instant, he had disappeared once again, only to reappear somewhere else just seconds later. He sent the Bwain fighters diving and looping around Nico's flanks, keeping them hidden until they were at last unleashed upon the unsuspecting ships.

The human ships fired back, but they were painfully slow. Carter fought at the speed of thought. He fought as he'd always wanted to against Cazador and all the others, unleashing all of his anger and frustration in a brutal attack.

"*Captain, I'm ready,*" Granger's Bwain announced to him through the Bwainsong.

Nico's ship launched a salvo of rockets. Carter waited until the last minute, then slipped away, and then suddenly reappeared again away from the incoming missiles. In the blink of an eye, the *Bwainhome's* laser fired, and tore into the side of the *Ninkovich.*

He'd come here to try to save everyone, and Nico had tried to kill him.

"*I've got the gravity drive,*" Pandith called through the Bwain near his elbow.

Carter could feel himself slipping into the Bwain's warlike energy now that their bloodlust had finally been released. This is what they'd wanted for so long. They wanted to rise up...to rebel...to purge their pain.

"*Bwainslayer, we are ready to stop,*" the aliens said.

A group of ships was turning, trying to press around Carter's flank. He directed the fighters to blunt their movement, and then he shifted the *Bwainhome* so that it was positioned behind Nico's battle line once again. These were the men who were wrong. They were corrupted, choosing to believe Phuri and Nico's lies instead of listening to their own consciences. They deserved to be punished.

"Captain, are you there? I don't have much time," Granger called.

"Bwainslayer, the plan," the Bwain echoed through his thoughts.

It was anger that fueled him, anger at his own failure. Anger that so many had to be sacrificed. Anger about the fact that no matter what he did, it never seemed to be enough. And then, finally, a single voice broke through the maelstrom.

"Atlas, I don't know if you can hear me, but I have to say goodbye," Mephista said, and her message tore through his thoughts with alarming clarity.

Chapter 19

The Refugee Fleet
Onboard the Tranquility

Mephista had once run from the pain of a hopeless battle, fleeing from the Bwain and the SSC as she made her way to the Sword Belt. For a long time, she'd held tightly to the anger she felt over her injuries, and the betrayal by a command that she'd obeyed, even though they'd knowingly sent her and her crew to their death. She used that anger to justify her raids against people who were truthfully no different than she was, but then slowly, because of her relationship with Atlas Carter, she had changed. She'd come to realize that people mattered more than anything else, and that you could only carry the past with you for so long. Eventually, you had to let it go, and focus on what was important.

And so, when the First Ones gathered in front of Decival's fleet, she asked him to turn and run for the anomaly.

"We won't make it," Decival had said.

"You will if you hit them with everything you have. The shuttles, the ships, all of it," Mephista responded through the restored communication link.

Lances of red and chartreuse struck out from the human ships. The First Ones reeled back, but more took their place. A dense pack of them burrowed right over their dying brothers like sharks that had caught the scent of blood. Mephista was racing toward them with the best speed the *Tranquility* could manage.

"Put all of the shuttles in an arc in front of us. Start firing everything we have the moment Decival's ships pass us," she ordered.

"What's your plan, Captain?" her navigation officer called.

"We're going to hold them off as long as we need to."

"Until Captain Carter arrives?" the officer asked.

"As long as we need to," she repeated as she stared at the writhing mass of horror they were rapidly approaching.

* * *

The Kuiper Belt

Carter pulled the *Bwainhome* out of normal space and forced himself to stop what was happening. He sat there for a moment, watching the destruction he'd wrought from within the *Bwainsong.*

Captain, are you there? Please...I don't have much time," a Bwain croaked out, passing along Granger's message.

Carter gathered himself, imagined the Mars rendezvous point, and felt the *Bwainhome* respond.

"I'm coming Granger. I'm coming for all of you," Carter thought as a new sense of hope and energy filled him.

* * *

The Shuttles

Bryon Purcell fought a desperate battle that he knew he couldn't win. In the corner of his eye he, saw the counter on the shuttles ticking downward. Where they'd started with nearly three-hundred, the numbers were now at two-hundred and fifty, and dropping steadily. There were simply too many of the First Ones to deal with, and his weapons weren't powerful enough to handle them all.

The craft he commanded was slow and lumbering compared to a fighter, but it was still much more maneuverable than the line ships it protected. He swung up through the fleet, firing continuously at a pair of First Ones that were diving at one of the heavy cruisers. He'd only lost two Bwain so far, though the third seemed to be doing quite well.

The larger ships were fighting as best they could, but they were much bigger targets and had fewer weapons to defend themselves. If the shuttles couldn't hold off the massive influx of First Ones, then the fleet was in serious trouble.

Bryon's cannon stitched a weeping red hole up the side of one of the creatures. Its tentacles lashed out at the shuttle as he passed, just nicking the edge of his hull. He scanned his readouts for a pressure breache, but it seemed as if he'd gotten away without severe damage.

"The *Maru* is in trouble!" someone called.

Bryon pulled up his right holo just in time to see a First One shape itself into a squid form before it squirted itself right into the back end of the ship.

"We've lost all propulsion. We're dead in space. Mayday! Mayday!" the *Maru's* captain called frantically.

Shuttle pilots swung into action, swarming the murderous First One as they bathed it in pink fury. The creature shuddered and dissolved, fading into blackness. A large section of the *Maru's* hull was melted. There was nothing that could be done. Unable to maneuver, the other First Ones swarmed in and rapidly consumed it. Bryon edged his shuttle's throttle to maximum, looking for a way past the swarm.

They had to find some way to get back to the anomaly, some way to escape. The last volley had been too much for the Bwain in the seat next to him, and as the creature slumped over and fell to the floor, the next alien stepped up into the seat, dutifully taking its place...but to what end? It was only a matter of time now before they all were torn apart, and they all knew it. It didn't stop them from fighting however. If anything, it pushed them all to fight harder.

Bryon glanced over at the seat next to him and smiled at the Bwain.

"You ready to do this partner?" he asked.

"Ready...partner," the Bwain hissed.

*   *   *

The Dauntless

The ship's constant evasive action was making Danielle nauseous, but she couldn't leave her post. If she stopped, the First Ones would have them in a heartbeat.

"The *Maru* is down captain," someone called.

"The *Husker* is failing."

"Ms. Hoff, do you have a solution for us?" Decival's voice boomed into

Danielle's ear.

She scanned her holoscreens. The entire fleet was surrounded by a white mass. The computer returned a warning for every input she tried.

"No sir. I'm still working on it," she responded as she worked her controls in a blur of frantic motion.

* * *

The Tranquility

Mephista hurled her rear guard into the creatures with all the fury she'd held back for years. The Bwain working with her weapons officers fired over and over again. First Ones broke apart, crumpled, howled, reared backward, and then flung themselves at the shuttles and cruisers once again. On her holoscreens, the human ships continued to wink out of existence, while the First Ones' numbers dwindled far more slowly. Still, she had to help the colonists. That was her one and only focus now.

"Mephista, you've cleared a path!" Decival reported, as if he couldn't actually believe the images flashing across the bridge's holoscreens.

"Get back to that anomaly as fast as you can, Captain," she urged, as the *Tranquility* surged onward toward the gaping, gnashing frenzy of the First Ones.

"Six of 'em coming from above. Engaging...," the weapons officer called.

There was no sound or sensation as the Bwain weapons fired, only the appearance of their projectiles on the holoscreen. Two of the First Ones flared and disappeared, but the other four came on.

Behind her, Decival's ships slipped toward the anomaly.

"Brace for impact," Mephista ordered, as her hand automatically reached for a nearby grip.

If it had been a human ship attacking, she would have heard the proximity warnings and felt an impact, but the ship's computer didn't understand what was happening when the First Ones consumed the rear decks of her ship. It simply reported a hull breach.

"We've lost aft generation!" her engineer reported.

"Trying to stabilize!" her navigation officer added quickly.

"Keep firing!" Mephista cried.

Four more cruisers slipped behind her flotilla. The fastest ships were nearly back in the anomaly.

"We just need to hold on a little longer," Mephista called out to her crew. They had made it this far; and there was no way she was going to lose hope now. They would continue to fight to the very last breath.

The holoscreens flickered. What looked like a massive shaft of light pierced the bridge hull over the heads of her crew and lopped it off. Several of the bridge crews' tethers broke, and they were sucked out with the rushing atmosphere into the maw of one of the creatures.

"No!" Mephista screamed inside her EVO suit. Hand over hand, she pulled herself forward toward the weapons controls.

A lone Bwain remained clutching the decking next to the weapons station. She wouldn't have thought that the creature would have had the strength, but it was showing incredible determination. Mephista reached the weapons and set them on auto fire. Then she felt an arm on hers.

The atmosphere had dissipated, and the Bwain would only have seconds left to live.

"I'm coming, Mephista!" it squawked before its eyes rolled up and the creature suffocated. Unfortunately, because the atmosphere had vented, she couldn't hear the Bwain's dying words. She couldn't' think of any reason it would speak though, unless it was relaying a message. Could it be? She didn't even dare to hope.

*   *   *

The Bwainhome

"Pandith, go!" Captain Carter's voice squawked through the Bwain beside him as soon as the *Bwainhome* re-entered the physical universe.

The environmental engineer rammed his shuttle throttle forward and shot out into the blackness of space. The gravity drive was attached to the rear of his shuttle, forcing him to head toward a First One, and then sweep over it in order for his attack to be effective. He headed for the most damaged capital ships first, but there was little to salvage, and nothing to accomplish other than scaring away the First Ones. After several close calls, Pandith realized that he could spin the shuttle in place and use the maneuver to clear the First Ones out in a wide area.

Whenever they came within a few hundred kilometers of the drive's exhaust, the creatures withered instantly. However, it wasn't long before the First Ones realized who their most dangerous opponent was.

"Captain, they've figured out what's going on. More and more of 'em are coming for me!" Pandith cried.

"Roger that. We're on the way!" Bryon called over the comms channel, his voice ringing out with all the force of an ancient warrior's battle cry.

A swarm of shuttles surrounded him, firing Hal's weaponry in all directions while Pandith simply spun in place, building up longer and longer trails of gravitons that tore at the First Ones.

On his holoscreens, Pandith could see the *Bwainhome* absorbing ineffective blows from the First Ones. The ship was having no trouble at all in holding them off. In fact, their attacks didn't seem to be doing any damage at all.

Pandith continued to spin his ship around as quickly as possible. He lost track of the number of the creatures he knifed through. He only remembered the elation he felt at seeing the devastation his efforts were causing.

"I think they're running!" Bryon called, his voice a mixture of incredulity and triumph.

Pandith couldn't believe what he saw on the holomonitors, but it was true. They had chased the First Ones away. They'd won a victory against a far worse foe than the Bwain...or so it seemed. His sense of victory diminished greatly when he looked more closely at how many of their own craft had survived.

At least a dozen capital ships had been lost. The *Maru*, the *Gonzalez*, the *Tranquility*...

"This is Captain Decival. All craft, all crew, make way for the next anomaly. We don't have time to waste. We need to get our civilians to safety. Move out ASAP."

Pandith slowed his shuttle's spin, and then lined up the craft with the rest of the shuttles. He kept glancing at his rear holos, not willing to trust that the First Ones wouldn't regroup and resume another furious attack.

They were nine hours to the next anomaly, and there was no time to think about anything other than getting to safety.

The ragtag fleet of survivors had won the battle for now, but the First Ones were still out there, and the battle for the survival of the universe itself was just beginning.

Coda

Earth

The man who walked into the president's office had a hard face. His skin looked like sun-dried leather, and a thick stubble clung to his cheeks, crisscrossed here and there by various scars. He circled the room, considering the furniture, the view, the clouds in the distance, the desk, and the man who currently stood behind it.

"This is your post, is it?" the man asked.

"No, it's been vacated," Phuri answered.

"For your Admiral?"

"For the most qualified man for the job."

"And what are these qualifications?" the man asked.

"A certain understanding of what power is, and how it will be used." Phuri said with a sly smile.

"Ah yes, power. Now that's something I'm very well acquainted with," the man said as he picked up a glass paperweight and hefted it as if he were weighing the power of the universe before him. His strong fingers gripped the object tightly, and his dark skin blanched with the effort.

"My name is Cazador," he said as he carefully set the paperweight back on the desk, and then sat down in the former president's chair. He shifted around a bit, testing it to make sure it was a good fit. A few seconds later he nodded to himself, apparently satisfied with the results. Leaning back comfortable, he clasped his hands behind his head, put his feet up on the desk, and smiled at Phuri.

"It will be a pleasure working with you, Mr. Vongsa," he said.

"I am at your service," Phuri said, bowing slightly as he returned Cazador's smile.

About the Author

J. Channing is an engineer and manager for a semiconductor company in Boise, Idaho by day and a dedicated entrepreneur and freelance writer by night. Born in Butte, Montana, he spent most of his childhood roaming around the northwest, living in eighteen different locations before getting through high school. When not at his day or night job, Channing is also actively involved in the community, with his church, and as a small business owner. He utilizes his business ties and proceeds to give back to the local community, having raised funds for Boise area charities.

J. Channing has been interested in military history, time travel, World War II, and weapons technology since he was a small child. The original story concept for *Forever* was outlined on one of his many solo bus rides from the Seattle area to Helena, Montana. It was adjusted and improved over decades and was finally, as a labor of love, completed. The book is a fulfillment of a story that has played out in his head hundreds of times; he hopes the world enjoys it as much as he always has.